MW01093309

XO, Willow Aster

the
BOOKWORM
box

Helping the community, one book at a time

DOWNFALL

WILLOW ASTER

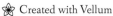

Thank you, Christine Estevez, for this brilliant idea.

PREFACE

This book is a romance based entirely on fictional places. It is set in the present where there are monarchies in a world that doesn't operate quite like ours. There are no dragons or fairies, but there is lust, greed, pride, and wrath...something that exists in any world and has since the beginning of time.

Any mistakes I make in properly conveying royal practices and whatnot, I hope you will excuse and consider that in the kingdoms of Farrow, Niaps, Alidonia, and beyond, perhaps it's just the way it is.

List of Characters:

Safrin Family of Farrow:
Neil & Kathryn, father and mother
Jadon, son of Neil and stepson of Kathryn
Eden, daughter
Bryson, son
Ava, daughter

Also in Farrow:

Brienne Jarvis, bodyguard

Catano Family of Niaps:
  Titus & Cecilia (Cece), father and mother
  Basile, brother to Cecilia
  Luka, son
  Mara, daughter

Also in Niaps:
  Elias Lancaster, advisor to Titus

Nearby country
  Forbrush Family of Yuman:
  Victros & Anais, father and mother
  Alex, son
  Nadia, daughter

Farthing Family of Alidonia:
  Vance & Jonquil*, father and mother
  Omar, son
  Delilah, daughter
  Caulder, nephew, advisor to Vance

*deceased

CHAPTER ONE

Today is the day I meet my future husband. It's a sobering thought and one that resounds with each step on the ancient path that leads to the university my brother Jadon, my parents, and my grandparents attended before me. It's as if I've stepped back in time to a place where cars and cell phones and jeans don't exist, and horses and carriages and petticoats do. Kings Passage University looms just ahead; a foreboding castle with the flags of each country doing little to soften its features. Kings Passage has students from around the world: princes, princesses, emperors, empresses, the extremely wealthy, and the few who have an IQ of 170 plus.

The flag of my country, Farrow, waves wildly on the right side of the entrance. I watch it proudly, admiring the way the colors stand out against the stone. To the left is the flag of Niaps, where I will call home as soon as I marry Luka Catano. I've never met Luka, but our parents have an arrangement—or should I say, *we* have an arrangement... thanks to our parents. I've studied everything I can about him, taking note of his chiseled jawline and piercing blue eyes, his startling blond hair. He is devastatingly beautiful. So beautiful it terrifies me. I feel quite lucky: if I have to be set up with someone I don't even know, at least he isn't hideous.

But what if he doesn't approve of me?

I turn around and am tempted to run, but the view stops me. The beauty of Pravia is unlike anything I have ever seen. Having grown up in the snow for at least six months of the year, the way the sun glints off the water and the feel of the tropical breeze wreaking havoc on my hair seems like a world away from my home in Farrow. I swallow hard and forge ahead, tempted to grab my mother's hand for comfort. I've never been the sort to do so—why start now?

I've been trained to be a lady, a perfect wife, a smart conversationalist...a queen. My body has been conditioned to be fit and alluring and to be the ideal womb for many babies...as well as you can condition for that sort of thing. I'm not sure what more Kings Passage can teach me that hasn't already been drilled into me by my tutors, but I think it's my parents' way of easing me into the marriage. Not that I've needed much coaxing. I'm ready, unlike my younger sister Ava, who denounces all things ladylike and noble. It's my responsibility being born into royalty, to do my part to carry on the traditions set before me. *I'm ready for all of it*, I think again and this time I feel my cheeks heat. The thought of being intimate with Luka is something I've tried not to obsess over, but it's hard to stop thinking about it.

"You're awfully quiet, dear. And you're looking flushed —what did I tell you about wearing sunscreen? You will burn in minutes out in this sun and freckle right up. Take my umbrella." Mother passes the umbrella and I dutifully carry it to block out the sun.

I did put on sunscreen and don't tell her I'm flushed imagining Luka Catano naked.

———

For centuries, Kings Passage was the metropolis of higher learning for royalty. A university for the future kings and queens of the world; it eventually expanded to a more diverse group but has retained the nostalgia of the past, while also staying cutting edge with modern technology and innovation. It is linked to the city of Pravia by a mile-long stone plank that can lift if necessary, creating its own island. Many people flock to Pravia in hopes of gaining employment at Kings Passage, but as soon as one enters the doors of Kings Passage, the noise of the city dies down, the pace slows, and if wealth were a smell, it would reek to high heaven.

Once we're inside, I stare transfixed at the ornate paintings on the massive ceilings until my mother takes hold of my elbow. I lower my head to see three people bowing and curtsying to her. My parents rule over Farrow and I'm used to seeing people bowing before them, but somehow I thought it might be different here.

Introductions are made, and Dean Hightower steps forward.

"Princess Eden, at your mother's request, Miss Brienne from your family court will show you to your quarters."

I look at the girl, who appears to be around my age, maybe older. She's taller than me, head lowered to avoid eye contact. I greet her and she nods politely at the floor. I vaguely remember her serving as a guard for my mother, but I never gave it much thought.

"Should you need anything, Miss Brienne will be able to attend to your every need," Dean Hightower says.

I sigh loudly and my mother gives me a stern look. I give her one back—she didn't tell me she was sending someone to look after me.

"Say the word and she will also give you privacy, should you want it. It is not our desire to be overbearing, but we also want you to feel at home here at Kings Passage. And safe." His tone reassures me.

The last thing I want is to be watched all the time. This was supposed to be a break from that. But the word *safe* is a reminder that I will always have a bodyguard close by. I study her. She's approaching six feet tall, and although willowy thin, she certainly looks as if she can protect me; hopefully, we won't have to find out.

"Thank you," I say.

She lifts her eyes to me and I nod.

"Supper will be served at seven o'clock. We are so honored that representatives from every country will be in attendance this evening. A tradition long-standing at Kings Passage. I do hope you get some rest before then, as the festivities usually go well into the night."

"We look forward to celebrating with you," my mother says kindly.

She is a beautiful, graceful woman, and the dean flushes a bit when she smiles at him.

We follow Brienne to my room. It's on the second level in the east wing, overlooking the ocean. I barely notice the spacious room with ornate furniture, looking at the vast blue-green water outside my window. I step onto the balcony and inhale the salty air. If everything else goes wrong, this view will be my haven.

The time drags before supper. Mother insists I take a nap while she leaves to rest and get ready at her hotel. I try to appease her, but sleep won't come. I'm too excited to see Luka. Brienne draws a bath for me—I don't even have anyone do that for me at home—and asks if she can do my hair. I show her a picture of the elaborate rose braid I want —it's actually called the Eden, not just in Farrow but around the world. I wore my hair that way to my prom and it has become my signature style. There are several variations.

"I've been practicing," she says shyly. "With your red hair, it's the perfect style for you."

"Thank you," I respond, surprised she's so vocal now that we're alone. "For tonight, I would like half of it in the rose and the rest of it in loose waves."

Brienne nods briskly. Her fingers move skillfully through my hair; she's done her homework. My hair is artwork when she's done. I thank her and ten minutes before my mother is set to arrive and escort me to dinner, I slip into my raw silk mauve dress. The neckline is lower than what I wear at home, but with the beaded and embroidered rosettes covering any cleavage, my mother won't make me change. I'll save those dresses for when she goes home.

Queen Kathryn arrives right at seven, ensuring we'll make a grand entrance. She kisses my cheeks and fawns over my dress and hair. I have no doubt I will miss her, but right now I can only focus on one thing: Luka.

"Exquisite," she murmurs, holding an arm out for me to take.

As we walk to the Great Hall, the anticipation is so thick I feel like I'm swimming in it. Two guards open the doors wide as we approach. I'm accustomed to us being announced, but here we enter without fanfare, and I'm grateful for it. It gives me time to look around the bustling banquet hall. A dignitary from Sojana stops my mother and I keep moving, searching the room.

I see his mother first and feel my nerves instantly kick up a notch higher. Queen Cece is even more beautiful in person and when she turns to me and smiles, my steps falter. She smiles wider and I walk toward her. When I reach her, she holds out her hands and grasps mine.

"Princess Eden, such a beauty." Her eyes shift behind me and she smiles wider. "Son, it's time you met your future."

I turn and look up into the eyes of Prince Luka of Niaps. His jawline is chiseled rock and seems to tighten even more as he looks at me. His eyes reach down inside me like they know every thought I'm thinking. His jaw ticks, one, two, three beats, and then he smiles. He reaches for my hand and I instantly sweat, feeling the heat between us.

"Hello, future," he says, his smile widening as he sees my quick intake of air. "I'd recognize that red hair and those innocent blue eyes anywhere." He kisses my hand and holds it in his. When he nods, I realize he's waiting for me to respond.

"Oh, hello. It's nice to finally meet you."

"Your babies will be glorious," his mother says, clapping her hands twice.

My eyes widen and he drops my hand.

"Mother," he says with an edge to his voice that has me looking between the two of them.

She waves him off and holds her arm to me. "I'm just saying what everyone else is thinking. I believe we're at the same table. Why don't we go sit down?"

"I'll be there in a bit. I need to say hello to some friends first," Luka says, motioning to a group behind him.

It takes everything in me not to wilt to the floor. My nerves are shot.

"Luka," Cece's voice lowers. "They can wait."

"Yes, *Mother*," he says.

We walk to the table and my mother joins us a few minutes later. Our mothers chat and Luka sits next to me, silent. I hear Cece saying something about how my beauty shouldn't be hidden away in Farrow and I feel my mother stiffen next to me. She smiles, but it's not a friendly smile.

Luka leans in and when I feel his breath on my ear, I don't move an inch. Heat rushes to my face and I resist the urge to lean in closer to him.

"How does it feel to only be seen as the uterus of a future prince?" he asks.

I gasp and try to face him, the venom in his voice making me shiver, but he's too close to move. His lips touch my ear and I swallow hard.

"I'm guessing you're used to being the most beautiful girl in the room. You are very pretty," he whispers, "but take a look around...you're just one of many here." His fingers run along my arm and I shiver. He smiles against my skin. "We'll have to see what you're made of, Eden..."

CHAPTER TWO

I was ravenous before I came, but now my appetite is gone. I don't even try to eat; my stomach threatens to turn at any second. I take small sips of water to try to dislodge the lump in my throat. It doesn't work. Luka eats everything on his plate and when I don't touch my food, he motions to my plate with his brows raised. I push it toward him and he demolishes it. According to the Internet, he's six foot three and weighs two hundred pounds. I've stared at pictures of him shirtless for hours, wondering what he does to look like a sculpted god, what he must eat to keep fit. Now I know that he eats like a pig.

When plates are cleared, I look at everyone around the table. "It's been a lovely evening. I think the trip is catching up with me. I'm going to head to my room now."

"You can't leave yet, Eden!" My mother puts her hand on my arm. "The dance," she says under her breath. "At least wait for one dance."

"Maybe I'll catch some fresh air then and come back in a few minutes." I stand up and avoid looking at Luka as I turn around.

I walk toward the glass doors on the other side of the room, hoping they're unlocked. There's a large balcony that overlooks the sea just outside and I exhale in relief when I'm able to open the door and walk out. The breeze carries the smell of salt water mixed with the fragrant trellises of jasmine. I stand there and breathe it in. The sound of the waves calms me.

When my thoughts take me to Luka, I push him back out. If I think about him, I'll panic. And nothing about the way I've been conditioned for this marriage allows for panic. My country needs the Catano wealth; Catano needs our oil. Only Sojana exports more oil than Farrow and all of their princesses are already married. I'm not sure it would matter if they had a princess to marry off—the Catanos and Safrins are certain that our union will fortify our countries more than anything else could. It seems Luka might be the only one who isn't convinced...and even if he is, he's not happy about it.

My mother steps beside me, snapping me out of my thoughts. She puts her hand on my back and says, "Come inside, dear. You won't win him over by hiding. It could be that he's resentful about this arrangement," she says in her most soothing voice, "but once he gets to know you, he'll be a changed man. You're every man's dream."

I groan. "Of course you'd say that, you're my *mother*."

"A queen never lies," she says, her lips twitching with a smile. When I level her with a glare, she sighs. "Eden, anyone with eyes can see your beauty." She rubs a lock of my hair between her fingertips. "And that's only the surface of who you are. Your father wasn't exactly head over heels for me the first night we met either, you know. But after we were married, we grew into our love."

I follow her in. I must have been outside longer than I

realized because the tables have all been cleared and the dancing has started. Couples seem to be forming already, the shy, heated look of interest apparent. Fathers and daughters are dancing together too and it makes me miss mine more than ever.

It doesn't take long to spot Luka. He's the one surrounded by all the beautiful girls. A few princesses that I recognize—the paparazzi has hounded all of us since we were born—and a couple of other girls that I don't. Luka's confidence, the glint in his eyes when he laughs, the way he looks as if he could either crush you or eat you alive—the combination of those things and all of the secrets underneath make every eye gravitate to him.

He looks my way, as if he feels me staring holes through him. His eyes roam down the length of me and back up, and with each second that ticks by I get increasingly antsy. When his eyes land on mine again, his lip curls into something between a smirk and a sneer. Even after our less than great introduction, I want him to come claim me right here, right now, in front of everyone, but he doesn't. I clench my hands into fists and watch as he turns from me and kisses each girl surrounding him on the cheek. They throw their heads back and laugh at something he says. He looks at me over his shoulder. *Is he talking about me?*

The next thing I know, he's stalking toward me.

"Dance with me?" His voice is silky smooth.

He holds his hand out and waits for me to take it. When I don't right away, he bends to eye level.

"Come on," he says, finally taking my hand in his anyway and kissing it. "Let's make the mothers happy. Send them on their way thinking their babies are going to be okay." His voice is mocking, but he pulls me flush against him and I forget to be annoyed with him. Our bodies fit together, getting along far better than *we* seem to be able to so far.

I sigh and he leans back a bit to look at me. "Why the disappointed face?" he asks. He laughs under his breath. "Surely you did not think we were going to fall in love at first sight?"

His words are cruel, but his accent is so alluring, it cuts some of the bite.

"I'm sure it's no secret by now that I'm not happy about this marriage," he says, smiling past me to someone else. Probably one of the girls giggling behind my back. I stop dancing and he pulls me closer, his hands gripping my hips.

When his attention focuses on me, he stops dancing too and we stand in the middle of the floor for a moment, studying one another. His eyes drop to my mouth and for a moment, I think he's going to kiss me. My insides tremble. He shifts to my ear, so close his lips touch my lobe.

"Such a delicate creature," he whispers. I shiver and feel his lips lift against my ear. "I want you to know that I'm looking forward to making every inch of you *mine*. One day. But we're *not married yet*. And know that I will *never* be yours."

I push his hands off of me and walk away. *What does that even mean?* My entire body is heated with his promise of making me his, but his last statement douses me with such cold fury I'm shaking.

My mom knocks on my door a few minutes later. "Eden? Sweetheart, open the door. I'm worried about you."

I let her in before anyone else can hear her. It's strange —I haven't seen anyone else in this wing so far. I look down the hall after she enters and all is quiet. She sees my face and her shoulders sag in worry.

I've gone along with our customs, never questioning my parents' wishes or even believing there is another way. Both of our countries greatly benefit from our marriage; therefore, it is the right thing to do. I've hoped that Luka has the same level of honor and commitment to his family as I do, but if tonight has proved anything, it's that I know nothing about *him* at all. Nothing but the list of his family's assets so long it could fill volumes.

"When our kids ask about the first time we met, we'll have a horrible story," I say, my eyes filling again.

"I have a feeling it will all turn around. Tonight was simply the prologue—you know how prologues are typically a bit troubling? Well, you have plenty of time to make your story a good one," she says.

Her brow creases when she sees my tears falling. Her arms wind around me and she holds me tight. "Oh, my sweet girl. We will miss you every day. It's hard to believe this time has already come." She leans back and puts her hands on my cheeks, studying me intently. "I know you are in good hands here. And that boy—he has some growing up to do, but you know your father and I wouldn't have agreed to this if we didn't feel it was a good match."

I nod. "I know you wouldn't." I give her a shaky smile. "Let's hope you're right."

Her smile drops a degree with those words.

Somewhere in the unspoken rules, I think it probably says: A girl does not question her queen, even if she is her daughter. Another case of *I've never been the sort to do so— why start now?*—except it's beginning to hit me that my entire future is in someone else's hands, and my marriage might not turn out as well as it did for my parents. Why have I not thought of this before now?

She kisses my forehead and pulls away.

"Everything will be okay," she says.

She turns and gives me one last hug. I try not to think of how long it will be before I see her next, the homesickness already settling in my bones.

I swallow my panic and dutifully kiss her on each cheek, my heart feeling hollow as she walks away.

CHAPTER THREE

And this is what I am still telling myself the next morning —*everything will be okay, everything will be okay, everything will be okay*—as I wipe the tears that keep falling. I've given up on sleep and walk out to my balcony to watch the sunrise. I barely slept at all, playing and replaying what was said the night before; the girls watching our every move; the way Luka looked at me; how his arms around me felt, despite his awful words...my mother leaving me in a strange country alone.

I've been without my parents a lot, but I've never been without my siblings. I think about everyone at home—my half-brother Jadon, and my sister Ava. Out of all of them, I'm closest to Jadon, but at the moment, all of them feel especially precious to me. I don't know if I can stand being without them.

My face feels raw from crying for too long. I step to the edge of the balcony and look out at the water, trying to think about something else, anything else. The water laps gently onto the sand and eventually lulls me into a more peaceful state of mind.

A girl's shriek catches my attention and I look across the way to the balcony to the left of mine. Any peace I'd found evaporates when I see Luka's blond hair. He's chasing Princess Nadia, one of the girls he was talking to last night— I only know for sure because I researched each girl after I came to my room. I avoid the tabloids as I'm in them most of the time, but I should've done my research before coming here. Everyone has changed considerably since I last looked, including Luka.

They're both in their underwear and she's laughing hysterically. He catches her and kisses her neck and she laughs harder, hugging him. I gasp when he turns to put his arms around her and sees me standing there, watching them. It's not close enough to hear what she says, but close enough that I can see his teeth clench his full lower lip. His eyes shine as his hands go lower and lower, until they cup her hot pink floral backside. My chest feels tight. She looks up at him, her back to me, and his eyes never veer from mine. I'm too stunned to look away. With one last glance at me, he pulls her tighter against him—kissing her, grinding into her.

I make sure I'm inside before he looks up again.

———

I don't leave my room for three days, and only then because it's the first day of classes. Brienne hovers over me, lamenting the fact that I barely eat the food she brings.

"You'll be starving by lunchtime if you don't eat a little something now," she says, setting toast and tea next to me. "How about I fix your hair while you eat the toast?"

I sit on the chaise lounge and think for a moment before I speak. I've had a lot of time to think over the past few days.

I clear my throat and pick up the pale pink boots Brienne has set out for me to wear with my short, flowy black dress. It's a stellar combo, one I would've worn but didn't expect her to choose. Once again, I realize she's done her homework.

"I know you're just doing your job, but don't worry about me. I'm going to be easy for you." I slip my boots on and look up at her. "It might take me a while to adjust, but I will. I'm fine running my bath, doing my hair—unless it's a special occasion, but even then, I'll be okay. Most of the time I'll eat in the dining hall, and if not, I can let you know ahead of time. How does that sound? Clean sheets once a week—I don't mind putting them on. If you just *want* to do something, you could keep things dusted or do the laundry —" I snort. "I've never done laundry, but I should probably learn, right?"

You could hear a needle drop, it's so quiet.

"Something tells me I wouldn't even be allowed in the laundry quarters, would I?"

She shakes her head solemnly, eyes wide.

I lift an eyebrow. "There's always washing by hand..."

Her mouth drops further the longer I talk.

"Honestly, if you just want to hang out here all day and read, I'm fine with that. When Dean Hightower or Mother asks how we're getting along, I will tell him 'beautifully.' I vaguely remember seeing you occasionally in Farrow, but it seems Mother has an attachment to you. I hope we can be friends too."

"Your mother saved my life. I owe her everything."

I stare at her. "I didn't realize."

She lowers her head again and it seems that's all she's going to say.

"Whatever arrangement you have with her, I'm letting you off the hook while you're here."

"I'll do my best to stay out of your way, Lady Eden."

"No, that's—" I sigh. "I just need this time to be...you know what? Never mind. We'll figure it out as it comes."

I stand up and smooth out my dress. I pick up the mini iPad the university gave to me when I arrived, tuck it in my small bag along with my lip stain, and walk toward the door. I give Brienne a tiny wave, and when I step out, I make sure Nadia and Luka are nowhere in sight.

Unfortunately, I can't avoid them any longer. They're in my first class, walking in at the last second and looking like the perfect couple. I feel him before I see him. When I look up, he's staring at me, his eyes doing their sweep up and down me. I can't tell if he likes what he sees or despises everything about me. He stalks toward me, Nadia following close behind, and when he sits down next to me, he leans near my ear.

"Next time I'm visiting Nadia, why don't you come over? I'll let you get a closer look. See the goods you're purchasing..."

"So far there's *nothing* about you that I want to buy," I tell him.

His head tilts as his finger traces a shape on my arm. I flick it off of me and he chuckles.

"Is that jealousy or just your temper on a normal day?" he asks.

"Are you a prick or is this just you on a normal day?" I turn and face him then. He's so close I can see his pupils dilate.

His jaw clenches and he slowly takes a step back. He laughs under his breath and it sends a shudder down my spine. I stare at him until he looks away.

"I should've known my dad would give me a pious bitch." His head tilts back and he glares at the ceiling.

Out of all the things I expected to feel for my fiancé, hatred was not one of them.

Toward the end of class I'm still so shaken, I try to get my things together so I can walk out quickly and end up knocking my iPad and phone off of my desk. I lean down to pick it up and collide heads with the person on the other side of me. I hold my head and look up and the guy is doing the same, looking apologetic.

"I'm so sorry," he whispers.

I shake my head. "*I'm* sorry."

His fingers lift to touch the spot on my forehead that feels like it's growing by the second and I hear a chair scrape behind me. Luka knocks the guy's hand off of me and I turn to look at him.

"Hands off," he growls.

I glare at him and he sits back down in his chair, glaring right back.

Still shaking my head, I turn to the guy next to me as he places my things back on my desk. The bell rings and I gather everything and put it in my bag.

"Thank you," I say to the guy on my left. "Is your head okay?"

"Much better than yours, I think. You might need ice. I'll never forgive myself if I've left a bruise on Princess Eden," he says.

I flush. He smiles and I like the way his smile brightens more when I smile back.

"I'm Thaddeus," he says. "Call me Thad."

"Back off, Thaddeus," Luka says. "She's spoken for."

Thaddeus looks past me at Luka and Nadia. I turn and see that she's clutching his arm.

"Greedy much?" Thad says.

I roll my eyes and duck out of the middle of them. I'm halfway to my next class when Thad falls into step next to me. He's cute, although a little on the short side for me. *It doesn't matter—you're spoken for...*flits through my brain. I stop at the door and Thad frowns.

"Looks like I'm next door. Maybe I'll see you at lunch?" he says.

Luka walks up and bumps into Thad. It looks accidental, but one look at his satisfaction is enough to know it wasn't.

"Move along, Thaddeus," he says.

I lift my hand to wave at Thad and he grins.

I want to run to my room and hide in there just to breathe. I wonder if he's going to be in all of my classes. If so, maybe I'll try to switch some of my classes around. Nadia isn't in this class, which makes me breathe a little easier, for some reason. A girl grabs the seat next to me before Luka can.

"Mind if I sit there?" he asks her, pulling a sweet act that has my eyes narrowing.

"I do mind actually," she says, avoiding looking at him.

I choke back a laugh, and Mistress Oleander begins class before he can argue. I look at the girl and nod gratefully.

After class, she puts her hand on my arm and says, "You are way nicer than I'd be. I was sitting behind you in the last class and when you called him a prick, I almost clapped right in his face."

I cringe. "Not my finest moment."

But she stands there looking at me, her grin so wide, that I smile the first real smile all day. "Oh yes, it *was*." She tilts her head back toward the door. "I'm Tysa, by the way. Sit with me at lunch? I've always wanted to meet the Princess of Snow and I have to say, you do not disappoint."

CHAPTER FOUR

"I'm afraid nothing can be done about your classes," Mistress Oleander says firmly. Her smile does nothing to soften her statement. She slams her heavy book shut and grins wider. "Under the request of both of your parents, you and Prince Luka are to have every class together, as well as take part in our marriage enhancement therapy."

"Marriage enhancement therapy? What year is this?" I lower my voice when she flinches, leaning in slightly. "We're not even married yet!"

She tilts her head to the side. "It sounds as if the two of you might really benefit from therapy," she states. "Now, why don't you get to lunch, you don't want to miss out on our delicious Beef Wellington."

"I'm not hungry and I don't eat beef," I whisper, tears threatening to spill over.

Her eyes grow wide as she reaches out to pat my hand and then stops herself, her etiquette taking over. "It'll take some time to adjust to being so far from home. I came from the snow myself and all this sunshine just doesn't seem normal at first!" She laughs, shoulders bouncing up and down. "Before you know it, you'll forget what the snow is like." Her shoulders stop mid-bounce when someone moves up behind me. "Ah, there he is. You have your work cut out for you, I'm afraid," she says to him, shaking her head. "You need to convince our beautiful princess here that these classes are meant to help you both, especially the therapy."

"We just got here. I hardly think we need therapy yet," Luka says, "though your class is a breath of fresh air." He winks at the lady who has more wrinkles than I've ever seen on one person.

She puts her hand on her chest, swooning right before my eyes. I roll my eyes and sniffle. I need to blow my nose and hide, damn it!

Luka holds his arm out and looks at me then, his cockiness choking the air around me. "I'll escort our delicate flower to the Grand Hall." He picks up my hand and puts it through his arm when I don't do it myself.

I pull my hand away. "You wouldn't know what to do with even one *night* in Farrow—the last thing you should call me is a delicate flower."

"Okay, *Princess* Eden. Settle down." His tone mocks me and I want to strangle him with his condescension. A frown creases his face. "I was only referring to keeping your virginal skin out of the harsh elements...like the sun. I'm also happy to eat your meat—at lunch and otherwise—as long as you promise to eventually eat mine." He checks to see if I'm paying attention to his innuendos then smirks. "And I stand corrected about you being delicate..." He leans close to my ear and whispers, "But I will not let Thaddeus or any other bastard touch one inch of you, even if that means escorting you to lunch when I could be fucking Nadia."

Mistress Oleander chokes back a cough to remind us of her presence, but we both ignore her.

Luka leans back and smiles, the color in his eyes exploding in hues of green and blue and making me sick in the process. "Watching your skin flush like this..." He runs a finger across the exposed skin on my chest and my mouth drops open. I hurriedly shut it. "—I'd say it's almost worth it."

Mistress Oleander clears her throat and gathers her things. I wait until she's out of the room before I speak. I lean up to whisper in his ear the way he keeps doing with me. "So you don't want me, but you want to make sure no one else has me? You're such a cliché."

"Never said I didn't want you," he says, turning so his lips touch my cheek when he speaks. My skin feels like it's on fire where his lips have been. "We could probably have some fun together, if you let loose a little bit. I can think of a few ways we could pass the time when your nipples pebble against your dress like they're doing right now..."

I gasp and step back, feeling an instant rush between my legs. "Not happening."

He shrugs. "Oh, it'll happen. It's just a matter of when —*before* we're chained to each other for the rest of our lives...or *after*."

I shudder and he laughs, pulling my hand back through his arm.

"Come along, Princess."

"Stop calling me that," I snap, but I don't pull my hand away. His shoulder against mine feels nice.

His laugh echoes down the ancient corridor and just before we enter the Grand Hall, he lifts my hand and gives it an open-mouth kiss. I swallow hard. "You're turning out to be more entertaining than I expected."

In the next moment, he's gone. One minute I'm looking at his lips touching my skin and feeling the flush of heat throughout my body, and the next I'm watching his back as he stalks toward a group of guys at a nearby table.

If this is the constant state of confusion he's going to leave me in, I'm not sure how I'll keep up. I'm momentarily frozen but then straighten my shoulders and ignore Nadia's table. She's surrounded by the girls from the first night. They all turn and look at me first then search for Luka, Nadia's shoulders relaxing when she sees him. She turns to me again and smiles and it almost looks genuine—but I know better.

I bypass the Beef Wellington and ask for the salad, cringing when I see how much dressing is on it. I miss Henri, our chef at home. He prepared all my meals and each was a masterpiece, so colorful and flavorful.

Tysa waves me over and I'm sitting down before I realize Thaddeus is across from me. He smiles when I look up, and I dig into my salad to avoid conversation. It feels like asking for unnecessary trouble to have his attention. I'm two bites in when I feel Luka's eyes on me. He squeezes between Tysa and me, glaring at Thaddeus.

"Are we gonna have a problem?" he asks.

I shake my head and forget about my plate, hurrying out of the room. Luka rushes after me, grabbing my elbow before I reach the exit. His eyes are flashing, as if he's angry with *me*. I scoff and he drops his hand.

"Where are you going?" he asks, his voice softer than this eyes.

"None of your business."

"Ahh, you're going to act like a child now. Why am I not surprised?"

I shake my head and walk out.

And this time he lets me.

Classes that afternoon consist of me ignoring Luka and not hearing a word the professors say. Luka sits by me and is quiet, which is almost more distracting than if he was being his normally obnoxious self. When the last class of the day ends, I hurry out of there and go to my room. Brienne is there, cleaning my bathroom that doesn't need cleaning.

"How did your day go?" she asks dutifully.

"It's been quite the day. I feel like I could sleep for years. I'm exhausted."

She sets down her cloth and picks up the container that holds all the cleaning supplies. "I'll let you rest. If you need anything—"

"I'll be sure to message you."

She nods and leaves the room, shutting the door behind her. I lock the door and lean against it, feeling the weight of the day on my shoulders.

How will I do this?

This marriage is a mistake.

I can't spend my life with a man that I can't stand. We'll kill each other in the process of trying to do good for our countries...

My room suddenly feels stifling and when I walk toward my balcony, I stop, images of Luka and Nadia rushing to mind. Instead, I open my door and look down the hall, and when I don't see anyone, I slip out.

The castle is still bustling with professors leaving for the day, the rest of the staff who takes care of the place, and students getting to know each other in the charming alcoves set up for such things. I skirt along the side of the room and when I reach the door, I'm relieved when no one stops me. It's not like I'm a prisoner here, but I'm not given much freedom at home, so I'd expect it to be the same.

I step outside and inhale the salty air, taking only a moment to let it soak in that I'm here before hurriedly walking toward the long plankway to Pravia. It feels like another world on the other side. The closer I get to the city, the louder it gets: cars honking, music playing in the distance. People are walking everywhere; some in a hurry to get to the next place, and others tossing balls on the beach and walking their dogs. When I step into the city, I go the opposite way I'd been with my mother, wanting to explore something different this time.

There's an older section of town that has cobblestone streets. There are the touristy horse carriages and quaint shops. Flowers climb up the stone archways, and on some pathways, I have to bend to avoid the blooms overhead. I step into a candle shop and feel eyes on me. I turn around, but no one is paying any attention to me—it's all in my head. I breathe deeply and tell myself to relax. I smell candle after candle and love one so much, I buy it. It's heavy, but the clerk gives me a sturdy bag to carry it in. I leave the shop and still feel strange. There's a huge man I hadn't seen before I went into the shop, standing outside when I come out. When I walk away, he follows. I stop in mid-step and he does too, looking away like he isn't following me. I turn and start running and feel him close behind me. When I start getting winded, I stop and step in a doorway. He walks forward slowly, stopping in front of me. He's huge and I don't think, I knee him in the groin and stomp on his foot with my heavy boot. He yelps and grabs my arm when I try to run. I maneuver out of his hold, grateful that my training has come back, but just when I think I'm free, his grip gets stronger.

"Miss, I'm not going to hurt you," he says.

I try to get away and realize it's futile. The man is a giant and all muscle. I'll have to choose the right moment to escape. God, this can't be happening.

"I swear, I'm not going to hurt you. I'm here to protect you."

I stop struggling and look at him.

"Let her go," Luka says.

The guard lets go of my arm and stands taller. I rub my arm where his hands were and shoot daggers up at him.

"My apologies for any pain I caused, Miss." He lowers his head and backs away as Luka steps forward.

He's furious, but so am I.

"What are you doing out here?" He steps closer and so do I, our chests nearly touching.

"Are you seriously having me followed?"

"Your girl was too slow and she can't protect you. Look at her—she missed the part where you kneed his balls because she was so far behind."

I look past him and Brienne is now glaring at the man, knife in hand.

"I can take a walk by myself. I don't need anyone tailing me. I need to breathe." My voice raises with each word and Luka rolls his eyes.

"It doesn't work that way in my family."

"I'm not in your family yet, as you so clearly let me know the first night. This town is safe. What I do is not your concern. I don't want to be followed, so get your guy off of me from here on. Are we clear?"

"We are so far from clear," he says, taking that final step that makes the heat of his chest hit mine.

We stand there staring at each other, chests rising and falling, and when he puts his hand on my waist and pulls me even closer, I get a rush of adrenaline.

My breath shallows and his eyes fall to my mouth. There's not enough air. He leans his forehead against mine and his words, as always, catch me by surprise.

"Have you saved yourself for me?" he asks, his voice low and raw.

I try to step away, but his hand at my waist tugs me closer, the hardness of his body nearly making my eyes roll back.

"When do you think I would have had a chance to do anything?"

"So that means yes," he says.

I sputter out my frustration. "Why are we having this conversation right now?"

"Mostly just curiosity." He grins and I groan, which makes him grin wider. He drops his hands then and my body feels cold when he steps away. He sobers and again I'm on the roller coaster of his constantly changing moods. "My family's enemies would love nothing more than to snatch you up and defile you in every way, making it impossible for us to marry. When we marry, our countries become allies and strong ones at that. There will be eyes on you at all times. I'd say I don't want any harm to come to you, but we both know I'm not the caring type. If you step outside of Kings Passage, you bring Brienne, and I will have Franco following you both." He lifts his hand when I start to argue. "This is not open to discussion. I will not have you get hurt on my time." And then he adds under his breath, "Too much money is riding on this."

"You really are a bastard, aren't you," I whisper.

"Yes. I really am a bastard."

CHAPTER FIVE

Brienne and I walk back to the university with Luka and Franco following. She tries to make conversation several times but gives up when I don't give more than one-word answers. I'm getting madder with each step back to the castle.

I won't live like this.

Not until I have to.

I walk faster, and when I reach the doors to the castle, Brienne opens them and I step through with resolution. I don't look back as I head to my room with her on my heels and Facetime my dad.

He picks up on the third ring, his smiling face filling the screen. "Let me step out of this meeting." He's quiet for a moment, walking out of the room and stepping into his office. "My beautiful Eden. How are you?"

"Not great," I tell him, eyebrows lifted.

His eyes widen. "What's wrong, sweetheart?"

"You didn't tell me I'd have to be followed here. I thought the whole purpose of this was so I could have a little freedom before being tied down to Luka Catano."

"Whoa, your tone, Cherie, dial it back. What has caused you to be so upset?"

"Luka is awful, for one. How could you force me to marry such a jerk? I don't think I can do it. He's insufferable and loves to antagonize me."

"Does he now?" My father sits down. His face is tight and I want to backtrack, knowing he won't put up with my sassiness. "What has he done?"

"He had someone follow me tonight. I didn't realize it was his guy and I attacked him."

My dad chokes back a laugh. "That's my girl. But really, Luka was just trying to protect you. What is the harm in that?"

"It's not just that—it's the way he acts. He's rude and inconsiderate and I hate him." My eyes fill with tears and they roll down my face. "I didn't realize he was such a terrible person."

"Give him some time. He's young. He's probably putting up a bit of an act, not sure how to be himself. I wasn't the nicest to your mother either, you know."

"She mentioned something like that. Doesn't make it right though."

"No, it doesn't."

The tears keep falling. "Dad, can we get out of this? *Please?*"

He's quiet for so long, I wipe my face and start to feel hopeful.

"Dad?"

"I'm afraid not, Cherie." He clears his throat. "Too much is at stake. Our countries need this. Give him a chance. Get to know him. Go to the counseling."

"So it's true? You did set up the counseling? This is crazy," I yell.

"Eden, you have always known the cost and you have always been willing. Don't lose your head over there. Your temper cannot get the best of you. We are in contract with his family and you know it. Break that and we will have a war on our hands."

"But I thought I had a father who—before anything or anyone else—would fight for *me*," I say quietly.

"You're completely out of line," he says sternly. "You're thinking selfishly here. You've come such a long way. Don't regress into selfishness."

"Goodnight, Father."

And for the first time in my life, I hang up on my father and despise the position I was born into.

I stay out of Luka's way as much as possible and he also stays at a distance—there but not vocal. Maybe he knows I can't be pushed right now because he doesn't even smirk my way. He looks at me; we make lingering eye contact, but neither of us seems up for a fight. After the last class, I fall into step with Tysa.

"I'm heading to the library. Wanna come?" she asks.

"Sure. I haven't been there since the tour."

"It looks the same." She shrugs, smirking. "The second floor is perfect for watching all the sex just waiting to happen—"

"People are having sex in the library?" I stop walking and look at her.

Her laugh is so loud, heads turn to see where it's coming from.

"You are so cute." She shakes her head. I know she didn't mean it as a compliment, but she's not being hateful either. "People are not having sex in the library...unfortunately. God, wouldn't that be a kick. No, it's where it all begins. The flirtations start—fluttering eyes, the brush of a hand here and there, and the occasional dry hump hidden behind the bookshelves."

"Dry hump?" I ask, frowning.

We turn the corner and enter the library, my mind full of images of couples and books. Tysa motions for me to sit at the table and pulls out a chair across from me.

"How do you not know what dry humping is?" she whispers.

I tilt my head and she leans in closer.

"It's when people come as close to fucking as they can with their clothes on..."

My face heats up and I look around to see if anyone could've possibly heard her. She laughs, eyes closing as she covers her mouth to be quiet.

"Ahhh, you should see your face. What hole have you been hiding in? I can see how you wouldn't have much chance to misbehave, being the sweet princess of the north, but seriously? No movies? Nothing?"

"I watch movies," I tell her. I don't add that the home theatre is stocked with movies that have been screened prior to me watching them. "I've seen things..." I add, rolling my eyes when she laughs harder.

"This is going to be so much fun," she says. "We need to find someone you can dry hum—" She cuts off when a loud clang sounds behind me.

We both turn around and see Ned Davenhall getting pushed down. I haven't met Ned yet, but he seems scared of his own shadow, and being nearly a foot shorter than even me, he appears to be at a disadvantage against the guy looming over him. I get up to see if Ned's okay just as the huge guy is pushed to the side. Luka is holding him up by the shirt, his feet lifted an inch from the floor.

"Pick on someone your own size," he tells the guy.

The librarian scuttles over to us and Luka backs away. He leans down and holds his hand out to help Ned up. Ned takes it and gives him a nod before scurrying away.

The librarian whisper-shouts to the guys and they both go sit in their respective seats. I can't help but watch Luka as he sits down, still breathing hard. That was decent. The guy has a temper that isn't pretty, but that was decent.

"Well, look at you, going all soft already. Is he getting to you?" Tysa asks quietly.

I flush again and she laughs. "No, I am not going soft. Just glad to see under all that Neanderthal, he has a heart."

Her lips pinch together and she nods like she can see right through me. "Mm-hmm," is all she says.

"Are we doing homework or what?" I ask.

"I'd rather pick the guy you're going to dry hump for the first time, but I think you've already chosen him," she says under her breath.

I roll up a piece of paper and throw it at her, laughing when it hits her between the eyes.

The librarian clears her throat and gives me a disapproving look. I fold my lips together and try to look busy. I didn't realize the library could be so exciting.

I glance over at Luka and my eyes narrow when he scoots his chair closer to the girl next to him. I don't recognize her. She's beautiful. Of course she is. I look around and don't see Nadia anywhere. I wonder how she'd feel about this and then feel ridiculous for thinking it a second later. It doesn't matter what Nadia thinks—I am his fiancé.

He catches me looking at him then, almost as if he can hear my anger ratcheting up.

His look is almost a dare...as if he wants me to confront him, as if he looks forward to it.

He turns to her and whispers something in her ear. His hand goes under the table and she leans into him, closing her eyes in enraptured bliss. Good god, what is wrong with him? And what's wrong with me? Why do I feel sick that it's not me he's saying sweet things to...

I can't watch anymore. I won't.

I lean forward and pick up my things. "I'm ready to go," I tell Tysa.

She shakes her head at Luka. "He doesn't deserve you."

CHAPTER SIX

My brother Jadon always knows the right thing to say. My hands shake as I Facetime him. He hates the phone, would much rather be outside practicing his sword work or riding his horse, visiting the poor people in our outlying villages and passing out food and clothes.

He's just that way.

Good.

Kind.

Always putting others first.

Where I was always selfish, as my dad so "lovingly" put it, Jadon has always been deep-down good. The antidote to my temper. When I can't see straight, I go to him.

"Edie," he says first thing. He's the only one I allow to call me that. His face crinkles up when he sees that I'm upset; his smile falls off of his face immediately. "What's wrong?"

I start to cry and feel terrible because he looks so worried. It just makes me cry harder. "Did you know Luka Catano is the worst kind of person?"

"What do you mean? What's happened?"

Jadon has spent time with Luka. They went hunting together with our father and Luka's two years ago. He assured me then that it was a good match, that I'd be safe with Luka.

"He chases anything in a skirt. The first day I woke up in my new room, I saw him and Princess Nadia in their underwear. You know, Nadia Forbrush? Why didn't his parents set him up with her? They seem like they've got a good thing going. Tonight he was flirting with someone I didn't even recognize and he can't stand me. He takes every opportunity to put me in my place. Saying *we're not married yet.*" I wipe my eyes. The tears keep falling and won't stop.

Jadon sighs. "I think he's had some sort of relationship with Nadia off and on, but it would never work. And I don't think he's interested in anything more than, you know... being a guy."

"You mean fucking around?" I say it with all the anger I feel and Jadon's eyes go wide. "You've always been so careful with me. You especially, but all of you. You think I don't know what's going on despite being sheltered my entire life? I've saved myself for him and he's slept with half the female population by now. I expected some of that, but not right in front of my face. How is this right?"

"It's not, you're right. Once he got to Kings Passage, he should've cut off all ties with anyone but you."

"How about when he signed a contract to be engaged to me? How about then? I guess it'll be okay then if I just go out and dry hump everyone in sight."

"Eden!" Jadon's voice cuts through and makes me jump. "Dry hump? What are you learning over there?" He chuckles and then swipes his face with his hand when he sees the look on my face. "Focus on school. You've wanted to go there your whole life. This is your chance to study with the best of the best. I'll talk to Luka. I can't promise he'll listen, but I'll try. Are you sure you're not reading into the situation?"

"No, it's all clear as day, trust me."

"I'll talk to him, and listen, if things don't change, we'll talk to Dad, okay? Keep me posted. I love you, Edie."

"I love you, Jadon. Thank you."

As always, by the time we hang up, I feel calmer.

I was just shy of fourteen when the contract was signed. We would marry at the completion of our first year at Kings Passage. Luka's family countered with the amendment to marry when Luka and I turn twenty, which would be upon the completion of our second year. Our third and fourth year would be almost exclusively spent learning together, our classes specific to the industries of our countries. Agriculture, finance, and sociology based on the statistics of our countries would be the main courses, so we'd both be versed with the best approach to leading them.

At fourteen, having seen Luka's pictures and watching video clips of him surfing in the Labyrinth Sea—well, I was spellbound. Under the notion that all of this was so romantic.

A fairy tale.

I would've agreed to anything just to be Luka Catano's queen.

Joke's on me.

———————————

The next week passes without any altercation. I keep my head down and my focus on schoolwork, just as Jadon told me to do. He's right about one thing—I've always wanted to study here and I don't want anyone, especially Luka, to divert my attention from that. I've been stuck with Farrow tutors up until now and while they were brilliant, I grew bored early on, my mind bursting with the need to expand past what they could or *would* teach me.

Luka attempts to stop me one day after our last class. He calls my name and I ignore him, walking faster. I think I've lost him and turn back to go to my room. He's standing there leaning against my door when I walk up.

I sigh and punch in my code, making sure he can't see it. "What are you doing here?"

"Why are you ignoring me?"

"It's easier to not hate you if I don't have to talk to you," I tell him.

His head tilts to the side. "You don't hate me."

I bite my lip and open the door. "Pretty sure I do."

"It's all the sexual tension between us," he says, smirking. "You don't know what to do with that." He runs his fingers through his hair and I watch the way his bicep bulges with the lift. He gives me a deadpan expression and I turn around, frustrated that he caught me looking. He puts his hand on my arm and I look at him over my shoulder. His fingers run up and down my arm and I wonder if he's aware of my whole body tensing with his touch.

"You know nothing about me." I walk away from him, setting my bag down and go out to the balcony.

He follows me out. "You're right. So tell me something about you."

I turn to him, a sharp retort ready, but he looks sincere and I swallow down my anger. "You don't want to know anything about me," I whisper.

"I do." His voice sounds raspy and he swallows hard when I study him. "Come on, just one thing..."

"Autumn in Farrow is my favorite time of year. It's the

last hurrah before winter begins and once winter arrives, it's there for what feels like forever. We have bonfires in the mountains and dare each other to get in the already frigid water, roasting marshmallows and shaking as we try to dry off. My brother always wins the challenge in the village to swim the farthest, but last year, my sister pushed him in the water after he'd finally dried off because she was so mad he'd beaten her again."

Luka chuckles. "It sounds like you miss them."

"I do. More than anything. I've never been away from them. I don't like it."

"I've never been close to my family. Well, except my sister, but even so...I wouldn't know what missing feels like."

"It's an ache that never goes away. A feeling here," I put my hand in the middle of his chest and tap three times. His hand comes up over mine and holds it. "A constant emptiness right here. Like a part of me is missing."

He assesses me, his eyes not giving away what he's thinking. When he swallows, it draws my attention to his throat and I pull my hand away.

"Sounds bloody terrible," he says and I laugh.

"It is. But better than not having them at all. I don't know what I'd do without my family."

"You'll miss them then...when we move to Niaps."

The word *we* makes my heart stutter, and the fact that he's talking about us being together with anything other than dread...

"I will," I say quietly.

He nods. "We could stand to learn some of that loyalty in Niaps."

He seems like he wants to say more, but he doesn't and we both turn to look at the water, watching the waves crash against the shore. It's the most peaceful feeling I've had with Luka since we met.

After a few minutes, he pushes away from the balcony and turns to me. "Did your parents say anything to you about the obligations you'd have to fulfill as my fiancée? The meetings, banquets, charity lunches?"

"They mentioned it, yes. When will it start?"

"This Friday night. There's a welcome reception at the conservatory at seven. Formal attire. Can you be ready to leave at 6:50?"

"You sound like you're making a business transaction." I try for a joking tone, but it comes out plaintive.

"It's what we are, right?" His eyes are back to being bottomless oceans of blue that want to bury me and I turn back to the real ocean of water.

"Right." I stand there for a moment feeling lost and decide I've had enough. I walk to the door. "I need to finish up some homework."

"I'll see you Friday."

And just like that, all the peace is gone. The moment we had is lost.

CHAPTER SEVEN

When Friday rolls around, I have more homework than ever, have slept maybe a total of five hours over two nights, and the last thing I want to do is go out with a fiancé who hates me. Brienne hovers, knowing I have to be ready in half an hour and I still haven't decided what I should wear.

"Why don't you sit here and I'll help," she says when I've sagged against the armoire yet again. "First, your hair..."

I fall into the chair, grateful. When she starts her magic on my hair, I settle into a dreamlike state. "You really are good," I whisper.

She holds up my makeup palette and I nod, happy for her to take over. I close my eyes, feeling more relaxed by the moment.

"Okay, open," she says. She's turned me away from the mirror and when I try to peek, she shakes her head. "Not yet." She grins and I decide it's not so bad having her around all the time.

"There's a dress I can't wait to see on you—one sec, I'll get it." She goes to the armoire and shifts the hangers to the side as she searches for it. Finally, she holds up the dress.

"This one."

It's a dress I managed to get past all the overdone dresses my mother's seamstress made for me before I left. I smile and nod and Brienne lights up. She helps me put it on and it's the perfect satiny glove for my curves. She steps back and laughs.

"Not exactly the reaction I'd hoped for," I mutter.

"Oh no—I'm just imagining Prince Luka's face when he sees you!" She claps her hands and I can't help but get caught up in her excitement. "Here…" She turns me around to face the mirror.

I blink slowly…shocked by what she's managed to create in such a short amount of time. I have the perfect smoky eye, red lips, and my hair is twisted into a low sweep of curls and twists. It's the perfect juxtaposition to the sexy low-cut black dress with the high slit that nearly reaches my lacy thong.

There's a knock at the door and Brienne steps back as I go to open it. Luka is looking down the hall when I open the door and when he turns to look at me, he seems to freeze. He stares into my eyes for the longest moment and when his gaze finally lands on my lips, they stay there for five long seconds. My heart must be beating out of my chest. His Adam's apple bobs as he does the slow descent down my body. My skin feels every drag of his eyes.

He holds out his arm and I step forward, feeling like I'm sleepwalking.

Neither of us says a word as we walk to the waiting car. Out of the corner of my eye, I've taken in the details of his suit, the way he suddenly oozes power and intrigue, the intoxicating scent of him, his full lips puckered in thought, his brow furrowed ever since we got in the car.

I wish he didn't look so perfect.

And that my heart didn't pound every time I look at him.

"Are you okay?" I ask.

"I'm fine." He hasn't looked at me since we left my room.

"You look nice," I tell him. I fidget with the clasp of my shoe and the slit in my dress widens, exposing my skin up to my thigh. He stiffens next to me and looks out the window.

"Cover yourself."

"What?" I think I must have heard him wrong.

He motions with his finger, turning to look at me after he's waved it around my leg. His eyes are breathing fire. "Cover. Yourself," he orders between his teeth.

I stare him down. "No." My insides feel shaky, but I don't look away. "If you can't handle yourself, look away."

His eyes flare brighter and his whole body turns to face mine. One finger lands on my thigh and skates up my skin, slowly, slowly, until every inch of me is gooseflesh.

"You want to play with fire?" he asks, his fingers softly tracing their way up my leg.

His eyes drop to my cleavage and his tongue snakes out to lick his bottom lip. I watch every movement entranced, aching for something *more*.

Every part of me is reaching out for him without me moving an inch.

More.

I don't dare move.

More.

My body begs for more and my heart begs for less.

He lowers his head and runs the tip of his tongue up the valley between my breasts, and I stop breathing altogether. When he makes his way up my neck and veers off to my ear, I turn, and his mouth is so close if I even inhale, our lips will touch. I test it out, breathing deeply, and our lips brush for the tiniest second, sending a jolt through me nonetheless. He stays close, his mouth hovering so it brushes mine with every breath, and when his lips finally claim mine, I collide into him.

It isn't a soft, sweet first kiss.

It's a crushing flood, a storm, an arrival.

My fingers grip his hair, pulling him even closer.

His fingers move up between my legs and I gasp when they swipe underneath my lace. I groan into his mouth when his fingers rub over me and then he slips one finger inside, thrusting one, two, three times, as he pulls back and stares at the way my lips fall open.

More.

Just as I choke down a moan, he lifts his finger to his mouth, popping it inside and licking it clean.

"I knew you were wet for me." He leans back in his seat, leaving me cold and empty. Mission accomplished.

I stare at him waiting for him to say more, to come back and finish what he started, but he's done. Point proven.

Humiliated, I turn away from him. The rage inside burns as I hold back tears for the next minute it takes to arrive at our destination.

When our driver opens the door, a crowd of people are waiting; photographers snap pictures, some getting in our faces, and the guards push them back at the last second. It's more extreme than what I'm used to—Farrow is more subdued than Pravia.

"Is it true you're engaged to be married?"

"When can we expect a wedding?"

"Have you chosen a designer for your dress?"

So many questions are shouted at us, but neither of us answer the reporters.

We haven't given a statement about our engagement yet, but the rumors have been swirling for over a year now about it. I don't know if it was my family or his who leaked it.

We get to the end of the walkway, and under an arch heavy with flowers, we stand and pose for what will be our first official photograph together. Since I still want to kill him, it takes everything in me to put on a smile and lay my hand on his chest as he winds his arm around my waist. When his hand ventures south, I grit my teeth.

"Move your hand an inch lower and I will make you suffer," I tell him, never letting the smile leave my face.

"Don't pretend you don't want it." He chuckles under his breath and squeezes my waist tighter.

The doors open and we're greeted by another slew of people. The queen of Pravia waits on her throne, looking regal and stunning with her blood-red dress. When we meet her, she looks at me with interest, but when she turns to Luka, she looks like she might inhale him.

"Such a beautiful couple," she says, her eyes still roaming Luka. "Are the rumors correct—will you be marrying?"

Luka lowers his head and kisses her hand. "According to our fathers, yes."

"And according to you?" she asks.

His voice softens and I can't hear what he says next. Whatever he said makes her smile. Louder, he says, "If she'll have me." He looks at me then. "And on the way over here, she finally let me know she would." His mouth twitches as he struggles not to laugh and all the blood rushes to my face. His grin widens as he watches my fury and then he turns to the queen. "You are the first to know." He lowers his head once again and then moves by my side.

"I'm honored," she says, still looking amused. "Enjoy your evening. Thank you for coming."

"What did you say to her?" I ask when we walk away.

"You heard me."

"No, when she smiled. What did you say?"

"I said since she wasn't an option you would do."

CHAPTER EIGHT

The dinner is mostly bearable. Good food, tolerable people, and then there's Luka. Once we're done eating, the music begins and most couples step onto the dance floor for at least one dance. When I've sat there for nearly an hour with Luka chatting up the couple next to him and acting as if I don't exist, I decide to walk to the dance floor. It doesn't take long for a guy to come up to me and ask me to dance.

"James Follows," he says.

"Eden Safrin."

His eyes widen, but he doesn't comment on my name. "Would you like to dance?"

He holds his arm out and I accept gratefully, comforted when he places his hands on my waist. I let the music take over my mind for the few minutes we move around the floor and am in a daze when James suddenly freezes. The next thing I know, Luka steps in to take James's place. I turn to thank James for the dance, but he's already halfway across the room.

"You like to dance?" Luka asks.

He puts his hands where James's had been, yet his

hands feel completely different. I don't want to think about how he makes me feel.

Yearning. Breathless.

"Yes."

He steps closer to me then and I lay my head on his shoulder, giving in to the pull of his body. I can't look at him right now, so this is better. Safer. And yet, the closer I am to him, the harder it is to think clearly. The ride over comes back to me with sudden clarity. His hands on me, his fingers dipping into—God, what am I doing?

I step back and push his arms off of me. He steps forward, hands going to my arms to hold me still.

"Let me go."

"What's wrong?" he asks.

"Let me *go*."

He lifts his hands up and keeps them up as I move off of the dance floor. I make the mistake of looking back and see Nadia walk up to Luka. He smiles down at her and I see red. I rush outside and turn in circles until I see Luka's driver. I hurry to him and he stands straighter when I approach.

"Would you take me back to Kings Passage, please?"

"Alone?" he asks.

"Yes, Prince Luka is staying a bit longer and said I should ask for your help."

He studies me then and I'm certain he knows I'm lying, but he doesn't hesitate for long. "Certainly. Anything you wish."

"Thank you."

He opens the door for me and I step in. As we're pulling away, Luka comes out and watches us drive off. I can't force an ounce of pity for him. He deserves to walk a thousand miles in the intolerable heat...without any water...for days.

When we reach the castle, the driver opens my door and smiles as I step out. "I've worked for the Catano family for as long as Luka has been alive, you know," he says. He leans a bit closer and lowers his voice. "I think he's finally met his match."

"I'm pretty sure he would disagree."

He waits to see if I'll say more and I don't bother to explain myself. Finally, he shuts the car door and tugs on the bill of his cap. A car pulls up behind us and Luka steps out seconds later.

"As I said..." the driver says with a smile.

Luka storms up to me.

"You left," he says, his forehead furrowed.

I brush past him and walk inside the castle, heading to my quarters as fast as I can. He grabs my arm.

"Slow down. Talk to me. You can't just leave me at an event...the night we practically announce our engagement, no less. You made me look like an asshole. We're in this together."

"Since when?" I shrug his hand off of me. "Because it seems like you're just making up the rules as we go along. Fact is, I don't want to see your face any longer tonight, and I'll do just about anything to get away from you."

He stops walking behind me as I continue to race down the hall, and then I hear him jog to catch up. I feel his eyes on me, but I don't look at him. When I reach my door, I stop and turn to him and the look in his eyes stops me cold. He looks confused, like a little boy whose favorite toy has been taken away. I sigh in frustration and open the door, and when I see his mouth open, about to speak, I slam it in his face.

Not married yet, I remind myself again. The words bring more comfort every time I say them.

Brienne isn't in my room yet, probably expecting me to be back much later, or annoyed if she's been tailing me tonight. I enjoy having the room to myself as I strip out of my dress and take my makeup off. When I hear my door open, I throw my short purple robe on and turn, smiling, trying to put on a happy face for Brienne.

"I'm back earlier than—" I stop in mid-sentence when I see that it's Luka.

He stalks past me, glaring.

"You can't just barge in here." I put my hand on my hip and his eyes run down the length of me and back up again, excruciatingly *slow*.

"I don't need an invitation to come into my fiancée's room." His gaze is still wandering and I roll my eyes and walk past, muttering under my breath about changing my code.

His hands grab my waist and he pulls me flush against him. He stares at my mouth as I try to catch my breath, my chest heaving into his more than I'm comfortable with.

"We need to set a few ground rules," he says.

"Nope."

"Yes," he grits through his teeth. "I don't like the way things ended with us tonight. It does not set a good precedent for our marriage if you think you can treat me like that."

I want to pry his fingers off of my waist, but then he lowers his head and I'm so certain he's going to kiss me, I stop breathing. He hovers by my mouth for what feels like an eternity. When he pulls back just slightly, my breath shudders out and I collapse deeper into his chest. His hands wind tighter around my waist and I have to tilt my head back further to look in his eyes.

"This is much better," he whispers. "You think I can't

feel how much you want me? I can smell your desire."

"I'm not your whore," I seethe.

"Are you sure?"

I pull back and slap him. "Get out."

"Eden—"

"Go." I point to the door and he walks slowly to it, giving me one last look before walking out, slamming the door behind him.

The next day, Nadia is hanging on him again and he lets her. She juts her chest out and he traces his fingers along her neck and down to her cleavage as I walk past them in the corridor. His stormy eyes shift to mine, yet he doesn't release her. He continues staring until I have to look away.

I hate him. I hate him. I hate him.

I feel on the verge of tears, even after Tysa tries so hard to make me laugh during lunch. I end up going to my room for a few minutes before my afternoon classes, desperate for a break in seeing him. My phone rings and it's Dean Hightower.

"I need you in my office as soon as you're able, Princess Eden."

"It'll be okay that I'll miss class?"

"I'll send an excused absence. Just get here, please."

I hurry to the office and when I get there, I'm shocked to see my mother and Queen Cece already inside.

"What is going on?" I ask my mother as she rushes to hug me. When she pulls back, I study her eyes and she averts hers, clearing her throat.

"I'm sorry I didn't have time to warn you I was coming," she says. "No time to warn you at all."

"You're scaring the girl," Cece says, chuckling behind us. "Marrying my son is nothing to be scared of. Most girls would kill to be in your position."

"*What is going on?*" I repeat to my mother.

"Have a seat, Princess," Dean Hightower says, motioning to the chair next to my mother and Cece. I see another empty seat next to Cece and wonder if Luka is coming.

My mother turns to face me. "King Farthing of Alidonia is threatening Farrow and we need to make our alliance with Niaps public," she says. "Today."

"Threats? But what—" I clutch her hand and squeeze it.

"I was hoping my son would be here so we could tell you together, but you'll need to be married sooner. This weekend," Cece says.

"*What?*"

"I know it's not what we planned and you wanted this time at school, but I'm afraid we can't wait." My mother smooths my hair down and I lean away from her.

"We can announce our engagement today," I tell her. Tears start running down my cheeks and I fling them off. "Luka told the Queen of Pravia last night. That should be enough to make them back off."

"Your father thought you'd say something like this and I told him I'd come and help you see reason. The wedding must happen immediately." My mother's voice barely lifts with inflection as she speaks, but I hear the underlying anger in her tone.

"Since we are closer to Niaps, the wedding can be there," Cece says. Her eyes sweep down me, reminding me of her son's in the way that I feel she can see right through me. "I have a tailor who started working on your dress the moment he knew I was coming to get you."

"But I want to get married at home and in the dress I've picked out..." I put my head in my hands and cry harder.

And that's when Luka walks in.

I lift my head up to him and his face goes white. "What's wrong?" He rushes over and squats down in front of me, grabbing a tissue from Dean Hightower's desk and dabbing my face. "Someone tell me what's happening right now," he demands. "Are you hurt?"

I don't know if I'm more in shock over his soft, caring voice, or the fact that by this time next week, I'll be his wife.

"She's just fine," Cece answers, standing up and moving behind Luka. She puts her hand on his shoulder and he stands up, looking angry.

I wipe my face and press my lips together, trying to will my shallow breaths into calming.

"You'll need to be married this weekend, rather than the date we agreed upon," my mother says. "Eden is just in shock and doesn't want to get married in Niaps."

"I don't want to marry him *at all*," I spit out.

Cece's gaze sharpens on me and she turns to her son. "Luka?" she asks, as if he'll clue her in on why I'm being so unreasonable.

Luka lowers his head and I watch as the color returns to his neck and cheeks. "We've had our differences," he says, shrugging. "We needed this time in our engagement to get to know one another. What's going on?"

"There's not much time to talk about it now. Our jet is waiting to fly the four of us to Niaps so we can start preparing for this wedding."

"No," Luka says.

"What do you mean *no*?" My mother stands up and moves closer to him. "It's in the contract. You will marry."

"I'm not disputing that, but we will do it when we're ready."

"Tell him, Cecilia—"

"—Father told me a little bit about what's happening with Alidonia," he interrupts. "We'll announce our engagement tonight, but I want Eden to have the wedding she wants. We'll do it in Farrow or not at all."

I look at him, and my heart skips a dozen extra beats. *More.*

"And I'd prefer her to *want* to marry me before we exchange vows, but we can't always get what we want, can we?" He smirks his Luka Catano smirk at me and I want to rip his head off and also kiss him until he can't say another idiotic, infuriating word.

I turn and stare straight ahead, unable to look at him another second. "What is another year or two?" I wipe my face and stand up, walking quickly to the door. "If it really will change things for us, I'm willing." I have to force the words out, but I say them anyway, knowing that my world is about to turn upside down.

Later, on the jet to Farrow, as I sit next to my mother and across from a sleeping Luka and his mother, I replay his comment and wonder when he changed his mind about wanting to marry *me*. Or if that was even what he meant.

I hate that I feel the slightest twinge of hope.

His eyes open and he stares at me for a moment, almost as if he can hear my thoughts whirling about him, then closes them again and goes back to sleep.

I've turned into a stupid girl with stupid dreams, none of which included marrying a man who doesn't want me.

CHAPTER NINE

When we near Farrow, I sit on my hands to stop fidgeting. It hasn't even been that long, but it feels like forever since I've seen my family. The mountains and water feel like security blankets wrapping around me, cradling me home. I stare out the window, soaking it all in, anxious to hurry up and land.

"You seem happier," Luka says.

Startled, I turn to him. I take in his amused expression and turn back toward the window. "It's been a long flight. I'm ready to get there already."

"Did you sleep?"

"Who can sleep when they're about to get married?" My tone is dry and he chuckles. "Although, you didn't seem to have any trouble," I add.

"I'm accustomed to not getting any say in the direction my life goes...especially the life-altering choices." All the humor has left his voice and I turn sharply to look at him. Cece frowns and his eyes drill into her, daring her to argue. "You'll get used to it too," he says, turning slowly to face me again.

It's the first time I've thought that maybe Luka is an old soul underneath all his swagger.

"I didn't even get to tell Tysa goodbye."

The pilot interrupts us then, reminding us to fasten our seat belts. "We're making our descent into Farrow, where the weather is sunny but a brisk six degrees Celsius. We should be landing in about ten minutes."

"We're gonna freeze our asses off, Mother." He turns to Cece and nudges her.

"This is nothing," I say. "Next month and the one after that are when you'll feel the cold."

"You must be sweltering in Pravia," Cece says.

It's the first time she's said a full sentence to me since I said I didn't want to marry her son. It's been a quiet plane ride.

"I've only been into town once and I did get pretty hot, yes." I don't dare look at Luka. That afternoon still makes me livid every time I think about it.

She doesn't respond but studies me for a few piercing moments then looks out the window. She's an unusual woman. Intimidating and quick with the retorts. I was swept up the first time I met her, I realize. Infatuated with the glamour that is Queen Cecelia Catano. Now I wonder who she really is. Someone I don't need to push too far would be my guess.

The rest of the flight is quiet except for the flight attendant bustling around and the pilot giving us final instructions for landing. And then we're in my country again. I immediately feel calmer.

From the plane, we get into a helicopter that takes us the rest of the way. Our landing pad is on the roof of the east wing of our house, and pride swells inside of me as we glance down at the breathtaking mountain peaks and see the Safrin home—what some would call a castle—nestled in the crevice of one of the mountains.

"It's beautiful," Luka says.

I glance at him, grateful for the kindness, and then I regret looking. His jawline is sharp, his nose slightly pointed but perfect for his face, but his full lips and the shocking depth to his blue eyes mixed with his light hair all lend to such beauty, it's hard to look away. I feel my face flush and I force myself to think about everything but him.

When we land, the family is waiting to greet us. Jadon and Ava stand in the front, and Father is just behind them. Father steps forward as we step off, clutching my hands before hugging me. I keep my hug brief, still too angry about the situation to linger. He greets Luka and Cece as I make a beeline for Jadon.

"You okay, Edie?" he whispers, pulling a face.

"No."

"We should raid Alidonia and be done with it," Ava says.

Everyone stops and stares at her.

"This is the twenty-first century. It's ridiculous that my sister should have to marry anyone for political gain. We really should be more progressive than that." Her dark eyes burn into Luka's and he grins.

"What are you, twelve?" he asks.

She stands up taller—it's really getting to her that she's not had a big growth spurt in a long time. "I'm fifteen." Her voice is indignant and it just makes him laugh.

"Right. Well, I happen to agree with you, Ava Safrin," he says and offers her a killer smile.

She pinches her lips together and tries to keep her smile down. Her eyes are gleaming when she looks at me and I want to yank her out of the room and warn her to not be lured by him. It's already too late—one tiny exchange and my contrary little sister is won over by Luka.

Luka and Jadon do the man handshake, bumping and clasping and a one-arm hug. I want to pinch Jadon too. Where is the loyalty? But it hasn't been that long before I was a swooning girl who couldn't wait to marry Luka, and he and Luka seem to have some sort of friendship on their own, so I guess I can't blame them.

We all make our way inside, where Mother is waiting. She shows Cece to her room and leaves me with Luka. I don't bother saying anything, simply holding my hand out when I open the door to his quarters. He stalks in and turns around to face me, reaching past to shut the door behind me.

"Did you mean what you said about getting married this weekend?" he asks. He stands so close I can feel his breath on my forehead.

I stare at his neck and nod.

"Are you certain?" He waits for me to nod again and then nods himself. He takes a step back. "We should come to an agreement now so there's no confusion later. We're too young to be married. I want to be honest with you and let you know that I will pursue other interests."

I swallow hard and raise my head to the ceiling, willing my emotions to not take over. Tears threaten to spill and I don't want to risk that humiliation. "I wouldn't expect anything but that from you." I skirt past him and walk to the window, looking out at the vast mountains spread out around us. I gave him the room with one of the best views. "As long as you're okay with me pursuing mine."

I feel him move behind me and it takes a moment for him to speak. "Of course. However, I won't be humiliated, so you'll have to learn to be discreet...something I'm not sure you're capable of—"

I don't say anything, measuring my breaths and trying to shove my anger back down.

"Eden?" He steps closer, so his chest is against my back. I close my eyes and try to drown out the heat that comes whenever we touch.

"There are a lot of things I'm capable of that you'll never experience."

"I guess we'll see about that."

I press my lips together and turn around, nodding briskly. "Okay then. I better go see what the plan is." But neither of us move.

"I can come with you..."

"Not necessary."

He opens his mouth to say something and I shake my head, finally moving past him. He walks over and holds the door, watching as I walk away.

When I reach my father's study, I hear my mother talking and she sounds worked up. I tap on the door and open it without waiting for an invitation.

"Will you at least tell me what is happening with Alidonia to warrant such a drastic change in plan?" I stand over my father's desk and he stands up to walk around it, putting his arm around my shoulder.

"Trust me when I say I wouldn't have asked this of you unless it was urgent. We need the joint forces of Niaps— they need to know we have powerful allies."

"That tells me nothing."

"Eden!" my father spits out in frustration. "We do not have time for a temper tantrum. You wanted nothing more than to be married to Luka a couple of months ago. I ask you to look back at the sacrifice you were willing to make then and make your peace with it now. You speak about wanting to serve your country—it is time."

"I will marry Luka. Tonight. Will my dress be ready in time?" I ask my mother.

She smooths her dress down and stands up, thrown by my sudden change of heart. "Adrian is working on it now. I need to take you to her for a fitting and any last-minute changes. But it's getting late. We can surely wait until tomorrow?" She looks at my dad and he says nothing.

"Seems paramount that we do it tonight." I can't stop the bite in my voice and I ignore the look my dad gives me. "Let's find Adrian."

She hurries over to me and we leave the office. She takes my arm as soon as we shut the door. "It will all be okay, Eden. I have to believe that the good feelings you had about this in the beginning are key."

I ignore her and let her lead me to where Adrian is working. When we enter the room, she is standing in front of my beautiful white beaded gown. The sleeves are long, but the neckline is low; the intricate diamonds glistening in the light make it glow.

"I would like to be married outside by the waterfall. It's not frozen yet, right?"

"You'll be chilly, Eden. Why don't we have it in the ballroom? We have plenty of flowers to make it beautiful."

"I'd like a white fur stole, faux is fine, to wear over my dress," I speak over my mother and her brows furrow in the center as she frowns down at her hands. "That shouldn't take long. The dress looks ready. We can still be married by eight."

Adrian clasps her hands together. "A fur wrap will be perfect over this. I have just the piece."

"Hear that, Mother? *Perfect*." I turn and leave the room.

"Wait, don't you want to try it on?" Adrian asks.

"I trust you got it right," I tell her and she beams.

I walk down the dark hall to my bedroom, shut the door behind me, and lie down on the bed.

I've dreamed of my wedding countless times in this bed.

Now that it's happening I feel nothing but dread.

Naive for thinking anything close to a fairy tale could ever come true.

Shame...for the way my body constantly betrays me when I'm around him.

I don't stay idle for long. I take a long bath and after I've applied my makeup, I start on my hair. I decide to wear it up the way Brienne fixed it for the conservatory gathering, and realize I haven't seen her since we got here. I've gotten used to having her company. Maybe she could help calm me down from this madness.

My mother raps on the door while I'm spraying a light mist over my body and hair, the smell of jasmine and vanilla filling the air. She walks in with my dress and a fur stole over it, looking subdued. Ava steps in behind her and sits on my bed. They're both dressed in new gowns that Adrian must have already been working on for another occasion. Brienne stays near the doorway.

"Come in, Brienne," I say over my shoulder.

"I'm good here, Lady Eden. Thank you."

"You're a valued part of our family. Come on in," Mother tells her and then faces me. "We came to help you get dressed. It's time."

Ava hops down from the bed and comes to stand by me. "Your hair looks pretty." She looks at me in the mirror and then turns to touch the diamonds in my ears.

I let them help me into the dress, numbly going through

the motions. When the wrap is placed around my shoulders, I turn and walk to the door.

"You're a vision," my mother whispers. She shakes herself a bit and holds out her arm for me to take. "Come, let's not keep your Luka waiting."

I fall into step beside her, feeling like a puppet walking numbly to my fate.

CHAPTER TEN

When I step outside the family castle into the crisp air, I feel my identity fall off, just like the leaves of the trees as they die every year.

I'm shedding my old life, leaving it to become part of the earth around me. I will be leaving my heart here while carrying a shell of myself to Niaps.

Seeing Luka snaps me out of my morbid thoughts and I stop mid-stride. He's a stunning solitary figure against the dark mountain behind him. Lights are hanging overhead, casting a spark on him that has nothing to do with marrying me. He's already let me clearly know that he will be sleeping with other people—I can interpret pursuing other interests despite my inexperience—which is already incredibly demeaning. To know the last thing he wants is to be stuck with me leaves me feeling desolate. More alone than I ever thought possible on my wedding day.

A cello plays a woeful tune as I walk toward Luka Catano, my father by my side—fitting, considering the solemn mood of the evening. My father kisses my cheek and puts my hand in Luka's. We turn and face the priest, but I look over my shoulder and see Jadon's reassuring smile. I turn and try to pay attention to the priest's words, but I can't focus. The ground blurs at my feet and I wonder if I'm going to pass out. Luka nudges me and I realize it's my time to speak. I only know I've said the words when Luka nods; I barely hear him say, "I do."

A ring is slipped onto my finger and the priest produces one for me to put on Luka's finger.

It's the kiss that forces me out of my stupor. When Luka's lips touch mine, my nerve endings wake up and I lean into him. His hand clasps my cheek almost tenderly and my eyes pop open. His eyes are clenched closed and he looks as if he's in pain. I break the kiss and back up, breathless.

I'm married—I should be elated, floating on air. But I'm empty.

It's all a lie. A façade. I want to run and never look back.

But I can't. It's hopeless.

Our priest announces us and everyone claps. The cello swells into a happier tune, Luka takes my arm, and we face our family. It's then that I realize Luka's father is standing next to Cece, a forbidding figure with a cold stare; Cece seems warm in comparison. I shiver when I see him, and Luka squeezes me closer through our linked arms. I glance at him and he gazes down at me with an unreadable expression.

"Hello, Mrs. Catano," Luka whispers.

I feel like the wind has been knocked out of me.

"You should eat something." Luka hands me a slice of bread and butter. "You'll need your strength," he says under his breath.

My eyes snap up to his. "I'll pass."

"We'll see," is all he says.

I used to dream of that smirk being directed at me, and now every time I see it, I want to smack it off his face.

"Settle down," he says. "Your face is doing that red thing it does when you want to choke me to death. I'd like to live today, please. We should at least have a truce on our wedding day."

I take a sip of my family's vintage wine and turn to face him. "Quickest way to have me choke you to death is to call me out on my red face. Little tip there for your future, Prince Luka."

He snorts. "You're funny." He chuckles and then goes completely straight-faced. I resist rolling my eyes because I've done far too much of that around him and I don't like letting him know when he bothers me.

I'd rather him think I'm completely unaffected by him—the opposite of how I truly feel inside.

He unarms me. I'm intrigued by him, yet I loathe him.

I eat a few bites of the risotto dish specially prepared for me and talk to Jadon, who is sitting on the other side of me, for the rest of the meal. I'm dipping my spoon into the exquisite raspberry tart when the explosion sends me to the ground.

The priest falls near my feet and I shriek.

Father runs to our table and yells. "Get to the tunnels and as soon as it seems safe, go with the Catanos. The rest of us will go to our safe house."

Another explosion goes off in the distance. Jadon and

Luka both put their hands on my arm, each trying to pull me to safety. We crawl to the side and Luka's parents and Ava are not far behind us. Jadon leads us to the tunnels, lighting a torch as we step inside and handing it to Luka.

"I'll be behind you. Follow this to the end and there will be a boat to the airstrip. Go with him, Eden, and I will send word to you when we reach our hideout."

I hug Jadon and Ava quickly, wiping my streaming face as we make our way through the barely lit tunnels. It feels as if we'll never get there, my heart rate still in high gear, and just when I think I can't stand the dark another second, we turn a corner and the opening is just ahead.

"Careful, son," Titus says before Luka steps out. I notice he doesn't offer to step out himself, but Luka doesn't hesitate. He walks out of the tunnel and looks around quickly before peeking his head back in.

"I see the boat and everything looks calm. I don't see another soul," he says.

We step out gingerly but then quickly move to the boat once we're all outside. I release a shaky breath of relief when we're all on the sand and I see that Brienne is with us.

"Your mother sent me to watch out for you," she says loud enough for everyone to hear. At this moment I've never been more grateful to have her by my side. I clasp her arm and nod.

No one speaks as Luka takes the oars and rows us at least ten minutes past the tunnels. The night is still, leaving no hints that explosions ever happened.

When we reach the airstrip and I see the plane waiting for us, I start to cry again. "I can't leave my family," I whisper to Luka when he helps me off the boat.

He makes sure his parents are off and the boat is secure then puts his arm around me and guides me to the plane.

"You're following your father's wishes," he says. "He wanted you to go with us."

"But why can't we all go to the safe house? I need to make sure everyone gets out of here safely."

Samuel greets us, a longtime employee of my father's. "I will be your pilot this evening," he says, motioning for us to climb the stairway up to the plane.

I take one last look around and Luka puts his hand on my shoulder. "They'll be fine, I promise," he says, tucking a strand of hair behind my ear. "We need to get out of here, though. I'll make sure you get to safety. Okay?"

I let out a long exhale and step onto the plane. It takes a moment for my eyes to adjust to even the dimmest of lights. Luka helps me with my seat belt when my hands are shaking too hard to clasp the two ends together.

Brienne sits alone across the aisle and Luka's parents face us. I feel like I'm on display as I sit there trying to not break down again. Luka takes my hand in his and it's then I realize I'm wearing a beautiful stone. I hold my hand out to look at my wedding ring. A large oval diamond with tiny diamonds surround it and under that is a diamond wedding band that sparkles like crazy.

"Do you like it?" he asks.

"It's beautiful," I whisper.

I lean my head back against the seat as the image of the priest falling at my feet plays through my head over and over. I feel Titus' eyes on me and it's unsettling. Something about him sets me on edge.

Tears keep falling and Luka squeezes my hand tighter. We take off and once the seat belt light goes off and Samuel tells us we are free to move around the cabin, Luka whispers into my ear, "Is there a bedroom on this plane?"

Alarmed, I pull my hand from his and look at him.

He smiles. "I just want to get out from under these watchful eyes." He leans back and waits for my nod before standing. "We're going to rest a while," he says to his parents.

Titus nods and Luka holds his hand out for me to take as we walk toward the back of the plane.

When he shuts the door behind us, I collapse onto the bed, sitting there in a daze.

"I wish we had something for you to change into," Luka says, pulling the covers down on the bed. "You must be ready to get out of that."

I don't hear any sexual undertones in his words for once and I'm so grateful. I look at him and try to smile. "Thank you." He looks confused, dropping the pillow and then putting it back in place. "For being kind," I add.

"I'm sorry this day has turned out to be such a nightmare." He pats the pillow, motioning for me to crawl into bed. "Come on, why don't we try to get some sleep. I don't even know what time zone we're on right now, but I'm exhausted."

I nod and drape my stole onto the back of a chair. My dress is bulky but not so full that it takes over the bed. I lie on top of the covers and Luka stands over me, studying me carefully. He takes off his jacket and puts it next to my fur. And then he lies next to me and says gruffly, "Would you be comfortable lying on your side?"

I turn to my side and feel his hands on my waist, pulling my back to his chest. I feel his breath on my hair when he sighs and I close my eyes. His arms feel so good around me, I think I'll never be able to sleep. I'll never be able to turn my mind off.

"Take a deep breath," he whispers in my ear.

I do.

"And another."

Luka has been so different today, almost sweet, I think as I slowly inhale and exhale one more time. Exhaustion suddenly takes over, and right before I fall asleep, I wonder which Luka I will wake up to.

CHAPTER ELEVEN

The pilot's voice wakes me and I sit straight up. Luka follows, his arm still grasping my waist.

"What? What is it?" His voice is raspy with sleep and the sound makes my stomach flip-flop.

"We're getting ready to land."

He rubs his hands over his face and puts his feet on the floor, getting his bearings. I put the stole over me like a blanket. It's chilly without his arms around me. He eventually steps next to me and we stand at the door, pausing before facing his parents.

"You slept?" he asks, his eyes grave as he looks at me.

I wipe under my eyes, hoping I don't have mascara everywhere. "Yes, thank you. You?"

I don't know why I'm suddenly shy with him, but I am.

"Like a rock. Woke up like a rock too." I think that's what he says, but I can't be sure because the pilot speaks again.

When we step out of the bedroom, Luka's parents are talking and don't acknowledge us, which is a relief. I expected them to tease us for sleeping together. We buckle up quickly and our landing is smooth.

"We'll be taking a short flight with one of our planes from here. Just a short flight," Titus says briskly. He turns to Samuel when he steps out of the cockpit. "Thank you for getting us here safely."

"My pleasure," Samuel says. He turns to me then and gives me a slight bow. "I wish you the utmost happiness, Lady Catano. I hope to see you again in better circumstances."

"Thank you, Samuel. I appreciate that. I hope so too."

He opens the door to the plane and when I reach the top of the stairs, I'm hit with scorching heat. Another plane sits a few hundred meters away and I follow Titus and Cece. Luka walks beside me, Brienne behind us. I don't know what to make of Luka's new demeanor. If this is him as a husband, it's not bad.

When we get on the Catano family plane, I am shocked by the extravagance. Our jet is lovely and spacious, but simple. Theirs is three times the size and feels like stepping into a luxurious living room. It doesn't even feel like a plane.

We buckle up and it seems we've barely taken off when we're landing again. This time I'm not so startled by the heat as I step off of the plane. We have no belongings with us, so it takes no time to get into the waiting car and drive to a deserted house nestled in the palm trees and overlooking the ocean.

"This is one of our family homes that is remote enough to be considered a safe house," Cece informs me as we step inside the home that looks like an extension of the jet, only less colorful. Everything is white but manages to look even more inviting. "It is yours now too. As long as you remain loyal to us, of course," she adds, smiling her enigmatic smile.

I swallow hard and nod. "Thank you. I don't suppose—there hasn't been any word yet from my family, has there?"

"Your father let me know when they arrived at their location," Titus says. "He said they will wait a week and make sure everything is clear before returning to Farrow."

I deflate, putting my fist across my mouth when my eyes well up again. "Thank God," I whisper.

"You should have told her as soon as you heard," Luka says, his words sharp with anger.

"I didn't want to disturb the two of you." Titus never seems to get ruffled. His tone is cool and unaffected. I wonder if he ever shows any emotion other than annoyance or disinterest.

"We will leave at nightfall so you and Luka can get to know one another better," Cece says. She goes to the refrigerator and opens it, showing me that it's fully stocked.

"You're leaving us here?" Luka speaks up before I can, and we both turn expectant eyes on her.

"Of course," she shrugs, "it's your honeymoon. What better place to be than a deserted tropical paradise? There are enough provisions to last you the week. You'll find clothes in your room." She points to a door. "That's the pantry and there's enough food in there to feed an army... otherwise known as Luka." She laughs and it makes me jump. I'm still shaken from the events of the night before... it's too soon to be so lighthearted. "There is also a full-time housekeeper and chef on-site who will take care of things should you wish to not lift a finger." Her lips jut out with an exaggerated smirk. "I'm sure they will be happy to serve you in bed."

"*Mother*." Luka puts his hands on top of his head and gives his hair a hard tug. He looks at me and I don't know what surprises me more—the apology in his eyes or the tinge of embarrassment on his skin.

She goes to him and lifts up to kiss each cheek. "Your father and I are no strangers to honeymoons. Enjoy your time here. We will send a plane to pick you up in a week and then depending on how stable everything is with Alidonia, we'll go from there with a new plan."

Luka looks at his dad, waiting for him to add to the conversation, but Titus has stepped to the windows and is looking out at the water.

"In fact, don't worry about us now. We will make ourselves busy until we leave tonight. Go, have fun. You deserve some fun after the stress of yesterday." She waves her hands, effectively shooing us out of the kitchen. "Your things are set up in the master bedroom. You can thank me later." She winks and I want to groan but manage to contain it.

Titus turns and clears his throat. "Don't forget—you must consummate the marriage for any of this to be valid."

"What?" My mouth drops open. "Is that true?" I turn to Luka.

He shoots his dad a look and grabs my arm. "Come on. I'll show you around."

We walk up the dark, planked staircase. When we reach the top, he stops and faces me. "It's true." He lowers his head and doesn't look at me. "I will make it good for you. I'm sorry it's all happening like this, but I promise I'll do my best to make you comfortable."

"I don't know why I didn't think it mattered, what we did once we were married." I shake my head, frustrated with myself. "I do trust you won't intentionally hurt me." That's the best I can do to be conciliatory.

He nods and leads me to the room at the end of the hallway, and when he opens the door, I gasp. The room is huge and bright from all the windows. To one side, there is a massive four-poster bed draped with white intricate lace and soft linens. On the other side are two white chairs sitting side by side, overlooking the water. But the show-stopper is the infinity pool. It travels the expanse of the room then leads outside, connected by a passage you can swim through, all jutting out over the ocean.

"The bathroom is just over there." Luka sounds almost shy as he points behind him. I can't stop looking at the pool.

"I've never seen a view like this, ever."

"It's always been my favorite of our houses," he says. He bends down and puts his hand in the water. "The water is perfect if you feel like a swim."

"I—I don't know how to swim."

"What?" He turns to look at me, the shock dropping when he sees my embarrassment. "It's okay. I can teach you. I've been swimming for as long as I can remember. Niapsians are practically born in the water. I suppose it's not like that in Farrow..."

"I've been *skiing* for as long as I can remember...and avoiding the water except to admire how pretty it is. Too cold." I scrunch up my nose and he stares at me, his eyes shifting from my eyes to my mouth. I lick my lips and his pupils dilate, his tongue reaching out to wet his mouth.

He clears his throat suddenly and I blink.

"You'll need to learn how to swim, living in Niaps. How about we try now? It will get our minds off of...everything."

"Shouldn't you be with your parents while they're still here?"

He scrunches his forehead. "I haven't spent time with my parents in years. No reason to start now. You've seen enough to know what they're like, haven't you? Cold, heart-less, controlling?" His eyes aren't as light as his voice.

"I hardly know them after one eventful night. Even the dinner with your mother the night we met, we were surrounded by other people. You're not close with your parents?"

"Is any prince close to the king?"

I think about that and about my own relationship with my father. I'd say he's closest to Jadon, and I'm closer to our mother. But I've never doubted his love for me or my siblings. It saddens me that Luka doesn't have that. What a lonely existence.

He goes into the closet and comes out with a deep blue bikini in one hand and a white bikini in the other. He shakes them and grins. "Look what I found!"

"Oh, great." I level him with a look. "Your swimsuits."

He laughs. "My Speedo is in the closet. These are yours."

My eyes widen and he laughs harder, tossing the white swimsuit to me.

"I'll be right back," he says, widening his eyes to mimic me. He stops right before he reaches the closet. "Do you need help with all those buttons?" He waves his finger at my dress.

I lift my hair and turn my back to him. When his fingers brush over my neck, jitters swirl inside my chest. He unbut-tons slowly, carefully.

"A lot of buttons..." His voice is hoarse and I look at him over my shoulder, causing my hair to fall down my back.

He steps closer and moves my hair forward. Neither of us moves for what seems like an eternity. I feel his chest moving up and down against my back, and I wait with bated breath to see what he'll do next. He lowers his head and I feel the softest whisper of a kiss against my neck. Goose bumps erupt on my skin and my nipples harden into a deep ache. When he reaches my waist and unbuttons the last button, he takes a deep breath and puts his hands on my hips.

"Or we can just stay right here," he says, turning me around.

I hold my dress so it doesn't gape open at my chest and his eyes fall to my nipples.

He steps closer and I lower my head to his shoulder. "We should wait until your parents leave," I say into his chest.

He lifts my chin so I can't look away. "Consider every moment until then preparation," he says. "Until you're so wet you can't think straight."

And then he kisses me senseless, stealing another piece of my heart.

CHAPTER TWELVE

One kiss and I'm lost.

He pulls away and rubs his thumb across my lips, his chest rising up and down against me. "You should put on that swimsuit before I rip this wedding dress off of you."

I pick up the suit that he must have dropped when he started kissing me, still clutching my dress to my chest, and rush to the bathroom. I shut the door behind me and lean against it, trying to catch my breath.

What was *that*? How is it possible that he completely blindsides me with one single kiss? What kind of game is he playing?

And what am I in for next...

I need to get ahold of myself before what I know will happen tonight.

I can't let him get in my head.

I can't.

I won't.

I open my eyes and see the bathroom for the first time. This place. There's a crystal chandelier hanging over the round jacuzzi tub—the largest I've ever seen. The shower looks like it could fit six people and still be spacious. More windows and not a single piece of fabric to cover the view. The blue water stretches out as far as I can see.

Even though we're about to go swimming, I take a quick shower, needing the cool water to bring me back to my senses. There are bowls of bath bombs near the tub and glass decanters of delicious-smelling shampoos and body washes near the tub and shower.

I could stay in this bathroom forever and be happy.

With clumsy fingers, I put on the tiniest scrap of white and stand in front of the full-length mirror. *Oh God. I can't go out in this.* I'm from the north and have extra insulation for all those cold months. He's used to rail-thin model types and I've got curves for days. My skin is so pale it's blinding.

He knocks on the door when I've been in there a while. "Did you fall in?"

I smile in spite of my nerves. "No, I'm still here."

"Let me see you."

I shake my hair out, letting the curls fall to my waist. I should probably put it back up...

"Eden!"

I jump and then relax when I hear him laugh. I go to the door and crack it open. He's standing just outside the door bare-chested and in his swim trunks, his hair already wet. He must have showered in one of the other bathrooms.

"No Speedo, thank God," I whisper through the crack.

His lips pucker as he holds in a grin. "You can't handle me in a Speedo. Tomorrow maybe." He eyes me lazily and I like the teasing glint in his stare. "Are you going to hide in there forever? Open the door and let me see you."

I open the door wider and his face goes slack. His eyes roam down the length of me and linger. I feel my skin flushing and put my hands on my chest, trying to hide some of it.

"Drop your hands," he demands.

I don't hesitate. I drop them.

He takes a ragged breath and holds out his hand to pull me the rest of the way out of the bathroom. Once I'm out, he grabs our hands up over our heads and turns me around oh so slowly. His eyes scorch me, roam every part of my body, heating me from the inside out.

"*Fuck. Me.* Where have you been hiding?" His voice is a husky rasp that I feel right between my legs.

He takes a strand of hair between his two fingers and gives it just enough of a tug to see the curl bounce back up, his hand brushing my stomach as he lets it go and I swallow hard. He doesn't miss a thing, his eyes tracking the pull of my throat. He puts his hands on my hips and pulls me against him. My head falls back at the feel of him and his tongue traces a line up my throat. Up and down, up and down.

His hands go lower and lower until he's got both hands on my cheeks, kneading them and then squeezing hard. He rubs up against me and my eyes close. "See what you do to me?" he asks, grinding into me once, twice, three times. I gasp and he leans back to look at my face. "You like that?" I can't form words. He puts his fingers on the exact spot I've been craving him and barely applies pressure there while I shudder to hold in a moan. "So responsive," he whispers. "I'm going to enjoy undoing you."

I duck my head, unable to look at him. He tilts my face up, and when my eyes reach his, I'm surprised by the softness there. The lust is still thick, and I can't help but smile at him. His lips tilt up and his fingers start moving over me, rubbing slow circles at first and then faster and faster. I lean my head on his shoulder and cry out when I can't take it anymore.

"That's it," he whispers.

His hardness bobs against me and just as I'm about to reach out and touch him, he backs up, holding his hands out for me to take. I do and he guides me to the pool. My eyes drop to look at him and my mouth waters. His thick tip is peeking out of his tented shorts. It will most certainly hurt, but I think I might welcome the burn. He adjusts himself and grins.

"Don't look at it, it'll just keep showing off." He winks.

I laugh and he grins even wider, his eyes crinkling.

"I like it when you smile," I tell him impulsively. I enjoy the playful side of him. A little too much.

He does a mock bow and then drops my hand and dives into the water. When he comes back up, rivulets of water drip from his hair and down his face, the sunlight hitting his skin just so, I can't believe my good fortune. Even if he's a world-class bastard, I have married the most exquisite man. It might all go downhill, but what if it doesn't? What if we can have fun together? No feelings...just pleasure. A business partnership with extracurricular activities...

"What are you thinking? Your face has had a hundred expressions flit across it in the last twenty seconds," he says. When I don't answer, he adds, "You're beautiful, you know...I could lose my mind with you in that white bikini. Are you coming in?"

He moves to the edge and I sit down, putting my feet in the water before sliding all the way in. He watches me like a snake about to strike. He glides over to me and puts my legs around his waist.

"The water gets deeper on the other side," he says, motioning to where the pool continues outside. "So in here, don't worry. Just stand up. Out there, it gets to twelve feet —" He looks at my lips and his arms tighten around me.

It's hard to pay attention to anything he's saying; he feels like a rock underneath me.

"You know what? I can't concentrate with you bouncing on my cock. And these," he glances down at my nipples brushing against his chest, "are begging for me to suck them. You're dangerous."

I choke on a moan as he gently unwraps my legs.

"Let's get this lesson over with and then eat, yeah?" He lifts his head to the ceiling and lets out an anguished sigh then motions to the edge of the pool. He shows me what to do with my feet and walks me through a few basic strokes. I follow each one and he nods, pleased when I've accomplished it. "Are you comfortable holding your breath underwater?"

"Yes. That I can do."

"I think you've got it then. Let's see your dog paddle."

I attempt it, feeling foolish, but he grins like I've mastered a marathon.

"And your breaststroke..."

That one is a little harder for me, but I can do a few strokes on each side before my feet touch the bottom again.

"Are you sure you've never swam?" He tilts his head, giving me the side-eye.

"I promise. No. You're just a good teacher." I grin.

He looks like a different person than when we were at school. His eyes are light and his smiles are far quicker. I could get used to this. I look away and try to not stare at him again.

"I think it's time to try underwater," he says. "Remember how to move your arms?" He does the motions and I copy him, nodding.

"I'm ready." I take a deep breath and go under. It takes a few tries of getting my nerves to fully let go. It doesn't take long for me to realize that this is by far my favorite way to swim. It comes much easier and I glide everywhere, finding the passage and coming up for air outside. Luka is beside me and he runs his hand along his hair, smoothing it back.

"Nice work," he says. "If you're as fast of a learner with sex as you are with swimming, you are going to be one fine fuck."

My face flames and I go back underwater so he can't see me. It's weird to be talking about sex so nonchalantly with him, and yet, when I think of the way we've been with each other from the beginning, it's not so crazy. We've never struggled with being direct. I just don't know how comfortable I'm going to be with sex. I hate that I don't know what I'm doing and that I want him so much. It's embarrassing. I'm obviously not thinking straight. I take another deep breath above water and go right back down.

He takes my hand and pulls me back through the passage. When we're on the other side, he faces me and touches my hair again. It's flying out everywhere like Medusa's and he looks entranced. For a second, I wonder if it's all an act to make tonight easier for me, or if it's possible that I'm getting under his skin too.

He reaches out and twists one of my nipples, just enough for me to feel the twinge. My mouth parts and his other hand goes to my hip, pulling me tight against him. We shoot up out of the water, and his hands move to my face as he kisses me like he can't wait another second. Our tongues find each other and I feel like I'm still floating even though my feet are firmly on the ground.

He devours me. Consumes me.

His hands dive into my hair and then travel down my back and lower and lower...

He picks me up and carries me out of the water. When he reaches the bed, he shifts the sheer lace out of the way and lays me back, standing over me like a god. I swallow hard and lean up on my elbows.

"I thought you wanted to eat first..."

"I do." He leans over me and plays with the string to my top. "Do you mind if I just...untie this?"

I shake my head and he unties the strings around my neck and then the ones around my back. When he tosses the top, I watch his eyes drink me in. It's a heady thing watching his face fill with lust...for *me*. I have a moment where I can't believe Luka Catano wants me and then it's all forgotten when he leans down and pulls my nipple into his mouth.

I can't breathe, can't think straight.

My eyes roll back.

His hand moves between my legs and when it dives beneath the material, I'm gone.

"Luka," I whisper.

His mouth lifts off of me with a pop. "Yes, Princess?" His eyes find mine and he moves to the other side, his tongue flicking me.

"When do your parents leave?"

He grins so wide it takes over his whole face. "You ready to get after it?" His tone is teasing, but his eyes are deep pools of want.

"Yes," I whisper.

"They left when you were in the bathroom earlier. I was just trying to not jump on you the minute they were gone. Give you some time to—"

I pull his mouth down to mine and kiss him hard. He

pulls down my bikini bottoms and tries to remove his own, but I move his hand, pulling them down and sighing into his mouth when I touch him. He takes a shuddering breath and then his hands are everywhere. He shifts out of my hand and moves down my body, his tongue leading the way. When he reaches between my legs, I'm so shocked I clamp his head between my thighs and he chuckles into me, his tongue lapping me until I shake.

He shifts up until he's lying beside me and puts his finger where his mouth has been. "You okay?" He adds another finger and then pulls out slowly, rhythmically, while he watches me.

"Mmm...ye—" My eyes squeeze shut when he rubs his other finger on the outside of me. "How do you know?" I whisper. And then I feel stupid. Of course he knows exactly what to do.

"Open your eyes. Look at me."

I open them and his face is over mine, his breathing coming out in slight pants now. He rubs against my thigh and I struggle to keep my eyes open.

"Your taste is my new favorite addiction." He pulls his fingers out, sucking them one by one, and shifts so he's lined up with me, then teases me by not moving. He leans down and kisses me. "My favorite poison," he whispers.

He slides into me slowly and I moan. His fingers move to rub between our legs where we meet and he pushes further in.

"Don't stop kissing me." The urgency in his voice is like the key to his invasion, opening me right up.

He dives in and I take all of him. Everything he has to offer.

I don't expect it to feel so good the first time, and it does hurt. But every time it gets painful, he's there kissing, soothing, and it changes into a good pain. When I start thrusting in motion with him, his head rears back and I feel him get even harder inside me.

"Oh," I moan.

"You feel so good," he whispers. He leans up on one hand, his other still moving between us, and stares at me like he's seeing me for the first time. I pulse around him and his eyes close. "I'm not going to last long with you doing that..."

The way he says it makes me feel like I'm doing something right. He starts moving again, faster this time, and I watch his face in wonder. He looks agonized but determined. I feel the flood of him inside of me and am completely ruined.

He will demolish me.

In a way, he already has.

CHAPTER THIRTEEN

"What do you think?" he asks, a few minutes later. He lies facing me, the closest thing to pillow talk I've ever had.

"It didn't hurt as much as I thought it would."

"Because you wanted me so bad," he says, grinning.

"You don't suffer much from humility, do you?"

"Not when it's obviously true, no."

I flush and look at his chest instead of his eyes. His fingers are lightly tracing over my skin, making goose bumps pop up everywhere despite the sweat we worked up.

"Hey," he tilts my face up, "where did you go?"

"I must seem so backward to you. So stupid. You hated me in the beginning; now you're being nice...I'm just wondering who you really are."

"I'm the bastard, remember? Still the asshole. You might be growing on me a *little* bit." He tweaks my nose and his grin drops when he sees I'm still not smiling back. "Did I rush you?" He leans up on his elbow and looks worried.

"No. I wanted to, remember?"

He drops his head back on the pillow and tucks the

edges under his face, his eyes wide. "You were like a vise around my cock. Next time will be even better for you..."

I don't have any complaints, but I don't tell him that.

"I'll run a bath for you and ring the chef. Are you hungry?"

I nod and he gets up and goes into the bathroom, while I watch his backside like a hungry lioness. When he's out of sight, I put my hand across my eyes and remind myself that I cannot fall for my husband.

I get up before he comes back and look at the sheets, realizing there's a cloth that contains all the proof of our consummation. "They really think of everything," I mutter out loud, pulling the fabric off to a spotless bed underneath.

Luka comes out and sees me holding the cloth. He walks over and takes the cloth, depositing it outside the bedroom door without a word. I hurry to the bathroom so he won't see me streaking across the room and step into the bath, sighing as I lean back into the fragrant water. I wash my hair and as I come up from under the water, Luka is sitting on the ledge watching me.

It's the way his eyes linger—take their time tracking every detail of me—that makes the blood rush to my head. I like his eyes on me. He reaches out and glides his hand down my body, and just like that, I'm ready for more.

"Your body is a revelation, Eden. I've never seen another so beautiful. I'm afraid it will haunt me—" He stops, as if he realizes he's speaking too freely.

"—When you're with another?" I say it boldly, like it doesn't shred my heart to say those words.

I watch his neck rise and fall when he swallows and looks away. "We won't speak of others on our honeymoon." His jaw ticks and I wonder if I've angered him. "Our food will be ready in half an hour. I'll give you some privacy until then. After we eat, I won't be so generous."

Dinner is a feast of fresh seafood grilled to perfection. I dip each bite in the lemon butter sauce and sigh in bliss. The meat of the fish is succulent and exotic compared to what I'm used to from home.

"I could eat this every day." I wipe my mouth with the cloth napkin and Soira, the woman who has served our food, asks if I would like more. I hold my plate up to what she is already dishing out and Luka watches us, amused.

"Me too," he says, grinning wider.

"Your wife is very beautiful and has a good appetite." Soira beams. "I'll bring the dessert tray out, but you keep eating this as long as you like."

"Thank you, Soira." Luka's eyes never leave mine, as he sits back sipping some sort of expensive scotch.

By the time Soira steps out with the desserts, I'm full, but they look too delectable to not at least have a bite. I pick out a small cake with fruit and chocolate drizzled over it. I take a bite and close my eyes, moaning over how delicious it is. I hear Luka laughing across from me and smirk when I open my eyes. Caught.

"One would think you've been schooled on the fine art of seduction," he says, eyes gleaming. He leans forward and when he can't quite reach, he shrugs and stands, leaning over to lick the chocolate that is still on my lips. He puts the next bite in my mouth and watches as my mouth closes over the fork. As he slowly pulls it out of my mouth, I lick my lips and he pounces.

He picks me up and puts my legs around his waist,

sitting back down with me on his lap. His lips tease me with little nibbles and licks and I squirm on top of him. I'm the greedy one.

"You want another bite?" he asks against my lips.

I give his lower lip a bite and his eyes widen before his tongue dives into my mouth. I'm wearing a short dress that I found in the closet...very few clothes in there, but more swimsuits and cover-ups for the week. He reaches under my dress and feels my damp scrap of lace.

"I want to care that you might be hurting from earlier, but the thought of you aching where I've been, remembering me long after I'm there, makes me so hard, I'm losing my mind. Tell me to stop if you don't want this."

I bite his lip again and get lost in his kiss. He rips my lace with one hand and pulls himself out, teasing me with the tip. When I've soaked him, he lifts me up and sets me back down with him firmly planted inside. I feel so full my head falls back and he nips at my neck, tongue tracing up to my ear.

"What would you like me to do to you, Mrs. Catano?" His words are raw and dirty and I cry out when he pinches my nipple. "Do you want it slow?" He moves agonizingly slow. "Or do you want it like this?" He rocks into me even harder and I can't breathe.

I can't form a coherent sentence, but hearing his words drives me crazy.

"Ride me." He gives my hair a tug and I start moving. His fingers move between us and work me until I go off like a rocket. He doesn't let up, thrusting up into me—faster, harder, and I see stars. Neither of us last long and I don't even care that I'm practically screaming as I squeeze every drop from him.

"Excuse me, Prin—"

Luka and I both go still when we hear a man speak. Who did Cece say would be here with us? I try to lift off of Luka, but he holds me firm.

"Leave us," Luka barks. "Can't you see we're—"

"I am so sorry, sir. It is an emergency. I would not interrupt if it were not urgent. Please meet me in the study when you are able. Both of you."

I hear him shuffle behind me and then it's quiet.

"I apologize for that. You're covered, he couldn't have seen much," he says, lifting me carefully off of him. I stand up, knees still wobbly and smooth my dress down. He adjusts himself and stands up, eyes worried. "We should hurry."

"What's going on?"

"I have no idea. The plan was we wouldn't have to speak to anyone but Soira all week...and she was to make herself scarce."

We go inside and I barely see the rest of the house as we walk to the study. When we step inside, the man is waiting. Brienne is next to him and my face flushes when I see her. I wonder how much she's seen or heard since we got here.

"This is Drake, head of our security when we're here," Luka says. He motions to me. "My wife, Eden." His voice is formal again. Back to cold Luka.

"Very nice to meet you," Drake says politely. "Please forgive my intrusion. I need you to return to Niaps. We have the jet waiting."

Luka's brows furrow and he shakes his head. "Why? Has there been a breach here?"

"No, nothing like that. I am afraid I cannot tell you the details, but your father will as soon as you've landed. He barely made it home and sent the jet right back."

"This makes no sense." Luka's anger is bouncing off of him.

I put my hand on his arm and he turns to me.

"Something must be wrong. We need to see what's happened. He wouldn't just do this for no reason."

"You don't know my father," he snaps.

"If it's nothing, maybe we can come back." I feel ridiculous as soon as I say it. And fearful...that the hope was heard in my voice, that he would know how desperate I am for more time with him, *just* him...

But he puts his hand on my cheek and nods. "You're right. We should get going. Let's go as we came, with nothing. It will all be here when we get back."

Drake opens the door and holds his hand out. "Right this way, Lady Catano."

When we climb on the plane and as I look out the window, I say a wistful goodbye to yet another place that now holds a special part of me.

CHAPTER FOURTEEN

"Thanks for teaching me how to swim." I lean my head against the seat and look at Luka.

"That's what stands out about our time in paradise? *'Thanks for teaching me how to swim?'*"

I shrug. "It was nice." I press my lips together and hold back my smile.

"*Nice.*" He shakes his head, a mock glare on his face.

It's strange—I feel I've gotten to know him far better since we got married. And not just that he can make me melt with one scorching look, but when he's teasing me, when he feels something, even shyness, and doesn't want me to see it. When he wants me as much as I want him. When his walls crack a little more...I wish we had the days at the Catano safe house so I could unravel more of him. I'm afraid he won't be the same, that the magic of that place holds a part of him he won't show just anywhere. And that thought has me wishing we could go back, or rewind time. I'm already mourning the loss of our time alone together.

"Nice," he repeats. He reaches across the plush chairs

and unbuckles my seat belt. "Come here. I'll show you how nice I can really be."

Brienne walks to the front of the plane and goes inside the cockpit, closing the door behind her. She's so quiet and still as a statue, I have a hard time remembering she's here.

I bite the inside of my cheek and shake my head. "I don't want to get caught again tonight, thank you."

"There's always the bedroom, but by the time we get in there, it'll be time to land." He tugs my hand and I make a show of acting put out over having to move. "I'll make it worth your while..."

"Don't mess me up when I'm about to see your mother." I sit on top of him, knees pressing against the back of the seat.

He lifts a mocking brow at my nerve and I know I'm in trouble. His hands find my ribs and he tickles me until I'm gasping and yelping. I laugh until I cry and he's laughing just as hard, both of us practically wheezing to catch a breath.

"Uncle!" I yell.

"Your uncle cannot save you." He can barely get the words out.

I finally get my hands on his side, tickling him, and he violently jerks to the right.

"Oh, you're not immune either, are you?" I dig into him and he sounds like a little kid, howling.

He captures my wrists and our laughter dies down. We're both breathing hard and can't look away from one another. He leans in and kisses me slowly, reverently, and I never want it to end. This kiss is everything—like a puzzle piece just clicked into place and I feel complete.

This time it's different and I wonder if he feels it too.

The slow, the sweet, the burn that is always ready to combust.

The pilot announces that we're about to land and I reluctantly move off of Luka. He reaches out and takes my hand in his and we're quiet until we touch the ground. So quiet I'd worry if he didn't smile at me when we stand up.

"Shall we do this?" he asks, motioning for me to go first.

My nerves ratchet up to an uncomfortable level. I'm at a disadvantage walking into Luka's home during an emergency, or whatever this is, having never been here and not knowing his family well.

A driver takes us to the family castle that looks like it could safely house the entire Kings Passage University and then some. I'm blown away by such displays of wealth. I wonder how it felt growing up never worrying if the winter would be too long, how the crops would survive, how the people in the villages nearby would make it. I've had a very comfortable life, and I've still never seen anything close to this degree of luxury.

We pull around and are greeted by the staff of House Catano. Once I've been introduced to the dozen staff members there, we move to the study and are given refreshments. It's all so formal and I watch Luka carefully for my cues. He seems to have gone further inside himself the moment we stepped into his home and I don't try to bring him out of it. We're both quiet and exhausted.

Titus comes into the room and Cece isn't too far behind him.

"Thanks for getting home so quickly," the king says.

"We didn't really have a choice," Luka responds, running his hands through his hair and looking at the floor.

"We both know the last thing you wanted to do was get

married, so I didn't think you'd mind being interrupted on your honeymoon."

My throat closes and I wish I didn't have to hear this.

Cece makes a face, making it seem like she's not in agreement with her husband.

Luka leans forward, his elbows on his knees. "Why don't you just let us know why we had to come here in an almighty rush, Father." His knuckles are white as he grips his hands together tightly.

"Your sister Mara is in trouble. She's offended the people with her disregard for the church and they have been going after her hard in the media. I need you here to show a good front...distract them with your marriage...get their minds off of her for a while. And with the threat to Farrow with Alidonia, it would be a good thing to have your faces showing up in Niaps anyway. We can't take the Farthing family lightly."

"So we basically came home from our honeymoon to do a few photo opps. If you'd told me this yesterday, we could have arranged for photos there and still been on vacation. What's really going on?" Luka gets up and walks to the bar. "Gin and tonic, anyone?"

"I'll have one." Cece perks up.

"Eden?" Luka raises the decanter and I shake my head. "What about school? Was that just for show too or can we go back?"

"I'd like to do a wedding reception for you here, let everyone feel a part of this marriage," Titus says, ignoring Luka's question.

"Eden, are you okay with that?" Luka asks.

I'm so surprised he's asking my opinion that it takes me a moment to speak. "Um, sure?"

"Very well. In two weeks...to give us time to prepare."

Titus leaves the room and Cece takes her drink from Luka, holding it up to clink his.

"Basile will show you to your rooms...room? I'll let the two of you sort that out. Titus saw the proof and confirmed it with your father, Eden, so what you do from here on is your concern." She winks. "Although, you know, an heir will be expected next."

My mouth dropped open when she mentioned proof and further drops about an heir. She leaves the room and Basile comes in, a man that comes to my chest and his eyes do get stuck there for a few seconds before Luka snaps his fingers in his face.

"Eyes off my wife, Uncle Basile."

"So it's like that—wife—hmm." Basile grins. "Good to know." He reaches out for my hand and then kisses the top of it. "I'm pleased to meet the lovely Eden. You're even more beautiful in person."

"Thank you." I smile shyly.

Basile holds his hand out for us to follow him, elbowing Luka. "Does my sister think you don't know your way around your own home? Or does she just want to make me feel like a servant?"

"Probably the latter, Uncle."

Basile chuckles, but it doesn't ring true, and it brings up even more questions about the weird family dynamic vibe I'm getting. He leads us to two rooms side by side.

"Obviously you know your own room, Luka, but we've cleared the room next to you for Eden. I'm taking it you'll be in Luka's room though."

This is all so awkward, I pause in front of my room as Luka touches my arm.

"Stay with me," he whispers.

The relief I feel from his words is ridiculous, but I don't

dwell on my feelings. Basile claps, ecstatic that we're a "real couple" and I can't help but laugh. We step inside Luka's room.

"Clothes and anything you could possibly need are in your room, but there's easy access. We'll get everything moved in here, if you'd like."

I start to answer that it won't be necessary to move my things, but Luka beats me to it. "As soon as possible, please."

"Very well. I'll tell Hanna to do that right away. I hope you'll feel welcome here, Eden. If you need anything, don't hesitate to ask me. And whatever you do, don't put your guard down around our dear king and queen. They will eat you alive," he warns, baring his teeth.

He shuts the bedroom door behind him and I don't know whether he was joking or not, but his last words make me shiver. I turn to see if Luka's expression can tell me anything, but he's staring pensively out the window.

"So what is the deal with school?" I have tons of questions, but this is pressing at the moment.

"We won't be going back to school." His mood has done a complete turnaround since we got here, exactly what I was afraid of. "My guess is Father will hire the best instructor from there to come tutor us. Unless it's a better media approach to go back to Kings Passage." He laughs bitterly. "I wonder what Mara has done now."

"I'd like to call my parents. I need to check in and see how they're doing, and I'll also need my things if we're not going back to Kings Passage." We left Farrow in such a hurry, neither Luka or I have had anything but what has been provided.

Luka nods. "I'm sure there are new phones ready for us. If not, it won't take long to set up. I'll go see about that now. My mother has probably set you up with a new wardrobe—

she's more likely to do that than send for your things. I'll make sure we get whatever you need though. Don't worry."

He leaves and I take a look around his room. A lot of dark wood and masculine furnishings. It's simpler than the rest of the house and far more comfortable. Not the colors I would choose, but nice. I sit on the bed and jump when the door bursts open.

A beautiful blond, green-eyed girl rushes through, her hair bouncing behind her. "Making yourself right at home, I see." She eyes me with such contempt I want to shrivel into the bed, but instead, I stand up and reach my hand out to her.

She doesn't take it. I drop it limply at my side and sit back down.

"Hello, Mara. I'm Eden. Nice to meet you," I say it mechanically...mere words without any feeling.

"I know who you are." For someone so beautiful, her face can sure do horrific things. Her sneer is terrifying. She points at me. "Don't get too comfortable here. This isn't going to last. Nadia deserves him far more than you ever could."

CHAPTER FIFTEEN

There's a tap on the door and Mara flings it open. "What do you want?"

A girl not much older than me, whom I assume to be Hanna given her arms are laden down with clothes, wilts and takes a step back. But then gathers her nerve and steps forward.

"I've come with Lady Eden's clothes," she says.

"Come in." I smile at her, but she's so busy rushing to the closet, she doesn't notice.

"Let me see that." Mara snatches a dress from the top and studies it. I don't recognize the dress, but I didn't recognize half the things Mother sent with me to school. "This can't be one of your dresses. I'd recognize Teresa's work anywhere." She drops it to the floor and rolls her eyes, moving toward the door.

Brienne steps into the room and sets her steely eyes on Mara. I grin when I see Mara swallow hard, but then she carries on like she's not affected by her in the slightest.

"First you move into my home and now you're going to be copying my fashion?" She turns to me. "I'm going to make sure this marriage is over before it ever even really gets started. It should've been me getting married first anyway. I'm the oldest, and it's only a matter of time before El—"

"I see you've met already," Luka interrupts the last part of her rant. He waves a phone toward me and I take it.

Mara's shoulders are still tight, but her face transforms into a sweet, softer expression. She goes to Luka and wraps her arms around him, laying her head on his chest. "Congratulations, Luka love. Thank you for coming." Her voice is like syrup and I can't believe that Luka seems to be softening mush right before my eyes.

He wraps his arms around her and her eyes flit over to me, triumphant. So that's how it's going to be. I turn and walk to the closet, which is the size of a nice bedroom, and run my fingers through the exquisite fabrics and colors that appear to be mine. She's right—they look more like her clothes than anything I've ever worn. Far more revealing. Beautiful, but out of my comfort zone.

I decide to go outside to call my mother and step out of the closet. Luka and Mara are quietly talking now—I can only imagine what they're saying, and they stop and look my way when they see me.

"I'm going to call my mother, see how everything's going."

Luka gives a faint nod and turns back to Mara. I feel a pain in my gut but ignore it and leave the room, shutting the door behind me.

Basile falls into step beside me and looks behind me to grin at Brienne. It's strange how quickly I've become attached to her.

"You met the toxic sister, I see," Basile says, grinning up at me.

"If you mean Mara, yep." I grin back. "Where is the best

place for privacy around here? I'd like to make a phone call."

"You'll never have privacy again." His words are ominous, but he chuckles as he says them, leaving me in doubt of what is true. "Follow me."

We wind through the dark hallways, and when we don't run into another person in that whole time, I begin to worry. Can I trust Basile? I don't trust Luka's parents, and I can't tell if I should trust his uncle yet.

"You're probably starting to wonder if I'm taking you to the dungeon." He winks and I blanch. "Oh dear girl, you really were, weren't you?" He puts his hand on my arm and gives it a quick squeeze. "I assure you, there will be no killing...today." He winks again and shakes his head when I don't laugh. "I can see that we'll have to work on your sense of humor. I've heard those from the north struggle with humor. Tis a shame."

"My humor is intact, I assure you. Forgive me if I don't quite trust all of you yet, not to mention the threat to my family—the very night that I married your nephew—still has me shaken. I haven't gotten my bearings yet."

"You're right, my beauty. I am expecting a lot from you. Forgive me for that. It's just that I like what I see in Luka in the short time he's been with you. I might have gotten a little bit ahead of myself." He lifts an arm when we turn a corner, and just past the vast windows and a large door, are the gardens. "See? I brought you to the most beautiful place on the Catano estate. No dungeon anywhere in sight."

This time I grin back at him. "Thank you, Basile."

He gives me a mini bow. "You're most welcome."

My mother answers on the second ring. "Hello?" She sounds tired and scared.

"Mother? Are you okay?"

"Oh, Eden. Are *you* okay, sweetheart? I've been worried sick about you. It was so hard leaving you like that."

"I'm okay. Once I found out you were all safely back at Farrow, I felt a lot better. Has everything really resolved that quickly with Alidonia?"

"It seems to be. I hear that you're having a wedding reception in a couple of weeks. We're supposed to come, show our support and all that," she says, sniffing. "I'm horrified that your wedding reception here was cut short. How are things with Luka?"

I pause before answering, unsure of what to say to her about these things. It's too embarrassing to talk about. "Good. He's been nicer."

"That's all you're going to say? I've been worried sick and you're just going to say he's been nicer?" She raises her voice, but I know she isn't angry.

"Not sure what you want me to say. As you know, we consummated the marriage." The anger does come into my voice then. "Was that *really* necessary?"

"Ah, you know what it's like here, Eden," she says softly. "We've come so far in so many ways, but at the heart of it, there are some customs that are as old as time. This is one of them. You must respect your father."

"I do. I *do*." Tears fill my eyes and in spite of being angry with my parents, I miss them. I don't agree with everything they do, but I have always respected them with everything in me.

"I know, sweetheart. Listen, I have a meeting to attend, but I will see you in two weeks, yes? I'm counting down the days. Oh—how is Brienne?"

"She's been great. It's nice to have her with me. Thank you."

"Please give her my appreciation for taking care of you."

"I'm glad I will see you soon," I whisper. "Love you."

"I love you. Until then."

The click of her line going dead is loud in my ear and I swallow back a sob.

My life at home will never be the same again. The thought is both heartbreaking and terrifying. Because this place...and Luka? Neither feels certain.

Luka finds me wandering the gardens. I've been walking through the flowers and barely seeing their beauty. The thought going off in my head as loud as a gong is: *I don't belong, I don't belong, I don't belong.*

"Eden?" he calls.

I turn and he's hurrying toward me. He looks angry.

"Where have you been?" he asks, wiping the sweat off his forehead. "You've been gone for almost two hours. I've looked everywhere."

"I've been here, in the garden."

"Next time let me know where you are going."

I scrunch my forehead together. "*Why?*"

He steps forward and pulls me to his chest. "I was worried." He winds his arms around me and runs his hand through my hair, pulling it back so I'll look at him. "It's too soon after what happened in Farrow for you to disappear on me. We need to stick close to one another. I don't—I don't feel com...you know what? You need to just trust me on this and don't go off on your own."

"I thought Basile would let you know where I was if it

was important." I'm not sure whether to be moved that he's concerned or to be annoyed that he's not telling me something. Maybe both.

"Basile has already had enough red wine for the week. He won't be telling anyone anything useful for a while."

"Really. He seemed sober when I saw him."

"A lot can change very quickly around here."

I sigh and he takes my hand, walking toward the house. "Do you think you can be comfortable here?"

"I...don't know."

He nods. "If you said yes, I think I'd worry." We reach the door and he turns to me, his face serious. "Listen, your best way to survive here is to not interact with my family. Mara will come around, but the others...just stick with me, okay? We'll do what we have to do this week and then I will start demanding for us to either go back to Kings Passage, depending on what's happening with Alidonia, or for us to get started on our schooling...in our own home."

"Our own home. Is that really an option?"

"It will be. I'll make sure it is."

Dinner that evening is by far the worst part of the day. No one seems to like each other. The only ones closest to having a normal relationship are Luka and Mara and Luka and Basile. The rest of them trade insults with one another and no one is laughing. It's not a sparring contest, more an utter contempt for what anyone else says or thinks. I sit there, leg bouncing underneath the table, a jittery ball of anxiousness.

Luka puts his hands on my shoulders and rubs them and the whole table comes to a halt. They watch us, I guess in shock or something close to it, that he's touching me with any consideration. I wonder if they think I'm the enemy or if it's just Luka's behavior that shocks them.

"Well, my wife and I have had enough dysfunction for the night. We have a honeymoon to catch up on."

The heat rises in my cheeks. I look at each face at the table. Mara looks furious. Basile, gleeful. Cece looks vaguely disgusted, and Titus looks curious. He studies me like he wants to unbury any and all secrets I am using to manipulate his son.

"Goodnight, everyone. Thank you for dinner." I take Luka's hand and we walk out of the room. I have no doubt we will be the topic of discussion as soon as we're out of there.

"God, they're so dull. Come on. Let's go fuck in the pool, give them something to really talk about."

I laugh but am shaking my head the minute he says the words. "No way."

"Oh, you know I do love a challenge."

"Not. Happening."

"We'll see."

The pool doesn't happen. But we do christen his shower, his closet, and his bed, all before midnight. And I fall deeper into his web, knowing what he considers just "fucking" is a risky game for me to play.

CHAPTER SIXTEEN

The next morning, I wake up on my stomach, naked. Covers at my feet. I stretch out and turn my head to look at Luka. Last night was...incredible. I can't get enough of him.

He's not beside me.

I sit up, look around.

Empty.

Disappointed or disoriented, I'm not sure which, I get out of bed and take a shower, slipping into one of my new outfits: wide-leg camel-colored pants and a white blouse, all the while wondering where he could be.

I don't spend much time on my hair, leaving my waves to do their thing in the humidity...my decision is easy when I see the perfect hair product for that in the bathroom. There's also the perfect product for straightening, deep conditioning, and anything else I could possibly want to do to my hair. I wonder who picked all of this out, especially when I see the elaborate makeup palettes taking over a whole drawer in the bathroom. It's all a little strange, but mostly thoughtful that they would go to so much trouble.

Once I'm satisfied with my appearance, I peek out of

the bedroom door—coast clear—and I head to the kitchen.
I'm not sure I even remember how to get there. I pass the
study and hear arguing. I pause when I hear Luka.

"I've done everything you wanted, I don't understand
why you're doing this." His voice is strained and angrier
than I've ever heard; it frightens me. As if I'm not already
fearful enough of my new surroundings; hearing the anger
in his voice shakes me.

Basile rounds the corner and stops when he sees me
standing outside the office. My heartbeat kicks up and I put
my hand to my throat.

"I was looking for the kitchen and heard arguing." I
decide to go with honest.

He hears their raised voices and nods. "Lot of that
around here between the two of them, I'm afraid. Best you
learn to just ignore it." He holds an arm out and I loop my
hand through. "I'll show you the quickest way to the
kitchen. You missed breakfast, but the chef will be happy to
prepare you whatever you'd like."

"Can I just make some peanut butter toast on my own?"

He looks up at me and gives me a sideways grin. "I
would've expected someone of your caliber would have
more refined tastes."

I shrug and grin back at him. "There is nothing finer
than honey drizzled over toast and peanut butter on top. I
dare you to find anything."

"Honey, you say?" He scratches his chin like it's a great
mystery and I laugh. "You will teach us things, Lady Eden. I
can see that now."

I roll my eyes.

"I'm serious." He laughs too and then points at the
doorway just ahead. "Here we are. We'll have to ask
Chelsea where those ingredients are. Here she is." He

waves Chelsea over and she smiles timidly. "Chelsea is our head chef during the week. Can you believe I don't even know where the bread is?" He scrunches his nose. "Too many more important things to do."

I know he's joking now; part of me wonders if he's ever really serious. I nearly ask him to keep me company while I eat—he's the easiest person to be around that I've met here so far. But he puts his hands on either side of the doorway once I enter the kitchen and gives it two taps.

"I really do have a meeting—not an important one, mind you, but if I don't show, Titus will have my head." He mimics slicing his throat and I grimace. "Before I forget, you're supposed to have a fitting in the parlor in half an hour. I wanted to be sure to remind you, in case Mara might have forgotten."

"Oh. Thank you. She must have...forgotten." We stare at one another for a moment and he nods, eyes serious now.

"Well, enjoy your breakfast. Chelsea, fix our girl up here, please."

When I find my way to the parlor, Cece and a woman I haven't met yet are already there.

"This is Teresa. She needs your measurements for the reception," Cece says.

"Wonderful. Thank you."

Teresa nods and smiles but doesn't say anything. She motions for me to hold out my arms, puts the tape around them, then my waist, and hips, until she's got all the measurements. When she's done, she shows me a few dress ideas and they really are beautiful. I choose the one I want and go with the palest creamy pink.

Mara comes in as I'm finishing up with Teresa and looks at what I've chosen.

"You can't choose that dress," she cries, snatching up the notes Teresa's taken, and waving them around in front of my face. "No. This is my dress." She looks at her mother, eyes blazing. "We picked it out for my engagement party, remember?"

Cece's lips thin and she holds her hand out for the notes, handing the paper carefully to Teresa. "You're not engaged, Mara. There's no reason this dress should go to waste when you're nowhere near an engagement. Eden picked this one out of all the dresses Teresa showed her and she will wear it to her reception." Mara sticks her lips out in an exaggerated pout and Cece gives her a sympathetic smile. "By the time you get married, there will be an array of other beautiful dresses to choose from!"

"I can pick out another," I say, despite loving the dress and not wanting her to get her way. It seems reasonable though, if she had her heart set on this dress before I ever came into the picture. A nice gesture to my new sister-in-law. "I like this one very much." I point to another photograph of a dress almost as pretty.

"That won't be—" Cece says.

Mara claps. "Thank you, Eden. That will be very slimming, perfect for you." She smiles sweetly and I want to go full catfight on her.

"I'll need to change the color to black," I add.

"Black? At your wedding reception?" Cece scowls, her head tilting to the side. "Absolutely not." She shakes her head and clasps both hands on her left hip. "We cannot have you looking so morbid on what is supposed to be your wedding reception. No."

"As you said—*my* wedding reception. I've already had a

wedding dress. *This* dress," I tap the photo, "was made to be in black."

Cece fumes, her eyes bulging and her lips working overtime, pinching together. She seems shocked and I think it's stunned her into silence. I hold back a grin.

"Oh, I agree," Teresa jumps in. "I have just the material. Well, would you be opposed to it having bits of silver too?" She hustles to her bag and pulls out swatches. A gorgeous black lace that has silver circles of various sizes embroidered into it. The effect is muted yet shimmery. "You will be a vision in it with that glorious red hair..."

"I love it. Yes, this is perfect," I tell Teresa, risking a glance at Mara.

She looks annoyed, and for a second, I think she's going to decide she needs this to be her dress too. But then she waves her hands as if to say "get on with it" and Teresa bends down to make new notes on her paper. I decide to get out of here while things are tolerable. I have a feeling it will only go downhill if I stick around.

When I reach Luka's bedroom—it still doesn't feel like mine—he's pacing the floor and stops when I come in. I attempt a smile, but I'm nervous. He looks angry, and I'm still feeling a bit off since he wasn't in bed when I woke up. It's dumb, I know, but I'm new to this honeymoon/wife business.

"Are you okay?" I ask when he doesn't smile back.

"I'm not. I need to be alone."

I don't know what to do with myself and take a few steps back.

Luka stalks to the window and puts his hands up on the doorjamb. "My father refuses to let us get our own home, even though I have the money. He says it's not safe and it defeats the purpose of us looking like a united front if we're not here in the family home."

"I don't see how that's showing a united front. If the objective was for us to be married, we're married. That should be enough."

He shakes his head. "He's just on a power trip, as usual. I'm so sick of being his pawn." The words are like angry stabs and I hold my stomach, feeling desperate to help. "You know what? It'd be best if you moved into your bedroom tonight. I-I need to think and I can't with you around every second."

I stare at him in shock then turn away before I lose it. I don't want to cry, the last thing I need to do is cry right now in front of him, but my heart is being ping-ponged at a rapid rate and I can't keep up.

"The least he could do was give me this…knowing how much I didn't want to get married…" It's like he's forgotten I'm in the room and is spewing what he's really thinking.

He's right. It's best I get out of here.

CHAPTER SEVENTEEN

I haven't even explored my suite when Hanna knocks on the door, carrying my clothes. I try to help, but she smiles and skirts around me.

"It won't take long," she says, putting the clothes in my closet. "Your bathroom is stocked similarly to Luka's; although, he might wish for you to take all the makeup." She laughs lightly and when she's done hanging up the clothes, she clears her throat. "One more trip should do it."

She's back in no time and I sit numbly on the chaise lounge by the windows.

When she's done hanging up the second batch of clothes, she looks at me expectantly. "Do you need anything else?"

"No. Thank you, Hanna."

"My pleasure."

She seems a little too happy to have the extra work. Maybe...maybe she's happy Luka and I aren't getting along. Maybe she wants him to herself. I close my eyes, fighting back tears. Now I'm going to be jealous too?

No, separate lives.

That's how it's going to be. The sooner I get used to it, the better.

It feels strange sleeping alone in a strange place after sharing a room with him. It didn't take long for me to get used to having his warmth against my back or waking up to him kissing me. My body heats at the thought. Why did I let myself feel anything at all?

I barely sleep but make my way to the dining room the next morning. Everyone is there already...everyone but Luka. They all stare at me when I walk in and Cece is the only one to speak.

"Good morning. Where is your husband?"

"Sleeping?"

Mara smirks. "I just saw him. He's *not* sleeping."

My face heats, but I pile my plate with eggs and then wish I hadn't once I start eating. My stomach is a mess. I hear a clatter behind me and turn to see Luka stumbling in.

"Mornin', my fine family. Scoot over, Eden, I need to sit by my wife."

I wrinkle my nose when I get a whiff of him. He reeks of gin.

"You're drunk at nine in the morning?" Titus shakes his head. "Get him some coffee now," he barks at the woman standing near him and she hustles to bring Luka a cup and saucer. It rattles in her shaky hand.

Once Luka has a few sips of coffee, he slams his hands on the table and everyone jumps, me included.

"Did you know my wife was a virgin when I married her?" he asks, nudging me with his elbow.

My eyes widen. "Luka!" I put my hands on my face to cool it and look around the table.

"She was. Not anymore. Because I'm the animal who married her against her will. I mean, I want to think she wanted to do it, but really, let's be honest, she was forced to marry me, am I right?" He laughs, but his head sags and I touch his arm. He flinches and turns to me, his eyes haunted. "I tried to make it good for you...God knows it was good for me. That's what all the bastards say when they take a virgin though..."

"Okay, that's enough," Basile jumps in. He comes around and takes Luka by the arm, dragging him out. "Let's get you sober, buddy. I'm all for a good buzz, but this is a train wreck."

I stand up and follow them out.

"Luka?" I call just before they round the corner.

"I can't even look at you right now," he says in a singsong voice. "Go away."

I fall back, uncertain what to do. I spend the rest of the day in my room feeling a strange sadness for Luka that I didn't see coming.

The next morning, he's at the breakfast table with Mara. When I walk in, she rolls her eyes and Luka avoids looking at me at all.

"Can you pass the butter?" I ask him.

"Can I?" he repeats. "I thought I told you to get out of my sight."

"What?"

"It's like you can't take the hint: I. Don't. Want. To. See. Your. Face." He takes a long swig of coffee and slams the cup on the table.

I'm still in shock when he leaves the room.

Mara twists her hands together in glee. "It's like I don't even have to do a thing. It's all falling into place. Brava,

Eden. You've brought a great deal of entertainment into our home...just by being *you*."

I swallow the lump in my throat and stand up, leaving before I embarrass myself further.

He isn't at dinner and I do my best to eat and leave without talking to anyone.

———

Each morning I don't know which Luka I'm going to get. It reminds me of being with him at Kings Passage and I wonder if he was drinking heavily there too. He's loud and mean when he's drunk, and sometimes even when he's not. It's all very confusing.

During the next week, it's not much better. After a particularly eventful dinner the night before where he yelled at his father and got thrown out of the room, I avoid going to the dining room the next morning. I'm starving when Basile knocks on the door and hands me a tray of waffles with fruit and whipped cream.

"You're a lifesaver, Basile. Thank you."

"I figured you might need a break from all of us."

"You figured right."

Before he leaves, he turns and says, "The longer you avoid talking to him, the harder it will be."

I nod. I know he's right, but I can only take so much. And really, what can I say? I thought I was starting to get to know him, but he feels like a stranger now. I don't know how to reach him when he's like this.

As soon as Basile leaves there's another knock on the door and assuming he forgot something, I fling it open. "What did you—"

It's Luka. My mouth closes and I stare at him. He looks down at my feet.

"I need to go out of town for a few days. I'll be back for our reception, of course."

"I'm staying here? I thought..." The alarm rises in my chest. My mind is going a thousand directions at once. "Where are you going?"

He still hasn't looked at me and that makes me more anxious than ever. Ignoring my question, he says, "Stick close to Basile if things get weird here. Everyone should be on their best behavior, but if they're not, he'll watch out for you."

The lump in my throat is growing and my eyes are overflowing now. Not knowing what to do with myself, I go into the bathroom and lock the door. I sit on the window seat in the dressing room section of the bathroom, looking out at the water, and take huge gulping breaths. Nothing about this marriage has gone the way I dreamed it would—the good, the bad, none of it.

He knocks on the door and when I don't answer, he turns the doorknob, cursing when he finds it locked.

"Open up, Eden."

"Why? You can't even look at me." I sound like a child, but I don't care.

He's leaving me alone with his crazy family and hasn't even told me where he's going. All that talk about returning to our honeymoon was either feeding my ego or trying to rile his father up. And the craziness of the past week...I don't know what to think.

"Don't be like that," he says softly. "Come on, Eden. Open the door. I want to talk to you."

"Why can't I go with you?"

There's a long pause and then, "It wouldn't be safe."

I scoff and stand up, unlocking the door and flinging it open. "Don't lie to me. That's the least you can do in this so-called marriage—be honest with me."

He looks me over, *finally*, his eyes assessing me as only he does. I turn away. I thought I wanted it, but I can't handle his eyes on me right now. He affects me too much.

He moves in front of me, rubbing his hand over his face. His eyes are stark when I look at him again. "You would do well to not develop feelings for me, Eden. It won't go well for you if you do—I can promise you that. This is not a typical marriage. I do not owe you answers, and I have been honest. From day *one*, I've been honest. You knew what I was all about."

"How can you not owe me answers when I've given up my whole life to marry you? Whether willingly or not, you're stuck with me. And if we're supposed to be all about getting our faces seen together, distracting everyone from who knows what with Mara—what has changed overnight that you need to leave?"

"It's a favor my dad conceded on when he said no to our moving out. He owes me this. This is something I need to take care of and then I will be here for our party, ready for our social media *splash*." His sarcasm is gone in the next sentence. "Our time together has surprised me, I'll give you that." He stretches out his hand and drops it when I step back. "But I've realized during the past week that I would be doing you a disservice if I acted like this was a normal marriage. It's anything but normal and my father agrees."

He steps back and walks out the door without looking back.

I decide right then and there that I will not succumb to Luka Catano's charm again.

My heart is mine and he can't claim it.

CHAPTER EIGHTEEN

I spend the next week hidden away in my room. Hanna brings my meals and I barely touch them. Basile tries to talk to me, but I tell him I don't feel well and he eventually leaves me alone. Brienne checks in throughout the day and I tolerate her more than anyone else. The nights are endless. What keeps me going is the thought that I will see my parents soon. I will try one more time to get out of this before leaving my fate in the Catanos' hands.

It's Friday, the day I've been dreading. Our reception is tonight. I'm stir-crazy, but I still don't want to face anyone. Knowing I have to see Luka tonight fills me with anxiety.

I think what hurts the most is that he pretty much admitted he'd been pretending with me. That the times we've had sex or when he was affectionate were just him playing a part. I think back to our time in his bed the night before he kicked me out of his room. The moonlight shone on his face and it felt like he was laying another part of his soul bare for me.

"You're perfect," he'd whispered after we both came down from our high. "I had no idea how perfect." He smoothed my hair back and kissed me slow, like he meant it.

He'd pulled my back to his chest and we'd fallen asleep like that, cocooned in a hazy afterglow.

All an act and one I don't intend on falling for again. There won't be a repeat.

Around four p.m., I begin getting ready for the party. The dress was dropped off earlier and has been hanging in the window. The silver threads catch the sunlight and I stare at it for a long time, feeling like a different person than when I picked it out. So much can change in so little time.

I fix my hair in a deep side part with sleek waves, and it falls against my pale skin like red ink spilling onto the snow. I'm heavy-handed with my makeup, creating a dark, smoky eye that looks more Maleficent than Little Mermaid. I step into the dress and wish that the princess feeling it gives me wasn't being wasted on the Catano family.

In all that time, I never see or hear from Luka. When he left, he really left. For the hundredth time, I wonder where he went, what he was doing, and what the urgency was— why did he run? Every time I think of him, I curse myself and try to redirect my thoughts to my parents. I wish they'd hurry and get here. My mom promised she'd call when they arrived.

It's a quarter to eight when she sends a text instead. *I'm sorry we were delayed a bit. We'll arrive a few minutes late, but we're here! Can't wait to see you.*

I fling my phone on the bed and sigh. Of all times for them to be late.

At exactly 7:59, there's a tap on the door and I open it to see Basile standing there. We speak at the same time.

"He can't even be bothered to escort me to our reception?"

"You look dressed to kill. Deadly and sexy as hell. Nice choice."

He doesn't answer my question and I nod my thanks to his comments. If I say another word, it will be vicious and he doesn't deserve that. As we're rounding the corner to go to the ballroom, Basile lets go of my arm and disappears, and Luka steps out of the corner, dressed in a black tux with a black shirt and black tie. We look like a matching set...and like we're dressed for a funeral rather than a celebration. How fitting.

His eyes drink me in from head to toe. He reaches out and runs his fingers down the deep line of my cleavage and I allow him the touch before stepping back. When his eyes meet mine again, he looks shell-shocked.

"How do you keep surprising me, Mrs. Catano?" He licks his lips and steps forward again.

I step back again.

His brow furrows. "No hello kiss for your husband?"

"No. Shall we go inside?"

"You're mad." He lifts his head to the ceiling and rubs his hand across his scruffy chin.

"You're astute."

"Will you be able to do this tonight? We're expected to—"

"I will play my part just as convincingly as you've played yours, don't worry about me." I smooth down my dress and press my lips together. "Now, *shall we go inside?*"

"You look like a wet dream I want to make—" he starts.

I hold up my hand. "No one is around right now. Save your lines for when someone else is around to hear them. That's what tonight is about, correct?" I crinkle my nose. "And seriously, a wet dream? That's the best you can do?" I shake my head. "Weak, crude *imbecile.*"

His mouth drops open and he stares at me for a long beat then bows his head and nods. "Let's go inside," he says eventually, his voice matching my coldness this time.

He holds his arm out for me and I take it.

When the doors are opened wide for us, we step through and the flash of cameras is blinding. I smile and look adoringly at Luka, and he stares back at me with what some could confuse for heat and lust, but what I know is really confusion and disbelief. The great Luka Catano has never had anyone put him in his place.

This might be more fun than I thought.

His parents allow me to kiss them on both cheeks and I do the same to Mara and Basile. We're one big, happy family. What a joke.

My parents arrive at a quarter after the hour and I rush to them, my eyes instantly welling with tears. I try to get a grip as I hug my mother and then my father.

My father holds me out and frowns. "What is this you're wea—"

"Neil, don't start," my mother jumps in. "You look beautiful, dear. I was expecting something more...happy bride... but this is...quite something." Her eyes fall to my cleavage and she looks away quickly, flushing.

"Thank you." I grab my dad's arm. "Do you think we could find a chance to talk somewhere later? I don't think I can do this. I really don't."

"Eden? Are they not taking care of you here?"

"Everyone has been fine. I have everything I could want. But I feel like a pawn. And I'm not sure you and Titus are on the same page. It feels like something el—"

"Welcome to our home," Titus interrupts, his voice booming across the room. "And welcome to our family." He kisses my mother's hand and gives my father's a hearty shake. "We are so happy you're here, and especially happy to have Eden as our beautiful daughter-in-law. She far surpasses my son's dreams."

I look at Luka standing next to him and he doesn't say a word. I wonder what his dad had to bribe him with to be quiet tonight since they always seem to be sparring.

My father looks at Luka and Luka seems to realize he should be saying something. He jumps to attention and gives a low bow to my father. When he reaches my mother, she holds up her hand and he kisses it, telling her she looks lovely.

When the whole awkward encounter is over and I'm sure the photographers have gotten their fill of pictures, we move to the dinner. We're sitting at a long table, facing everyone, both in the middle of our respective parents.

Occasionally, Luka will remember we're supposed to look like the loving couple and he will initiate wooden conversation.

"How is your salad?"

"Fine."

"Have you had a good week?"

"It was spectacular."

"Fantastic."

And then we're at another lull until he comes up with new tactics.

"There's something on your lip..." He reaches out and tries to smooth it away with his thumb. I jump in and dab with my napkin.

"I've never seen you in a dress like that. Did you pick it out?"

I nod and that stumps him for another few minutes. His jaw ticks and it gives me a tiny bit of satisfaction to see his growing frustration.

In one of our longer stretches of silence, there is a gradual dinging of the crystal that quickly sweeps across the room until everyone is holding their glass and looking at us expectantly.

Luka stands up and holds his hand out for me. I stand up and he puts a hand on my waist and another on my cheek and kisses me like he's consumed. I arch my back hoping to cut off the kiss, but he just leans in, his hand covering how deep his kiss goes. Flower buds are thrown at us as the crowd erupts in applause and cheers, a custom we don't do in Farrow. I pull back, more stunned by that kiss than the flowers surrounding us. He looks just as stunned as I do and we both quietly sit back down.

I don't know what to make of him.

When the music starts, Cece leans around Luka to make eye contact with me. "Why don't the two of you dance a bit? Others will join after your first dance."

"I don't feel like dancing," I tell her, smiling sweetly. "But, thank you for the suggestion. Feel free to dance yourself."

Her mouth pinches together and she takes a long swig of red wine. "Don't embarrass me, Eden. Get out there and dance with your husband and watch your insolent mouth."

I open my mouth to respond, but the look on her face is terrifying.

"You like dancing with me, remember?" Luka says, holding his hand out.

I glare at him *and* Cece but take his hand. When we get on the dance floor, he melds his body to mine and I shift woodenly side to side. He rests his forehead on mine and clasps me harder against him when I try to pull back.

"It hasn't been that many nights ago that you were

desperate to get as close to me as possible," he whispers. "You fell apart every time I touched you."

I push his hands off of me and he laughs, looking around like I'm playing a joke on him.

"You're making a scene. Dance with me and make it look like you want me as much as I know you do."

I grit my teeth and step closer to him, smiling at the photographers who are nearby. Inside I am fury and fire, but on the outside, I am serene and so very much in love. It's sickening, this game we're playing.

The dance feels endless, but eventually it does end and other guests start dancing, giving us the freedom to sit back down. I greet the guests as they come by to meet me, one by one. When the cake is rolled out, I clap my hands and exclaim at its beauty. I dig into it when I'm handed a large slice and am rewarded by its deliciousness.

"Oh my God, this cake." I look over and Mara has her nose curled up. "It's sickeningly sweet." She pushes the plate away from her and folds her arms.

Little piece of work.

When a photographer comes to the table and asks if he can have some time with me for solo pictures, Luka stands up.

"I'll be coming too," he says.

Cece laughs. "Surely your bride can leave your side for five minutes, sweetheart," she says loud enough for the whole room to hear. Or at least it seems that way. "It's Juan Salvo, the world-renowned photographer. He will capture a lovely likeness, I have no doubt."

"I *will* be coming too," he mutters under his breath.

I get up, my dress floating as I walk. I do love this dress. And Luka hovers like a protective husband, his shoulder touching mine as he takes my hand. I try to let go, but he won't let me. When I glare at him, he pretends not to notice.

Juan is actually quite good-looking. I notice more as we walk into a brighter section of the ballroom, where lights have been staged for photo opportunities. He walks past those and out of the ballroom and we follow him.

"Where are you intending to take these photos?" Luka asks, his tone biting. "In our bedroom?"

"By the water, if that pleases you, Lady Eden," Juan says, completely ignoring Luka. "When I saw your eyes for the first time, I dreamed of one day photographing you by the sea. You are very beautiful." His accent sounds like music and I smile, swooning a bit inside.

"Thank you." I duck my head, feeling a flush coming on.

"I knew I needed to be here for this," Luka snaps.

I turn to him. "That won't be necessary." I lean up and whisper into his ear. "We're living our own lives, remember?" I smooth out his tie when I pull away and smile. "Thank you for escorting me, sweet husband. That will be all."

CHAPTER NINETEEN

Juan grins when Luka stalks away. "He doesn't look too happy. Are you sure you shouldn't go after him?"

"Positive. Let's do this."

Juan is the consummate professional as he tells me where to stand for the best light and then starts snapping away. He shouts compliments as his camera clicks, but I don't take it seriously. It's what he does with everyone he photographs, I'm sure. When he lowers his camera and beams at me, I relax and smile back.

"I am so happy with these. You are a masterpiece of color. That complexion, your hair...as I said, your eyes—"

"If you're done coming on to my wife, I'd like to take her back to the party," Luka interrupts.

Juan just smiles bigger. "If I were coming on to your wife, she would not still be at this party." He laughs and Luka growls next to me.

I roll my eyes. "I'm going back to the party...alone... whether anyone is coming on to me or not." I poke Luka in the chest. "You're behaving like a child," I whisper-shout.

"But I wanted to get pictures of the two of you," Juan calls.

I turn around and reluctantly walk back. "Please hurry," I tell him.

"That will depend on how well my subjects behave," he teases.

"He's asking for a black eye," Luka says in my ear.

I turn to him, ready to give *him* a black eye and he's still leaning down, so our lips brush against each other. I feel a jolt and lean back, but he's leaning in and his lips are demanding more. Juan's camera goes wild, and I tell myself that's the only reason I'm kissing Luka like a woman obsessed. Not because of the magic power his tongue holds. Absolutely not.

When my knees go weak, he breaks the kiss and looks at me, eyes triumphant. He smiles and my eyes narrow, ready to let him have it.

"Relax your smile, Lady Eden," Juan calls.

I'd forgotten he was there and plant a smile on my face.

"That's it. Yes, perfect. I have the shot."

Luka takes my hand and pulls me away. I look back at Juan and he's watching us in amusement. He waves and I smile and let myself be dragged back inside.

"We've done all we need to do at this party. Let's go," he says.

"We can't leave. No." I smooth down my hair. It got slightly windblown outside. Luka's looks even better, tousled and like perfected bedhead. "I need to see my parents. Everyone is safe. I think Alidonia was bluffing. They have the oil they want, the forced truce. Everyone is happy but me."

He grabs my arm. "What are you saying?"

"I want out."

He shakes his head. "Impossible."

"I'll find a way."

He looks like he's about to explode, but what he does catches me by surprise much more than that: he picks me up and throws me over his shoulder and carries me out of the room. Explosive cheering erupts as we leave—everyone thinking we can't wait until the night is over to go have sex.

When we're outside the ballroom, I kick and yell and hit.

"You're behaving like a child." He repeats my words in a patronizing voice and I just about lose my mind.

"*Put me down!*" I yell, not realizing we've already reached his bedroom.

He puts me down all right, tossing me on our bed like a sack of flour. His bed, not *our* bed, I correct myself.

I scramble to the head of the bed and try to get off, but he's there, picking me up again.

"If you don't put me down and leave me there, I am going to lose it."

"Not until you agree to be still and listen."

"You're not saying anything I need to hear," I yell.

"You don't know that."

I still and take a deep breath. I'm so mad I'm going to cry and I really don't want to do that. "I'll listen if you don't say anything stupid."

"That will be difficult, but I'll try." I can hear the grin in his voice and hate what it does to my heart.

My foolish, lovesick heart.

He sets me down and I stand in front of him, looking at his chest and waiting.

"Did you read our prenuptial agreement?" he asks.

"No. I figured all of this was already out of my control. Why?"

"I looked into it further this week. It's ironclad. There's no getting out of it. We have to stay married for at least ten years. In that time, we will need to produce an heir. If we wish to divorce after ten years, we will have to do a year of therapy and only *then* could we have our marriage dissolved during the eleventh year. So...you can understand our predicament. We have a lot of time ahead of us."

I turn away right before the tears start to fall. I knew the agreement was probably something like that—it's not really a surprise to me, but hearing him recite the facts so coldly hurts. He's quiet, letting his words settle into me, I guess, and I'm grateful for the moment. Finally, I wipe my face and pray that mascara isn't dripping down my cheeks when I turn around.

"Let's just stay out of each other's way, okay?" I sidestep him and walk out of the room, shutting the door.

He's on my heels as I walk into my bedroom. "It doesn't have to be like this. We were getting along well before. I don't understand why that can't continue."

"You can't seem to decide what you want. One minute you can't keep your hands off me, then you say you shouldn't have pretended to have a normal honeymoon, then you leave without telling me where you're going...now you want to go back to pretending? This is ridiculous, even coming from you."

He stares at me, blinking slowly, then starts pacing and running his hands through his hair. After a few minutes, he starts to back out of the room, not looking at me again. My body goes cold.

He's becoming quite good at walking away.

I'll have to work on *my* exit strategy, so when the next time comes, I'll be the one walking away.

He mumbles as he goes, and when he reaches his room, he slams the door and all chaos erupts.

"Fuck!" he yells.

I flinch every time there's a new crash. *What is he doing over there?* Glass breaks and then there's a long silence.

I take off my makeup, still in a fog over the way this evening progressed. Luka's voice echoing in my mind: *There's no getting out of it. There's no getting out of it. There's no getting out of it.*

My phone dings with a text and I jump, my heart hopeful—for what I don't know. It's my mother. I sigh and read it.

Your father and I would like to give you a hug before we leave, but we don't want to disturb you. The plane will wait for thirty minutes. If you get this, let us know where to find you.

I'll meet you by the pool in five minutes, I text back.

I'm in lounge pants and a tank and throw on another light shirt. It's almost midnight and the sounds of the party are dying down. I look both ways down the hall to make sure no one is around and hurry to the pool. My parents are there with their guards and I rush to them, hugging them both for a long time.

"You're adjusting to married life?" My mom pulls away first. She sees my tears and frowns, wiping them off. "Are you homesick?"

"Yes. I mean, no, I'm not adjusting. Yes, I'm homesick. When can everyone come to see me?"

"Jadon has more responsibilities these days. Perhaps you can visit in a few months," my father says. "I signed a treaty with Titus tonight, Eden...you've done a beautiful thing for your country. Because of you, another channel has opened for our oil. We'll have more workers with the money

Titus provided. Families will be fed. Hundreds of lives changed, just like that." He puts his hands on my shoulders and I feel the weight of the world on them. "It is all thanks to you...and your husband."

My lips tremble and I lower my head as the tears keep falling. Finally, I nod. "That helps put things in perspective. Thank you."

"I'm sorry we can't stay longer," he says. "We have a meeting arranged in a month, so I'll be back then. I'll mention a visit to Farrow with Titus then."

"Okay. Tell everyone I miss them. And that they can call me! Everyone has been so quiet."

"So much is going on at home." My father doesn't elaborate and a prick of fear runs through me.

"What's wrong?"

"Nothing you should concern yourself with, dear." He gives my arms another pat. "Now, it's late. Best get back to that husband of yours and get some rest. We will talk soon."

"I love you, Father. Love you, Mother," my voice breaks and I try to hold it together for just a little longer.

"We love you, Eden," my mother says. "And we couldn't be more proud of you."

I give them another hug and watch as they walk away before breaking into sobs that nearly tear me in two.

I've never felt so alone.

I'm not sure how I'll survive this.

CHAPTER TWENTY

Luka is leaning against my door when I get back. "Where have you been?" He *dares* to sound accusatory.

"None of your business." I motion for him to move and he only steps closer to me.

"You've been crying. Were you with Juan? If he laid a hand on you, I will—"

"You think I'd tell you after your little break from sanity?" I stare him down and he swallows hard. "Move, please. I want to go to bed."

"Are you okay?" he says, softer this time.

"No. Now move, please."

He stares at me for another moment and with a long sigh, he moves out of the way. I go into my room and shut the door and it's several minutes before I hear him shut his.

I don't even want to begin to guess where his mind is right now. I've given up trying to figure him out.

———

After a long night of tossing and turning, I finally fall asleep just before the sun rises. I'm sleeping hard when I hear a knock on the door and before I can respond, the door opens.

"What—?" I'm lying on my stomach and lift my head, scowling at whoever would have the audacity to come into my room without permission.

Luka comes in with a towel around his waist, hair dripping wet. He hands me his iPad and I take it reluctantly.

"Could you not get some clothes on before coming in here?"

"You've seen it all anyway. And I know you liked what you saw."

I flush and focus on what he's trying to show me. We're all over the Internet. Not the pictures Juan took, from what I can tell, but from the other photographers who were there catching the candid shots.

"We look good together," he says, standing over me.

"Looks are deceiving, are they not?"

He sighs. "Can we call some kind of a truce? This snippy, irritable side of you is not attractive. I already know I can't deal with ten years, but it's going to be the worst kind of torture if this is how you're going to be all the time."

I feel a twinge of guilt, but it only lasts for a second. "You don't get to ask anything of me yet. That has to be earned. I was foolish letting you in as much as I did and I won't make the same mistake again. Lesson learned."

Once again he leaves my room in a huff and I just roll my eyes, done with his attitude. He has balls of steel and I'm learning I'll need to step it up to keep up with him.

I get out of bed and decide to go for a swim. I did my duty last night; I deserve a break today. I find a dozen swimsuits in one of my closet drawers. I hold them up, trying to figure out how they even work, finally trying one on. It's all straps and very little coverage. This won't do. I try two more and finally find a black lace bikini with Brazilian bottoms. I cringe at how little it covers, but it comes with black lace pants, so I throw those on, apply sunscreen, and wear a hat.

When I reach the pool, it's empty. I nearly do a dance right there to have it all to myself. I practice swimming and am happy that it comes back to me easily. I go underwater and get lost in my thoughts down there. All of my problems seem to float away when I'm surrounded by water. Eventually my stomach starts growling and I shoot up out of the water, smoothing my hair back.

Climbing the tile steps, I lean down and pick up my towel and when I stand up, Luka is there. *Right* there. I think I see the familiar want in his eyes, but there's something else too. He can't keep from looking me over, his tongue swiping his lower lip before he bites down on it. He shocks me by letting me pass without saying a word as I walk away. Grabbing my hat and pants, I feel the heat of his gaze and try my best not to stumble.

Once I'm in the safety of my room, I take a shower then crawl back into bed, reaching for a banana I swiped from the bowl in the dining room. I grab my phone and do a search for our pictures. I want to study them without his eyes on me. I see the pictures he showed me earlier, along with new ones, and one in particular catches my eye. He is looking at me while I'm looking straight ahead and the look on his face is like pure wonder. I stare at it the longest. That can't be real.

Someone knocks on my door and I sit up, chest heaving. "Yes?" I clear my throat and try again. "Yes?"

"I'm supposed to make sure you're ready in an hour for a family portrait," Mara says through the door.

I fall back on the bed. "An *hour*?"

"Yes, don't be late."

I groan. "Is this something else you were supposed to have told me sooner but conveniently forgot?"

I hear her chuckle. "I don't know what you mean. *Don't be late.*"

I grit my teeth together and force myself to get up. "What are we wearing?" I ask, but she's already gone...or chooses to ignore my question.

I pick out a white dress that looks classy yet modern ... it's one of the few that isn't revealing in one way or another. I allow my curls to do their thing around my face and do my rose updo so I don't have to dry my hair. The rest of the time I spend on my makeup.

Finally, pleased that I'm even halfway put together, I open my door and Luka is standing there, ready to knock.

"Very proper," he says, smirking. He's wearing a navy suit and looks so delicious it makes me angrier.

"Don't speak to me. Don't look at me."

I see his Adam's apple bob up and down as he looks in my eyes. If I didn't know better, I'd say he almost looks ashamed. But I do know better—he's not capable of true emotion.

"You know, it's customary to get irritable when you're horny. There's a remedy for that. A couple, actually. Would you like to hear them? Try them out later?" He's found his swagger again and is grinning wide, his blue eyes twinkling like I'm in on the joke.

I'm tempted. I am. What a fool. "Back off. Just stop with the innuendos, okay?"

He pulls back, serious again and his forehead creases in the middle. "We don't have time for an argument right now. Family's waiting. But we will continue this." He holds his arm out for me to take and I hold my long skirt as I swish past him.

I don't get very far before I realize I don't know where I'm going. I wait until he moves next to me. "Where?" is all I say.

He points ahead. "The gardens."

I speed-walk through the house and open the large doors; everyone is out there already. Cece acts deeply affronted that we've kept them waiting and I glare at Mara, who gives a little shrug and smirk. And then I see that they're all in navy.

"Why are you not wearing your navy dress?" Cece spits out. "You've already kept us waiting."

Juan steps out of the shadows, carrying one of his larger cameras. "It's perfect. She's the new bride. She *should* be the only one in white."

I smile at him in gratitude and Luka fumes next to me. Mara looks as though she's ready to trample me. I have to endure an hour of a prickly Luka. I cringe every time he touches me and he gets angrier as the hour passes.

Having to act like a loving couple is hard when I hate my husband. Or whatever this feeling is that is pulling me into a downward spiral.

The minute Juan says he has enough pictures, Luka grabs my arm and pulls me further into the garden, away from everyone else.

"What's going on with you? You're acting even worse than last night...or this morning. What's changed?"

My shoulders cave and I feel absolutely exhausted. "I'm tired. I can't keep up with your mood swings and I guess I'm acting the same way now. We're horrible together." I turn around and walk away. When I reach the family, they're all quiet, watching me, clearly eavesdropping. "Show's over," I tell them.

Mara does a slow clap and Cece taps her arm, stopping her.

Luka isn't far behind and he yells after me. "Eden, wait."

I hold up my hand and escape to my room. What could he possibly say that would be worth hearing? The tears start when I take my dress off. I remove my makeup in a trance and give up trying to be strong.

I shouldn't have to be this strong.

CHAPTER TWENTY-ONE

It's much later when I hear a knock on the door. I've napped and now I'm exercising along with online videos. I reach for a towel and wipe my forehead, opening the door.

Basile stands there, looking solemn. "May I come in?"

I open the door wider and step aside, making room for him to enter. Once he's inside, he moves to the round table with two chairs near the windows and takes a seat. I sit across from him.

"Did they send you to force me to behave?" I look out the window instead of at him.

"Something like that." He chuckles. "More like another event coming up. It will be at the Lancaster estate. You may have heard Mara mention Elias Lancaster a time or two." He gives me a deadpan look and I giggle. "He's an advisor to your father-in-law."

I *have* heard her mention him multiple times and have wondered if he's as obsessed with her as she is with him.

"When? What is the occasion?"

"Tomorrow night. It's Elias's twenty-fifth birthday and you and Luka are invited."

"This is the first I've heard of it, but okay. I suppose it's as good a time as any to figure out what is in my closet. Is it formal attire?"

He smiles. "Yes. My sister has a way of going overboard. Hopefully the clothes suit you. If not, you can always arrange a meeting with Teresa. I happen to know firsthand that she enjoyed working with you...and liked the way you stood up to Cece and Mara." He winks and my eyes widen.

Basile seems to know everything that goes on in this house, yet, he doesn't seem particularly close to his sister and brother-in-law. It's all very interesting. I wonder if I will ever find out how this family works.

"No time for a new dress tomorrow night but maybe for the next event..."

"Very well. And Eden? About behaving? You'll need to be on your best behavior with Luka tomorrow night. There will be eyes on you from all over the world."

I feel a chill at the thought. I'm about to ask what he means when he stands up and leaves. I wander to my closet and decide the rest of the day I will do beauty treatments on my hair and skin. I guess that's the bonus of not having to share a room with my husband. I try on a few dresses. There are so many lovely ones, but I settle on a royal blue dress that's fairly simple in the front—low cut but nothing too crazy—and then the back has the sparkle. The straps in the back are diamonds and it's cut out into a V low enough to be enticing yet still classy. I try it on and it fits like a glove. This is the dress.

I feel the best I've felt since arriving in Niaps. By the next day, I even feel somewhat relaxed. I received a massage after breakfast, which was served in my room. My skin feels like silk and my hair is extra shiny from the treatments. And the best part is that I haven't had to see a single member of the family all day. I'm saving up for tonight. When it's time to get ready, I sip champagne, turn on some music, and enjoy the time to myself. I was offered a hairstylist, but I said no.

When I see the finished result, I hate to admit it, but I'm the slightest bit excited for Luka to see me. I've arranged my hair in a side fall of curls to show off the back of my dress. My hair is cooperating and I have a flashback of Luka touching my curls when we were underwater. I shiver and press my lips together just as Luka raps on my door.

"Eden, are you ready to go?"

"One sec." I grab my jewel-encrusted clutch and open the door. He leans against the doorway and doesn't bother to hide the fact that he's checking me out.

"You've outdone yourself," he says. "Which Eden do I have tonight? Will you bite or will you purr?"

"I could ask you the same thing."

He holds his hands out. "What do you think? Am I suitable to be by your side?"

"You clean up okay."

He smirks and steps closer to me, pulling me flush against him. "Keep playing the cool act. I know it shouldn't, but it gets me so hard." He presses into me to prove his point.

"Have you been drinking already?" I frown.

"This is me stone-cold sober."

"So there's nothing to excuse your behavior."

His hands go lower and when he still feels my skin, he frowns. His hands go lower still until they find material, which happens to be hugging my backside. He thrusts into me again and leans his forehead against mine.

"You don't want to excuse my behavior. You like me best this way. Hot and salivating over you. Admit it."

I shake my head. "You need to take a step back."

He exhales a shuddering breath and drops his hands, stepping back. "We're going to be late. Let's go."

I shiver from the loss of his hands and the chill in his voice. I can't win with him.

I expect to see Mara in the car, but she must already be there. On the ride over, I relive the moments in the car with him the last time, in Pravia, and try desperately to rid myself of the memories. I grab a piece of paper and fan myself.

"There's no hiding from me, Eden. Now that I've had you, I know."

I turn to him and scowl. "What does that even mean?"

"I know you're dying to quench the ache between your legs. I know how wet you are right now. I know you think about me at night when you're lying alone in your bed and put your fingers where mine should be right this minute..."

"Stop. Why are you doing this?"

"There should be at least one thing beneficial to us... they've taken everything else from us. Why let them have this too?"

"It's not that simple."

"Isn't it?" He puts his hand on my cheek and the car comes to a stop.

I've never been so happy to step out of a car.

Elias Lancaster is a stunning man and I don't know what surprises me most about him—that he has manners and is a gentleman when we meet, or that Mara isn't gushing over him the way I expected her to. She is aloof and he certainly seems aware of her. Maybe she's right and there will be a wedding soon. He's friendly to everyone, though, so it's hard to be sure.

Luka and I find a tall table and he goes to get me a drink. He's gone so long I start to look around the room. I nearly choke when I see Mara and Nadia laughing at something Luka is saying. He's smiling—a smile brighter than I've seen on him in a while—and Nadia reaches out and grabs his arm as she laughs harder. Mara turns then and sees me looking and her smile gleams with malice. Nadia leans up and whispers something in Luka's ear and he goes still. He looks across the room and sees me watching and says something to her. She looks over her shoulder then, right at me. I stare at her brazenly until she looks away.

"I never imagined Luka would get married before me."

I turn and it's Elias, standing next to me.

"He's younger, never wanted to settle down...just seemed like it would be me."

"Our families had other plans."

"How's it working out so far?"

"Does the fact that he's talking to her right now instead of by my side tell you anything?"

We both turn and Luka and Mara are heading to our table. I don't see Nadia.

"The fact that he came running when he saw you talking to me tells me a helluva lot." Elias smiles. "Shouldn't keep a beautiful woman waiting, Prince," he says when Luka reaches the table. "You never know what kind of sharks are nearby." He grins when Luka's eyes flash and reaches out to take my hand, kissing it. "You come find me should your husband go missing again."

Mara chokes on her drink and Elias puts his arm around her. "Are you okay? You look pale."

"I'm fine." She shrugs his arm off of her and walks off. Probably to share grievances with Nadia.

Elias lifts his glass and goes to talk to someone else.

"What did he want?" Luka growls.

"I thought the two of you were friends."

"We are."

"Then why are you so angry that he's being friendly to your wife?"

"I don't like the way he's looking at you."

I shrug. "Someone has to look out for me while you fawn all over Nadia. It's embarrassing."

His cheeks flush and he looks down. "I've known her for years. Much longer than I've known you."

"You think I don't know that?" I take the drink he brought over for me and guzzle it down. "Makes it all the more humiliating."

He shuts his eyes and bites the side of his cheek. When he looks at me again, I'm scared of what I see in his eyes.

"What?" I demand.

"You don't need to worry about Nadia. It's...not your concern."

"Not my concern..." I repeat. "Wow. Sometimes I forget how heartless you are."

"I don't mean—I'm just saying...she's a friend, she's in our circles. She's not going anywhere. We'll run into her from time to time..." He swallows hard and I get a sick feeling in my stomach.

"I want to go back to the house."

"We need to at least stay until the cake." He attempts a grin, but it's not quite working. "You'll appreciate the cake."

We stand there, not speaking to each other, and barely

able to keep conversation going when people come by to talk to us. When the cake is cut, Luka gets us both a slice. I take a bite and it's delicious, but I'm too nauseated to eat it.

I'm not cut out for life in Niaps.

And I'm certainly not cut out for life with Luka.

CHAPTER TWENTY-TWO

Another car ride.

More awkward silence.

I don't even fully know why I'm angry with him tonight. Well, I do...seeing him laughing with Nadia stung, but it's more than that. I'm weary of the constant charge between us, tired of keeping up with his moodiness, unable to manage my own...and instead of falling into bed and sleeping due to this exhaustion, I lie awake night after night.

When we reach our bedrooms, he says, "Father says our instructors will be arriving this week. We can start classes on Monday."

"Okay." I turn the knob to my door and feel his hand on my arm. I look at him, waiting.

He hesitates before speaking, pausing so long I almost say something. "Would you want to go for a swim?" He sounds nice, sweet almost, and I'm tempted. So tempted. It feels like a peace offering...

"Another night, maybe? I'm really tired." And far too vulnerable.

He looks disappointed but nods. "Yeah, okay. Good night then."

"Night." I open the door and step inside, closing the door and leaning against it.

He's right. I *am* tired of the constant war between my brain and the ache between my legs. If this is what it's going to be like all the time, I'll go mad.

I listen for him to close his door, but instead, I hear his shoes clicking down the hall. I look out of my far left window and am about to turn away when I see him step outside and walk to the car. He gets inside and drives away. My heart falls to my feet. Is he going back to the party? Is he going to *her*?

It's dawn before I hear him come back and I finally give in to sleep.

I hardly see Luka for the rest of the week and when I do, it's in passing. Each night I listen for his door to open and watch as he walks to the car and drives away, not returning until early the next morning. More and more isolated, I venture into the halls, seeking any distraction to clear my mind. I'm not sure what the family does with their time. It seems they're always off to a luncheon or a charity and I wonder when I will be forced into the same hectic schedule of appointments.

Today the house feels empty and the marble floor feels cold against my feet. It's too hot to go outside, even for a swim. I've got to watch the sun; earlier in the week I didn't put on enough sunscreen and my shoulders are still burning.

I venture into a wing I've never been in and wonder if

this is where Luka was talking about when he said we could move to our own wing to get more privacy—that feels like forever ago.

I stop when I hear voices and try to turn around quickly, but the door opens and a good-looking guy my age or maybe a little older fills the doorway. He sees me and puts his fingers to his lips for me to be quiet. I stare at him and back away, quickly turning around and walking toward my room. But not before I hear Cece from the bedroom.

"Be quick with your exit," she says.

I round the corner and fly to my room and run straight into Luka. He holds my arms until I get my balance.

"Whoa, what's the rush?"

I shake my head and stutter. "No-uh...no rush. Sorry, I wasn't looking where I was going."

"You're shaking. What's going on?"

I hesitate for a moment and then come out with it. "I was taking a walk and saw a guy leaving. He startled me, that's all."

His face darkens. "My mom's boyfriend—brown hair, brown eyes, six feet or so?"

"That's him. Wait, what? She has a boyfriend?"

"She's acting out because my dad has had girlfriends for years. She decided this year to take a lover and pretends like she's not being completely obvious."

I lean against the wall and stare at the floor, trying to puzzle it out. Luka reaches out and smooths between my eyebrows.

"Does it make you angry?" I ask.

"I hate it," he admits. "But it's their life. Just another reason why I wanted to move out."

"If we moved out, I'd be even more alone than I am now."

Now his forehead creases and I want to smooth it, but I resist. "What do you mean?"

I shrug. "I at least see Basile a little bit each day, and your family in the dining room when I choose to go. I rarely see you and you're gone most nights, so...I imagine I'd go weeks without seeing anyone if it weren't for the events I'll eventually attend. If it weren't for Brienne—"

"Are you lonely, Eden?" He steps closer to me and his eyes are softer than usual. They make me want to open up and tell him things I have no business saying.

That I'm dying of loneliness.

That I miss the ease we had for those few days on our honeymoon.

That besides Basile and Brienne I am utterly alone.

That I'd do anything to get closer to him.

Instead, I say, "I'm okay."

"Our driver will take you wherever you'd like to go, just make sure there's a guard with you..."

"That sounds fun."

My sarcasm isn't lost on him. He bites the inside of his cheek and puts his hand on top of his head, slowly running his hands through his hair.

"How about we get out of here today? I'll show you some of my favorite spots."

"You don't have to entertain me. I'll adjust." I turn to walk toward my room and he catches up.

"I want to. Come on. It'll be fun."

I look at him to see if he means it and he seems sincere.

"Okay, sure. I guess we could..."

"Great. How long before you can be ready?"

"Ten minutes?"

He nods. "See you then."

I rifle through the closet and find a pair of flowy linen

pants. I'd prefer a bathing suit or jean shorts in this weather, and it would probably be okay here based on the clothes in my closet. I'd never get away with that in Farrow. I throw on a tank top and wide-brimmed hat, brush my teeth, put on a touch more makeup, and I'm ready to go. When I step out, Luka is too, and he's like my matching bookend in linen pants.

"We look like a married couple already." He smirks and tosses the keys in the air. "Let's do this."

I notice Brienne following when we step out of the house, and when Luka opens the car door for me, I'm surprised he's the one who will be driving. Brienne gets in the back seat and a guard pulls out ahead of us, while yet another follows.

Luka turns on some music and I look out the window at the water surrounding us on either side. I already feel better getting out of that house for even a few minutes.

"Do you ever get sick of being so closely guarded?" I ask.

His eyes flick up to the rearview mirror and Brienne is slowly nodding to the music.

"I don't mean her," I add.

"It's one of the biggest issues I argue about with my dad. I hate it. Fortunately, Franco and I are friends. The other guys are great too, but my dad doesn't even like that. He thinks if we're friends that keeps them from paying close enough attention."

"It's like that for me at home too. I think it's why I'm so close to my brother and sister."

"Yeah, I don't know what I would've done without Mara. Elias, too. We stuck together growing up and still do."

Just hearing Mara's name and the way he talks about

her unsettles me. I'm glad he's had her in his life, but I don't think she'll ever accept that I'm here. And I'm not sure he has a clue of what she's really like when she despises someone.

Like me.

"Are you hungry?" he asks.

"*Yes.*"

He grins. "Good answer."

As we get closer to the city, the houses are lined on the hills—cream stone and orange roofs in very crowded spaces. Some are large and spread out, but most are smaller and quaint. We drive into the heart of the city and the buildings are beautiful with tropical flowers in every color standing out against the stone.

"Do people leave you alone for the most part when you're here?"

A few people wave as we drive past.

"Most are respectful. There's usually at least one obnoxious photographer, but the majority of them stay out of my way."

We pull up to a beautiful, tall stone building with so many windows and hanging flower baskets at every column. When he parks, he holds up his hand. "Give me one second."

He jogs around to the other side and opens my door. I notice the guard smirk at Luka when I get out.

I see a sign saying it's a library and I'm surprised this would be Luka's favorite place. Until we walk inside. There are books as far as the eye can see. They reach the ceiling and tall rolling ladders are the only option for reaching the upper levels of books.

"I don't even know if you are a reader," Luka says quietly.

"I am." The words rush out quickly.

He smiles and holds out his hand. I take it and my heart feels close to bursting. *It's all the books*, I tell myself.

"This is heaven," I whisper.

"I agree." He motions for me to take a right turn and we go into a small tunnel with wall-to-wall windows.

I feel a bit like a gerbil, but I don't question him. When it opens up, we're in a large round room filled with greenery and tables with elaborate displays in the middle of each one. Delicious smells fill the room, making my mouth water. Only a few diners are here.

The staff practically falls all over themselves when they realize Prince Luka is in their fine establishment. We are asked if we'd like to dine on the roof. I look up and there's a glass elevator that leads to the top. Twinkle lights and greenery surround it, so I can't even see a table from here.

"Would you rather be up there or down here?" Luka asks. He looks like a doting husband rubbing my hand with his fingers and I remind myself that he's playing the part while we're in public.

"It looks intriguing up there."

"We'll go to the roof," he says.

We're escorted to the elevator and when we enter, I look at Luka. "No guard in the elevator?"

"There's one at the top already. He'll stay out of the way, don't worry. I had a feeling you'd want to be up there." He winks. "And I told Brienne to enjoy the books for a while."

When we step out, it's a wonderland. The view is extraordinary: we're up high enough to see the water and cliffs out one side and the other is a paradise of flowers and lights. A table is nestled in the middle of rose petals and a tree canopies overhead.

Wine is cooling in a bucket and Luka pulls a seat out for me. He takes his place across from me and we stare at each for a few long moments without saying a word.

I want to ask if he's okay, where he's going at night, why he's being so attentive today, but instead, I lean forward.

"Thank you."

My emotions are all over the place and I feel like I might cry if I say any more, so I don't. He seems to be clued in to my thoughts without me speaking them aloud.

He clasps my hands in his. "I'm sorry I haven't been more aware of what you needed. I'll try to do better, *be* better."

CHAPTER TWENTY-THREE

We've barely sat down and a huge wooden board is carried out, piled high with fruits and vegetables, olives and peppers, dips and cheeses...and meats to one side.

"It's like it's custom-made for us. I don't even have to touch the meat and I can still have all of this..." I wave my hand across the side closest to me.

"I might have called ahead and told them my wife is a veg head."

I roll my eyes, pretending to be annoyed but secretly pleased that he went to all this trouble.

"Save room for more food. This is just the appetizer."

"This is enough!"

"Oh no. Don't you know that with me there is always more?" His grin is wicked and I force myself to look away before I sink into his spell.

We clear the board quickly. I always forget how much Luka eats. Aside from the steak they place in front of him, everything else is catered to my tastes. I sample everything, moaning with pleasure every other bite.

"Everything is so good." I close my eyes and savor the flavors.

Luka smiles and tells me the history of the place. It used to be where the scholars went for higher learning. Large scrolls and manuals too big for one person to carry are still here and locked in glass.

"I'll show you after we eat." I make a disappointed face, so he adds, "But we can come back to look at the rest of the books another day. I really want to take you somewhere else today." He checks his watch. "After dessert."

They bring out mini cheesecakes and a pastry I've never had.

"Tarclova," he says and kisses his fingers like it's perfection. "Best ever. I'm already rock hard thinking about the noises you'll make trying this."

"Well, now I'll be sure to be silent." I laugh.

His eyes twinkle and he holds out the pastry for me to take a bite.

I do and my eyes close despite my efforts to not get carried away. "Oh my God. Mmmmmm," I hum, unable to hold it back. "That's the best thing I've ever tasted."

"I should have made you lick my fingers after I touched your p—"

"Luka!" Stunned, I open my eyes and he's staring at my mouth. I can faintly hear someone in the background, but I can't look away from him. He stands up and leans over the table, licking the edges of my lip with the tip of his tongue.

"Why can't I stay away from your mouth?" he whispers against my lips. He licks the seam then groans. "Let me in." His lips press against mine hungrily and I do just what he requests, I let him in.

We both hear something at the same time and pull

away. Our waiter is standing there wide-eyed and clears his throat. "Can I get you anything else?" he asks nervously.

Luka chuckles. "You don't have what I want." He gives me a hungry look. "I think we'd better take this elsewhere."

I put my hand over my mouth to hide my laugh and run my other across my cheeks. I feel them getting hotter and know I must be beet red.

The waiter puts the desserts in a little container and hands them to me. "Enjoy."

"Oh I will, thank you. Everything was delicious."

He bows and we get inside the elevator. All the way down, Luka stares at my mouth and when we arrive on the ground floor, he grabs my hand.

"Can I show you the scrolls on our next visit?"

"Sure." I hurry to keep up with how fast he's walking.

When we reach the car, the guard is already there. Luka opens my door, I sit, and he rounds the car, getting behind the wheel. He speeds through the streets and we head out of the city, in the opposite direction of the estate. We drive up through the mountains and then wind down until we're on the other side. When we reach sand, Luka parks.

He turns around to Brienne and says, "Keep the others back, okay? I don't want any eyes here."

She nods and relays the message to the others through her device.

Luka points out a cave. "That's what I want you to see."

We walk through the sand, a few hundred feet until we reach the cave. When we step inside, it's dark at first, but then we wind around and light from the opening on the other side is ahead. Water rushes through, first a trickle and then a loud rush of water. We're still on the ledge when Luka starts stripping. He leaves his underwear on and points at my clothes.

"You want to get your clothes wet?"

I'm speechless for a moment, watching him. He clears his throat to get my attention.

"No?" I frown at him. "But you didn't tell me we were going swimming."

He shrugs and I have to work very hard not to stare at his perfectly sculpted chest and enticing V when he's standing there looking so beautiful.

"Live a little," he says.

I pull my pants down first, watching his eyes widen when he sees my white lace. When my tank top comes off, he stares at my lacy bra until I put my hands on my hips.

"Right. Good." He almost seems nervous, but he's probably just momentarily lost all of his brain cells.

When he snaps out of his trance, he holds out his hand and I take it. We walk to the edge of the rushing water and look down.

"No way." I'm already shaking my head before I've even had a thorough look. "That's too far down."

"It's not very far and I'll be right there with you. I've done it a thousand times."

"No, you haven't."

"Okay, nine hundred times at least. Give or take a few hundred."

"I just learned to swim!"

"And you aced that in no time. This is next level."

"This is next level times one hundred."

"You ready? One, two, three."

And without thinking, I jump. Right before we reach the water, I remember to hold my breath and when I go under, Luka's there to help me reach the surface.

We're both laughing when we catch our breath.

"You did it! I didn't think you'd do it," he yells. He wraps his arms around me and holds me tight.

When I realize how long we've been holding each other, I pull away. "That was so fun." I look around and it feels like we're the only people around for miles. "How do we get back up to our clothes?"

His white teeth stand out against his tan skin when he grins. "We don't. I hope you weren't attached to those clothes." He backs away laughing when I splash him with water. "I'm kidding. See that little alcove there? We go through there and up the cliff. It leads to the car."

We swim for a few minutes, the water perfect for this hot day.

"I should get out of the sun, I didn't wear sunscreen because of the hat."

"You're right. Here let's go this way."

We swim to the shore and when I look back to where we jumped from, I can't believe I did it.

When we step out of the water, Luka picks me up and swings me around. I laugh, the adrenaline still rushing through me. He sets me down and holds me steady until the dizziness wears off before we walk toward the shade. There are odd formations of stone that resemble large boulders that we can walk between. There's a long one that looks as if it's been carved out in the middle and the sand under there is cool.

Luka turns and puts his hand on my arm. "Are you glad you came with me today?"

"It's been really nice. Thank you."

"You don't have to thank me. I should've shown you my city a long time ago. There's so much more to see. Tomorrow we can go to the flower fields. There's farsynthia as far as you can see."

"What's farsynthia?"

"The most beautiful, best-smelling flower in an array of colors. You've never heard of it?"

I shake my head. Luka reaches out and pushes back a long strand of my wet hair. My mouth parts and he steps closer, his lips brushing mine. It quickly intensifies and he holds me tighter. I can feel every sensation with only my thin lace and his wet boxer briefs between us. I push back every vow I've made to myself about not letting him in and succumb to him. If I can just hold on to my sanity this time. Stay levelheaded...

"I can't get you out of my head, Eden. Let me taste you. Please. I just need a little taste."

I moan as he kisses down my neck and falls to his knees. He pulls my lace down and looks up at me before taking a long swipe. I lean my head back on the stone and rock into his mouth. His fingers find me and rub quick little circles while his tongue drives into me slowly, and I look down at him, transfixed.

He's relentless.

Starving.

He looks up at me and that seals it. I'm gone. I shudder against him, my body falling limp against him. He stands up and I feel him hard against my belly. I can't stop myself. I pull his briefs down and touch him.

"I want to take you against this wall." He grabs my face on either side and pulls my mouth to his.

I stand on my tiptoes and he shudders into my mouth, lowering just enough to fit his tip inside. As soon as I feel him there, I want all of him.

"More," I whisper.

"God, I can't take this." He thrusts into me hard and I cry out. His eyes open. "Did I hurt you?"

"Harder," I practically scream.

In and out, harder, faster. I'm breathless and already so close.

He bites my lip and really drives into me. It's like he knows me inside out and gives me exactly what I need. Neither of us last long and when he comes, "Eden," in a long, drawn-out groan escapes his lips. It sounds so intimate...so meaningful...that I fear I'll never hear my name again without hearing him saying it just like this.

When he slips out of me, he holds my cheek and studies me. "Are you okay?"

I press my lips together and nod. "You?"

"You're wrecking me. I hope you know, you are *annihilating* me."

I grin and he presses a quick kiss on my nose.

———

He grabs our clothes while I wait in the trees, already hot again. I rest on a stone and fan myself with a long leaf. When he gets back, he's dressed and holds my clothes to his chest.

"I'm hesitant to give these back. You in all that white is too sexy to cover up."

I hold out my hand. "Give 'em."

He rolls his eyes heavenward and holds them out, watching intently as I pull my pants on.

"We should actually get going. It's supposed to rain soon."

We hurry the rest of the way and when we are about halfway home, it starts pouring.

"I wasn't quite ready to go home," he says, turning the windshield wipers to a higher speed. "Tomorrow, how about we spend the night in one of the inns nearby. Or maybe tonight we can move to the wing I was telling you about."

I'm happy he can't see my face because I'm flushing and fighting back the biggest smile. It might be the craziest decision to make, but today has felt *so good*.

I needed this.

Maybe I need him.

"I'd like that." I take a deep breath and force myself to ask: "Are you sure this is what you want?"

"I think you're getting in my blood whether I want you to or not."

I'm not quite sure what to make of that answer, but I know this much...

I'm not the only one affected by this pull we have toward one another.

CHAPTER TWENTY-FOUR

When we reach the estate, Basile is the only one who sees us come in. The guards disappear once we're inside and Basile nods as he keeps walking. He gives me a little smirk before he turns the corner and I withhold the building laughter in my chest. My heart feels like a different one than I left with, much lighter, more hopeful.

Something resembling happiness.

We reach our rooms and Luka leans against his door. "I'll tell Hanna to fix up the other room for us, but for now, come into mine?"

He pulls me by the waist until I'm lined up with him and opens his door. I fall into him and he lifts me up, sliding me slowly down until I feel him between my legs.

"Are you always ready?" I grin against his lips.

"Always."

He shifts behind me. "Take off your clothes," he says, his voice low.

I take my pants off slowly, and he helps, pulling the lace down for me. He pulls my tank top over my head, unclasps my bra, and with his hands on my waist, he pushes me forward, into the bathroom.

He turns the shower on and we step inside. He motions to the seat that lines one side of the shower. "Put your hands there."

My pulse pounding everywhere, I do what he asks. This time when he thrusts inside, it's slow and deliberate. When he's as deep as he can possibly get, he pulls my back flush against his chest and lets the water fall over us as he moves in and out, agonizingly slow.

"Look at me."

I look over my shoulder and the feeling intensifies when we're staring at one another. He grabs hold of my hair in his fist and covers my mouth with a brutal kiss. Releasing me, his hand slides down to my hip, digging his fingers into my skin. He snakes his other arm around my waist then travels down, down, down, flicking my clit until I gasp.

The sound of our moans and slapping flesh echoes. When I think I can't take another second, he pinches one of my nipples and I tighten against him and explode.

We are fury and fire in the calm, steady mist of water.

Nothing else matters. It's just the two of us: no doubts, no regrets, only our quiet breathing as he remains inside me.

He pulls my hair back and kisses me, both of us panting hard. "I don't want to fight anymore," he says hoarsely. "Please?"

I don't say anything back, but my heart shouts out its response. *Yes, yes, yes. I'm falling for you.*

"I want to finish this in bed." He pulls out and we step on a towel, him walking backward as he watches me, one hand holding mine and the other fisting himself. He is a sight to behold.

"On your hands and knees," he says when we reach the bed. I turn away, shy suddenly, but do as he asks.

He continues stroking himself, leaving me there waiting for him. "I wish you could see how hot you look right now, soaking wet, waiting for me. So fucking hot."

He isn't gentle when he enters me and I scream. It feels too right, too perfect; I can't even be embarrassed anymore. He's even louder than me and when I clench around him so tightly, he explodes and I drain him dry.

As I'm floating back to earth, I think about how grateful I am for birth control. That last time would have most definitely resulted in a baby.

"I feel like I need another shower." I giggle as I press my lips to his chest.

"You better go without me or you'll never get clean." He's closing his eyes, but his lips lift.

I think this might be the most content I've seen him.

I go back to the shower and wash thoroughly, unable to wipe the smile off my face. When I get out, I towel off and go through the side door into his closet for a shirt. I hear a knock and voices while I'm in there. It sounds like Basile. I find a pair of Luka's sweats, throw them on and roll down the top band and roll up the legs, eyes widening when I see myself in the mirror. *Hot mess.*

I step out of the main closet door and Luka and Basile stop talking, looking at me with something akin to horror.

"What's wrong?" I pull out the waist on the sweats. "Don't worry, I'm not gonna wear this in public. Ever." When neither of them laugh, I swallow hard. "What's going on?"

Basile looks at Luka and hands him an iPad. He swipes his hands over his face and sits on the bed, looking defeated.

"You're scaring me. Luka?"

"I don't want you to hear about this from anyone but me," he finally says, his voice flat. "Pictures have come out of Nadia and me. Incriminating pictures," he adds.

I feel an ache in my chest, but when it hurts too much, I shut it down, shifting into a cold, calm nothing. "Oh. When did you—?"

I don't have to clarify. He knows what I'm asking.

"That's where I was when I left...with Nadia. I—" He stops when Basile quietly leaves the room. "And also the night of Elias' party."

A knot that feels like a fist forms in my throat and I struggle to swallow past it.

"You knew what you were getting into—I told you—" he starts.

I hold up my hand, stopping him. I pick up my clothes and panties from the floor and walk out. He's on my heels, sheet wrapped around himself. When I try to slam my door in his face, his hand keeps it from shutting and he follows me.

"Get out."

"At least hear me out." His eyes are pleading with me and he puts his hand on my shoulder.

I shove it off.

"Don't touch me again. I won't just be another conquest for you." I hate so much that I cry when I'm angry, but I am furious right now and the tears threaten to spill over. "You couldn't at least spare me the embarrassment of cheating on me in our first month of marriage by being *discreet*?" I shake my head. "I don't even understand why coming here was such a big deal, if you were just going to get caught with Nadia. Did you *want* me to see that or were you really so stupid to think you wouldn't get caught?" I'm winding up even more now, the threat of tears gone. "Your dad making up the story about us taking attention from Mara? She's not even in the news right now. None of this makes sense. Or are you just missing Nadia so badly, your brain cells have disappeared, along with your integrity? What was today about? Why couldn't you just leave me alone?" I yell and choke back a sob. *"Get. Out."*

"But I can't. I can't leave you alone. That's the—" He slams his hand against the wall. "Today...I thought we moved past everything to—"

"I don't want to even hear the sound of your voice." I walk to the window and keep my back to him. I feel ridiculous in his clothes.

He doesn't belong to me and he never did. He never will.

"I won't stand in your way. If you want to be with her, go right ahead. Just don't make the tabloids. I think that's more than fair. Even your mother and father have figured that out." I put my hand over my mouth and squeeze my eyes shut.

"I've known that I don't deserve you," he whispers. "And who am I kidding? The apple doesn't fall far from the tree. But you—you make me feel like maybe I could be different."

"I don't trust anything that comes out of your mouth."

He sighs, and eventually, he walks to the door. When he opens it and walks out, I turn around and Mara is standing there in the hall, blatantly listening. Luka pushes past her and her grin is wide as she leans in my doorway.

"Your time is almost up," she says gleefully. "I'd start packing if I were you."

I move toward her so fast, her eyes widen and she backs out. I slam the door in her face and fall on the bed, screaming into my pillow.

Brienne comes into the room and sits by me on the bed, holding my hand while I cry.

When I've spent far too much time crying, I look for the pictures online.

The first headline says: *Trouble in paradise for the newlyweds already?*

I click the link and wait a moment for the pictures to load. *Groom seen at Princess Nadia's Halkar apartment in the days leading up to his reception with Princess Eden.*

I start to shake as picture after picture shows him entering her apartment, multiple shots of them on her balcony hugging, two of them kissing, and him leaving in the early hours of the morning.

And again a few days later...

There are more pictures of them the night of Elias's party. Heart pounding, I get to the end and click the next link, which shows more of the same. And another, and another...until I'm led to all the old pictures of them together. It seems he's never been able to stay away from her, even when he's seeing someone else. Apparently, he's not able to stay away from her when he's married either. His hot and cold routine makes more sense now.

Nothing about the way he's been today makes sense.

Nothing.

Tears stream down my face and I can't breathe.

I'll go home.

That becomes my overwhelming desire and I pick up the phone to call my mother, but I can't stop crying long enough to do it. Tomorrow. I'll call her tomorrow.

Hours later, Basile knocks on the door. "Can I come in?"

I open the door and his eyes are sad when he sees the shape I'm in.

I motion for him to sit at the table by the windows and I sit across from him.

"I know I don't have the right to ask, but I will anyway. For the sake of everyone in the house. For the sake of trying to dissolve this latest travesty." He shakes his head. "I'm not pretending to know the depth of your relationship with Luka; I don't know whether these new pictures hurt you or make you angry. Maybe you couldn't care less...but that's not the impression I'm getting." He pats my hand and my lips tremble. "I'm sorry you're hurting."

I look at him, wanting him to get on with it.

"I happen to think you're really good for Luka. I've never liked Nadia...or Luka for that matter. You make him infinitely more likable."

I sigh and he grins.

"However, I do love the boy, even when he is a pigheaded prat." He leans in and my heart starts to pound, knowing he's finally going to say what he came to say. "Can I ask that you be patient with him while he finds his way? I think it will be worth it."

I frown at him. "He's humiliated me, whether there are *feelings* involved or not. No matter what kind of pretense we're putting out to the world—what kind of start is that to a marriage? I don't understand why we even came here if he was going to run off and do that."

"Luka should be strangled for his egregious mistake, I grant you that. But I'm still asking for you to give him time. I think he'll come around."

I shake my head. "As if I *want* him to come around. No, thank you."

Basile tilts his head, his lips in a flat line. "That's too bad. Because I think he could love you."

I scoff, scowling at him. "He's incapable of love." I lean in closer to him. "And I'm not getting close enough for him to try it out on me."

Basile smiles. "It remains to be seen. I like your *fire*, Eden Catano—nice ring to that, by the way. My wager is on you bringing him to his knees, and I, for one, cannot wait to watch." He stands up and walks to the door. "All this lust and angst in the air are driving me to the wine. I'll be in the library should you care to join me."

"I think I'll hide here a little longer, thank you."

Luka knocks on the door not long after Basile leaves.

"Eden," he calls, "talk to me, please."

I shut myself in the bathroom and hold my knees to my chest, burying my head and wishing I could bury my heart.

CHAPTER TWENTY-FIVE

A couple of days pass before I see Luka again. It's quiet next door, so I'm not sure if he's even around. I don't venture beyond my room long enough to find out. I do search the web to see if any more pictures have come out, but they're still having a heyday with the ones I've seen already. Nothing new.

On day three of my hideout, our pictures with Juan are released. There are photos of the two of us and several of me alone. We look like a dream couple. Like the royalty we're built up to be. And under the comments of both our couple shots and my solo pictures, I'm made out to be a pathetic, blind, frigid princess who must not put out enough to keep the young prince satisfied. Many are rooting for him to be with Princess Nadia and never liked me to begin with; others think we are beautiful together and need to give ourselves time to grow in love.

It's all ridiculous. This manufactured romance that everyone can see right through—why bother trying to fool anyone?

Mid-morning, Basile knocks on my door.

When I crack it open, he says, "I've held them off as long as I can."

"Who?"

"Your in-laws. They expect to see you at dinner tonight. Normally I'd say do what you want in regard to where you take your meals, but this time I think you should be there."

I don't respond and he sighs before backing away. All of a sudden, my room feels claustrophobic. I pick up my bag and try to catch up with him.

"Basile," I call, pushing the strap of my bag up on my shoulder. He stops and turns around. "I'd like to use the car today, if that's okay."

"Sure," his face brightens, "let me just arrange for a guard to go with you. The driver will be ready to take you wherever you'd like to go."

"Great. Thank you."

Harmi is my driver and he and Brienne view each other with suspicion. I tell them where I want to go and Harmi looks at me from the rearview mirror.

"Are you sure? It will be crowded."

"Yes, I'm sure."

We stop by the art store and I pick up my supplies, smiling at all the customers and employees who gawk at me when I walk in. When I set my things down on the counter, it takes a few minutes for the girl to snap out of her fog.

"I-I can't believe you are in my shop," she says. She waves her hand across my items. "Take it. I cannot charge you. It's such an honor for you to step inside."

"Please let me pay. That way I won't feel bad about asking you to order certain colors next time."

She grins widely and nods, taking the money.

Brienne helps me with my packages and stares at me blankly when I step outside.

"Lighten up." I brush past her and Harmi holds my door for me. I hate the attention it puts on me to have guards, always have, but today I needed out of that mausoleum too much to mind.

We drive to the most crowded area on the beach and when Brienne tries to help me carry things onto the sand, I shake my head. "I'll make several trips. I need some time alone today."

"Lady Eden, you shouldn't be out here in the open without me by your side."

"Fine, but please don't be obvious."

She hands me the small easel and oil pastels and I walk out on the sand, setting it down near a few families with dogs. I go back to the car for the canvases and when I sit down on the sand, I savor the fact that no one has recognized me yet. The hat helps. It won't last, but for the moment, it's freeing.

I place the bag by my feet, open up the pastels, then put a canvas on the easel. And then I zone in on my subject. He's perfect: brown hair and dark eyes that are so expressive. It only takes fifteen minutes or so to capture his personality.

I'm assessing my work when I hear a little voice next to me. "Is that my dog?" she asks, her sweet voice in awe.

I point at the little dog I've been drawing. "Is that your dog right there?"

She nods slowly, her two front teeth barely growing back in. "Yes," she whispers. "Are you Princess Eden?"

I lean forward and whisper in her ear. "I am."

"Wow."

I add a few finishing touches to her dog and then hand it to her. "Here you go."

"I can keep the drawing?"

"Yes, it's yours."

She gasps and grabs it, running to her mom. "Thank you!" she yells over her shoulder.

I smile and set up a new canvas. Before long, I have a crowd of people surrounding me, asking me to draw their child, or themselves; a few couples shyly ask me to draw them. I draw until I run out of canvases and then say yes to every selfie request. By late afternoon, I've met a ton of the locals and feel a little better about humanity. Sometimes you have to stay away from the trolls behind screens and interact with real, genuine people. It's a good reminder for me to step out of my comfort zone more often. This day turned out so much better for me, and I daresay for everyone I met.

I get into the car, smiling and exhausted.

"Home?" Harmi asks.

Not my home.

"Yes, please."

It takes a while to get back because of an accident just outside of town and once we get around it, Harmi takes the curves like we're in a race. Way too fast for me. I hold onto the handle and yelp on one turn.

"What is your rush?" I screech.

"You are late for dinner."

"I won't make it to dinner at all if you don't slow down."

He slows down marginally, but not enough to settle my galloping heart. When we pull into the long driveway, I glare at him and pick up the things that scattered from my purse.

"My apologies, Lady Eden," he says when he opens my door.

"Luka will hear of this," I hear Brienne telling him.

Luka is there in the next second, hands on top of his head.

"Where have you been?" Luka's face is red and his hair is standing in every direction. He has a few days' worth of stubble and looks *frantic*. "Where have you been?" he demands once more.

"Out." I move past him and he jogs to catch up with me.

"Basile told you to be here for dinner."

"Did I miss dinner? I lost track of time."

"You can still eat, but you're *late*." He puts his hand on my arm. "Are you okay? I was worried."

I brush his hand off and wait as Brienne opens the door to the house for us. Hanna is hovering in the entryway and when she sees that I'm carrying things, she rushes forward, holding out her hands.

"I can put your things in your room. The king is waiting."

"We can't have that, can we?" I'm still living high on the beauty of my day and not willing to let this house bring me back down. Everyone looks at me like I'm possessed and I shrug. "I could use a shower, but I guess I could eat."

The dining room is frigid when I walk inside, not the temperature, the demeanor of everyone at the table: Titus, Cece, and Mara. Basile is the exception and he smiles indulgently when he sees I'm not properly dressed for dinner.

"Where have you been today, Eden?" Cece asks.

"I went to the beach."

"Please be more specific."

"I had Harmi and Brienne with me. They can give you the specifics."

She slams her hand down on the table. "This is a time when we need you to be showing a united front, not a time for you to go gallivanting into town on a whim and playing cozy with the locals. There have been pictures of you multiplying by the hour. What were you thinking?"

"Oh, so the question was rhetorical. You knew exactly where I was."

If fire could explode out of someone's head, it would be billowing out of Cece's. "I will not tolerate your insolence. As I said, you need to stick next to Luka for the next week at least, and act like the doting wife you need to become."

"He hasn't been sticking next to me like a doting husband though; he's been sticking his co—"

Luka places his hand over my mouth and just as hastily withdraws it. "I'm sorry. Trying to save you from more outrage."

"That'll never change, his cock will look elsewhere, especially if he's stuck with you the rest of his life," Mara throws in.

Luka levels her with a glare and she shrugs. "Just telling it like it is."

I ignore her and speak low so only Luka can hear me.

"I don't need you to save me from anything. You're the one who got us into this mess. It's not up to me to fix it."

He lowers his head. "You're right." He turns toward me then, his knees hitting my thigh, and leans in. "Eden, I'm so sorry. I thought—well, I wasn't thinking clearly. But now, I need you to he—"

"I don't want to hear the inner workings of your mind or the lack thereof." I raise my voice. "I married into a family of dysfunction—what's one more mess? It's not up to me to make your family look wholesome. That's impossible." I stand, looking at Chelsea and smile. "I'm sorry I missed your meal. It looks delicious."

"I'll bring a plate to your room later," she whispers as I walk past her.

"Not so fast," Titus says, holding his hand up.

In spite of all my righteous indignation, I stop.

"Luka has caused a great deal of shame with his actions. While I know he warned you of how a marriage to him would be, it is despicable that he was so careless in his indiscretions."

Cece rolls her eyes next to him and I have to bite the inside of my jaw to keep from going into hysterical laughter. I might lose it and never get it back if I start laughing now.

"He will make it up to you," Titus finishes.

He looks at me like I should be grateful and that's when it bursts out of me. I laugh until I cry, my shoulders shaking and every time I try to stop, it just wells up in me again. They sit there in confusion and don't know what to do with me, which just makes me laugh harder. When I can finally get a breath, I hold up my hand, as if that will make me stop. It doesn't. I wipe my cheeks and press my lips together until the mania in me slows.

"I'd much rather see the truth outright than have someone treat me like I'm clueless. Either way, it's gross. When you've made a commitment, you should keep it. But I can see that he comes from a long line of people who can't keep their word. At least the truth is out about him."

I don't stick around after I've said my piece. They can take their little family meeting and shove it.

I'm almost to my room when Mara calls after me. "Eden! I almost forgot." She holds a wrapped gift out for me to take.

"What's this?" My voice is full of suspicion.

"Just a little something I thought you might enjoy."

I unwrap it carefully and lift the lid to the box. Inside is a framed picture of Luka kissing Nadia.

"Tick-tock," she whispers.

I throw the picture down the hall and it breaks into tiny pieces. I sneer in her face and shrug. "That was an exquisite La Dora frame but not really my taste."

As soon as I close my bedroom door, all my bravado dissolves and I cry hot, salty tears until I'm a puffy mess.

What good is it to know the truth when I can't even admit the truth to myself?

Some secrets should never come to light.

This will never be my home.

They're not my family.

My heart is already irrevocably his…

Therefore I am chained to a life of heartbreak.

CHAPTER TWENTY-SIX

I start going out every morning. I set up my easel in different areas of the city and talk with people about everything from what they had for breakfast to the difficulties they're having with their mother-in-law. It makes me feel connected to something bigger than myself—a part of this new community that I'm supposed to have claimed. In getting to know the people of Niaps, I actually do become immersed in the culture and it's the closest to home I've felt since arriving.

Harmi and Brienne are growing on each other. Harmi is an insufferable grouch, and with Brienne, it's hard to tell what she's thinking, but every now and then they'll do something that shows a hint of their softer sides. Like when Harmi found a chair for a tiny old woman who wanted me to draw her portrait. She acted like she didn't need it and Harmi made sure he got her one anyway, ushering her into it like she was the queen bee. And Brienne played ball with a little boy while I consoled the boy's mother. She'd just found out her husband was cheating on her and—naturally—felt a camaraderie with me. I didn't tell her that our situations were not the same—my husband never loved me and we don't have a real life together—but just listened and let her talk it out.

Every day when I get back to the house, I'm greeted with hostility from Luka's family. They don't like that I'm doing my own thing, something they never thought of, and growing favor with their people.

It feels like I'm finally doing something right.

I left early this morning, earlier than usual, because I wanted to swim a while in the little private beach I found one of the days I'd gone exploring. Harmi passed a beautiful spot and I begged him to stop right there so I could go see where the path led.

"Lady Eden, I don't think it's a good idea for you to swim alone when you are so new at it," Brienne warned the first time we stopped.

"I'm never really alone, am I? Come in for a swim, if you like."

She leveled me with a look and ever since then she stands guard while I swim, barely tolerating the sun. The place has become my favorite morning and early evening spot ever since. There's never anyone here when I show up and the current isn't as strong as it is in some of the other areas.

I never leave without my hat and sunscreen. My skin is still getting a gradual rosy color and the freckles are popping up right and left, despite me slathering sunscreen on faithfully and covering up as best I can. This morning I don't feel like wearing my hat and run into the water, practicing a dive. It's a horrendous attempt and I get out, trying again. On my third attempt, I hear chuckling behind me and whip around.

Luka is standing there, pulling down his pants. "You have to hold your hands like this." He positions his hands and does the motions of a dive without actually going in the water. "And you need to be in deeper water. Trying to dive while you're already in the water..." He shakes his head, laughing.

"You're following me now?"

"I follow you every day," he says, smiling. "Gotta see what my wife is up to for myself. You've become quite the celebrity around here...in far less time than it took for the rest of us."

"That's an invasion of my privacy." I walk into the water when his eyes on me in my bikini become too heated.

"It can't be wrong to enjoy you doing your thing...I didn't know you were an artist. Why didn't you tell me?"

"We haven't really been on a quest of getting to know one another."

"Well, actually, I think we've done pretty well with that..." His eyes smile along with his lips and I shake my head.

"Don't do that. Don't joke about us having sex. I know it meant nothing to you, but I'm not quite ready to be the object of your jokes just yet."

"You think that's what I was doing? That wasn't my intention at all. I simply meant—"

"What do you want from me, Luka?" I interrupt.

"I want to start over." He says it simply, like it's the easiest thing to fall out of his mouth; meanwhile, it knocks me sideways.

"Why?"

"Because the more I find out about you, the more I want to know."

"Too little, too late."

He bites his upper lip and nods before clearing his throat. "You know our professor is waiting to teach us, right?

She's been here for a few days and might give up if both of us keep skipping out..."

"I forgot all about that!" I pick up my bag and wave to Harmi. He gets into place by the car and I hustle up the path.

"Hold on. Where are you going?" Luka calls.

"To apologize to the professor."

I get in the car and don't bother to look behind me.

When we pull into the driveway, I hop out and Hanna takes my things. "Where is the professor?"

"She's in the study, east wing," she replies.

"Thanks, Hanna."

I practically run to the study and stop suddenly as I reach the door. Luka bumps into me from behind. Groaning, I evil-eye him over my shoulder.

"Your stealth skills are way off today. You've really been following me for days? I don't buy it. You couldn't sneak up on a dead man."

He leans in and I feel his breath against my neck. "Maybe I wanted to be seen today."

I roll my eyes and knock twice on the door. A woman with white hair and steely grey eyes looks up from her desk and clasps her hands together when we enter.

"If it isn't the newlyweds. I'm glad you've finally decided to join me. My colleague Jesu chose today of all days to show up late, probably thinking you'd skip again."

"I apologize, Ms.—"

"Macardi," she finishes. "No apologies necessary. Your uncle filled me in on a little bit of what has been happening around here. And you're here now. Are you ready to study?"

"Yes," we both answer.

There's only one long table across from her, with two

chairs. I sigh and sit down, Luka scooting in next to me. At first I find it hard to concentrate when he's so close, but Ms. Macardi comes alive when she teaches. This is the way I've always learned—one-on-one or with my siblings—so before long, I relax and take notes while occasionally doodling on the edges of my notebook.

We fall into a routine over the next couple of weeks. Classes in the morning and in the afternoons I wander around town, trying to stay one step ahead of Luka. He doesn't bother hiding anymore. When I'm on the beach, he comes and watches me draw. If I'm swimming, he lets me swim for a while and then joins me, usually with some wisecrack about being the one to teach me how to swim.

Sometimes, when my guard is down, I start to have fun with him. He's like an obnoxious bulldog that won't go away. As soon as I'm done with him, he shows up panting, showing me his newest trick...which in his case lately, has been kindness.

I see him hand an elderly woman a flower. She flushes and puts it behind her ear as he beams, and it just makes me livid. How dare he act like a good person when I *need* to be mad at him.

At night, images of him with Nadia invade my mind, along with memories of us in his bed, on the beach, in the shower. I wake up, sweating and turned on. I listen for sounds of him leaving the house, but either he has become better at sneaking out or he doesn't go anywhere.

In my weakest moments, I search the Internet in the middle of the night, but Nadia is only seen with Mara or people from Elias's party. Eventually, she returns home to Yuman, and then I start thinking it's the only reason I'm seeing him so much —he doesn't have his sex buddy, so I'm on his radar again.

It starts to take its toll on me and my mind never seems to shut down.

This morning I have drifted off in class twice and both times, I come to with Luka and Ms. Macardi eyeing me with amusement.

She finally says, "I can't seem to hold your interest today, Eden. Why don't you go take a nap and I'll see you in the morning."

I flush and gather my things. "I'm so sorry. I will try to be more attentive tomorrow."

I leave the room as quickly as I can, embarrassed, but also relieved that maybe I can catch up on some sleep. It's been three nights since I got a good night's sleep and I can hardly keep my eyes open.

"Eden?" Luka rounds the corner when I reach my room. "Are you okay?" His forehead is creased into tiny lines of concern and for the hundredth time, I think about how beautiful he is.

"I'm fine."

"That's your standard answer for everything. I don't believe you."

I shrug. "I can't be bothered to convince you."

His shoulders sag and he steps closer to me. "When will you let me in again? I'm trying so hard to reach you."

"Is that what this nice act is? I wondered when you'd shed that. You can, you know...go ahead and let the real you come out to play. I know this is hard work."

He jerks back like I've struck him and his eyes are wounded. I would almost feel bad if I didn't believe it's all been a ruse.

"I hope you can get some rest," he says quietly.

He goes into his room and shuts the door.

———

I wake up and feel like I'm suffocating. I shake underneath the covers, but my skin is hot and my sheets are soaked with sweat. The room is dark; I can't tell what time it is. My head feels like someone is slicing it in two. I groan and put my hand to my head, realizing in that movement how achy my entire body feels.

I fall asleep again and wake to a rap on the door.

"Eden?" When I don't answer right away, the door opens and Luka peeks in. When he sees that I'm in bed, he rushes over. "Are you okay? You've been sleeping for a long time."

"How long?" I croak and put my hands to my throat. Everything hurts.

"I haven't seen you since yesterday. When I looked in here last night, you were sleeping hard." He puts his hand to my forehead. "Shit, you're burning up. How long have you been feeling sick?"

"I was just so tired..." My eyes close. It hurts too much to keep them open. "My head is going to explode," I whisper.

"I'll get some medicine for your head and we'll have Dr. Karibu come take a look. I'll be back."

I fall asleep and wake up to a doctor and Cece coming into the room. The doctor does some bloodwork, takes my temperature, and announces I have the flu. Cece backs out of the room and Luka climbs onto the bed next to me.

"What do we do?" he asks.

"Keep her hydrated. I will give her an herbal tea that should lessen the length of the sickness, but it will still take a couple of days to fully heal. She needs a lot of rest."

"Okay, thank you for coming. Will you come check on her tomorrow?"

I open my eyes to tell Luka that won't be necessary, but I don't have the energy.

"And the day after that." Dr. Karibu smiles kindly. He points to the door. "Is it okay if I go prepare the tea in the kitchen?"

"Can you show me how to do it so I can give it to her when you're gone?" Luka stands up and starts to follow the doctor.

"I was hoping you would," Dr. Karibu responds.

They leave the room and I go back into my dream world where Luka and I are swimming in the blue, blue waters.

CHAPTER TWENTY-SEVEN

I drift in and out of consciousness. Crazy dreams and stretches of time when I know I must be dreaming because Luka is forcing me to sip tea all the time. Other times, he has a cold washcloth on my forehead and is holding me while I shake with chills. Sometimes I think I hear him talking to me and I chase the sound, but the dreams pull me under again. I'm not sure what is real.

I wake up with a start and he's lying facing me, eyes wide open.

"Hey," he whispers.

"Hey."

He touches my forehead and takes a deep breath. "A little better. You scared me."

"How come?"

"You've been out of it for three days."

"*Really?*"

"Your temperature was up to 104 and I didn't know what to do. Dr. Karibu has been here twice a day and if he didn't assure me you were coming out of it, I would've lost my mind."

I swallow hard and realize just how dry my mouth is.

"Do you need water?"

I nod.

He leans over to his side of the bed and grabs a glass of ice water. A teapot is sitting next to that. He holds the water for me to sip and I drink it greedily. When I'm done, I lay my head back on the pillow, spent.

"The tea was real?"

"What?"

I motion toward the teapot.

"Oh, yeah. It's supposed to help you get better faster. It doesn't work fast enough, in my opinion."

"You look tired...I hope you don't get sick."

"I have the immune system of a dragon."

"I'm not familiar with the systems of dragons," I whisper.

"God, I've missed you." He grins.

"I need a bath."

"I'll go run the water. Bubbles?"

"Who are you?"

He laughs. "I'm really glad you're feeling better. I-I thought I might lose you. You were so out of it. My family even seemed concerned." His lips quirk up on one side and I smile in spite of myself. "Okay, water. I'll be right back to help you in there."

I feel like I've been hit by a truck. By the time he comes back in and says the water is ready, I'm rethinking getting up.

"I'm too tired," I tell him, nestling deeper beneath the covers.

"You can rest in there. I'll sit with you."

I lift my head. "Nuh-uh. No. You—" I point at him weakly and shake my head.

"I've seen it all, remember? And I won't cop a feel. Besides, there are enough bubbles in this bath to bury you, which is why I need to stay in there and make sure you've not devoured."

"It's like I woke up and you're...an imposter. I don't know what to do with this."

He laughs like I have a sense of humor and I frown at him. He throws back the covers and I curl up.

"Come on, loosen up. Let me pick you up."

I try to relax my body and he puts his arms underneath me and carries me to the bathroom. I vaguely remember him helping me to the bathroom the past few days and groan.

"Have you been in here while I go to the *bathroom*?" I shriek, albeit weakly.

"I feel the need to stress here that *we are married*."

He sets me down by the toilet and I shoo him out of the room. "That's not something you've ever wanted to admit, so I don't know why it counts now."

"This is how you sound from out here, *blah-blah blah, blah-blah-blah-blah*."

I flush the toilet and wash my hands, brush my teeth, and remove the gown I know I wasn't wearing when I went to bed a few days ago. I step into the bath and he knocks, coming in without waiting for permission.

"You were supposed to wait for help. You could've stumbled."

I roll my eyes. "When I get my strength back, you will pay."

He grins like he's so pleased and then just as quickly sobers. "When you were so hot and shaking like crazy, mumbling off-the-wall things, I thought I'd give anything to hear your smart mouth, but now I'm questioning my thinking." He picks up the shampoo. "Let me help you with your hair. You probably shouldn't be up too long."

I can't argue with him there. I already feel too weak to make it back to bed.

"Hanna is putting clean sheets on your bed right now." He pours water over my hair and scrubs my scalp. I close my eyes and enjoy the feeling of his hands on me. It feels wrong that I still crave his touch, but I do.

Every minute, it crosses my mind, how much I want him. How much I crave his touch. How I wish things were different.

I know it's wrong, but it feels so *right*.

I'm limp when he's done.

"Okay, sit up. I'll help you wash."

"I can do it," I argue.

"You're half asleep again. You do it, but if I hear too loud of a splash, I'm coming in."

"God, even my mother wasn't this much of a worrier."

He stands up and turns his back to me, waving his hand behind his back for me to hurry and wash. I grumble and sit up, quickly soaping up everywhere. One of the splashes sounds extra loud because I'm trying to hurry and he turns slightly, looking over his shoulder.

"I'm fine," I yelp. "So gonna pay," I mumble under my breath.

"You are definitely better—the attitude is back." He grabs a towel and holds it out, turning his head to the side and keeping his eyes on the ceiling. I step into it and wrap it around me and he swoops me back up.

"You can put me down."

"Don't wanna. I'll hand you a new gown once you're in bed."

"I need something to dry my hair."

"Okay, first things first." He sets me carefully in my clean bed and puts the covers up over my towel. When he comes back from the bathroom, he has another towel and he awkwardly wraps it around my head. "How do girls do that thing with the towel and the hair?"

I take the towel from him, turn my head over and have it wrapped in a turban in seconds. I close my eyes and fight the wave of dizziness when I come back up.

"Oh, see, you overdid it."

I'm too tired to argue with him now. I don't want to get my bed all wet, so under the covers I remove the towel and hand it to him.

"Fuck me. That was hot," he whispers.

I open one eye and shoot all the glares I can out of that eye. He holds his hands out.

"Just speaking the truth."

"Since when do you..." I can't even remember what I want to say.

I close my eyes and let sleep overtake me.

When I wake up naked a few hours later, I sit up, holding the covers to my chest.

"I wondered what you'd do when you realized you were naked." Luka's fingers skate along my back and he holds up a gown that may as well be invisible. It leaves nothing to the imagination.

"Could you get me something that covers a little more?"

"I don't know what you're talking about. There's also this." He holds up a white lace short set. He reaches over and grabs one more thing. "Maybe this one?"

It's a navy silk nightie, low-cut and too short to walk

around in, but in bed it'll have to do. I snatch it from him and put it on hurriedly, pulling up the covers as quickly as I can. Of course he sneaks a peek.

"Are you hungry?"

"I do think I could eat something."

"Perfect." He taps out a message on his phone and touches my forehead. "Now that's more like it."

"Did you let Ms. Macardi know that I'm sick?"

"Everyone in this house knows you are sick. She came to see about you a couple of times and told me to go to bed. I've been a wreck."

I feel a warmth surge through me and shove it down. He can be a caring person without me taking it to mean he has feelings for me.

"You should rest," I tell him. "I'm fine."

"Did you know I never believe you when you say you're fine?"

He's lying on his side now, facing me. "You look beautiful right now. Even after going through hell. When you were fevered, God, you looked like an angel...Eden..." He presses his lips together and I'm scared of what he's going to say. His eyes look so intense. "I want you to know, I haven't been with Nadia since that time we spent together...last—"

I start shaking my head. I don't want to hear it.

"Please, let me finish," he whispers. "It's different with her. She's a distraction, always available. You're nothing like h—"

My eyes fill with tears and he stops.

"I'm sorry. You should rest. I'll go see what's taking so long with your food." He gets out of bed and looks ten years older as he walks out of my room.

Tears fall back onto my pillow and I wipe them off with my fist. When Chelsea brings in a big bowl of soup and fresh bread with cheese, I sit up and grin. Luka follows closely behind her.

"Ah, there's that smile," she says, setting the tray over my legs. "We were all worried about you, Lady Eden. Especially this one here." She lifts her thumb toward Luka.

"I'm feeling a lot better. Thank you for the food and for your concern."

She smiles warmly and lifts her hand as she leaves. Basile sticks his head in the room.

"She's awake!" He puts his hands together and squeezes. "And looking like a vision. How can anyone pull off being as sick as you and still be a vision of beauty?"

"I said the same thing...only not quite as eloquently." Luka smiles at me.

"You're definitely cut from the same cloth." I tuck my head and smile, my mind full of conflicting thoughts.

I don't have to figure anything out right now, I remind myself. I don't know what I need to figure out really.

It just seems I need boundaries, even in my own mind.

To survive this house.

To survive Luka.

After another day in bed and being pampered by the still-attentive Luka, I am ready to break out of the house and breathe the fresh air.

Brienne sits with me in the afternoon and reads a book aloud when I'm antsy. When Luka steps out for a minute, she leans in. "Lady Eden, I've been so worried about you, but Luka has been so good to you. I wish you could see what everyone else sees when he looks at you. Trust your heart."

I stare at her and swallow. "That's the most you've ever said to me at one time."

She laughs and it's shocking how pretty she is when she smiles.

In one of the rare times Luka is not in my room—he's even showered in my shower—I put on my swimsuit and am in the process of rubbing sunscreen on my arms when he comes back. He stops dead in his tracks, taking me in with one long sweep. I snap and his eyes jerk up to mine. He grins.

"Oh, we're going swimming?"

"No, I'm going swimming. You're gonna give me some space. Go take a nap, clean your room, do homework...I don't care what, just go do something."

He frowns. "I'd rather go swimming."

I lean my head against the wall and laugh. He's been going nonstop for days and I know he must be exhausted.

"I'm worried you'll get sick if you don't take a break. Look at me, I'm f—"

"Don't say fine," he jumps in. "*Well, healing, better* are all acceptable words..."

"Very well. I'm better."

"And I am *fine.*" He smirks. "Unlike you, when I say it, I mean it. I've rested when you have. Some. I told you, I am resilient. And watching you outside in that bikini will cure anything that could possibly afflict me, I promise you that." His eyes gleam with mischief and I shake my head, grabbing a towel and walking out of the room. "Hold up," he calls. "I need to grab my suit, but also—I need to watch you walk away..."

CHAPTER TWENTY-EIGHT

"Does it ever get cold here?" I ask one afternoon when we're lying in the farsynthia fields. It's already snowing at home. When Jadon and I last spoke, he showed me the pile of snow that was growing by the minute.

"The nights get cooler in the winter, but the days are still warm enough to swim."

I nod, pleased.

"This place suits you." He plucks a few flowers and tucks one behind my ear and the other in my shorts' pocket. The last one he uses to tickle my cheek.

I brush his hand away, shivering.

"Do you miss the cold?"

"No. I miss my family, though. I've never gone so long without seeing them."

"We should plan a trip soon. Would you like to be there for Christmas?"

I sit up and stare down at him. "Do you think that would be possible? Is it safe?"

"As far as I know, the threat is gone and it should be safe to travel. Your parents came here with no trouble. We should be able to get there and we can stay as long as you like."

"What about Ms. Macardi?"

"She could come too..."

I grin. The thought of her amidst the rich history of Farrow—she would love it there.

"That smile. I think that's a definite yes." He bops my nose when I flop back down.

The flowers smell incredible. Sweet, almost citrusy, a scent all of its own. Luka was right about me loving it here. We've come twice in the past two weeks and I'm never ready to leave.

"I'll bring it up to Father later tonight. I think we have a charity to attend and you have a luncheon with my mother and sister this week."

"Don't forget the family ball." It takes an effort not to grit my teeth with the words. Mara and Cece bring up the family ball at every meal. I'm already dreading the event with a holy passion.

"Ah...the family ball." Luka does grit his teeth when he says it.

I've still never said a word against Mara, but he seems to be noticing more annoying qualities of hers as of late. I don't have to say anything—she can barely tolerate my presence. I have a feeling if I nudged back even slightly, she'd completely lose her mind on me.

"You really want to go with me for the holidays? You don't have to, you know. No one cares what we're doing as a couple, Luka. I don't think they ever bought it. And your parents probably wouldn't appreciate me dragging you away from them over Christmas."

"In the months you've been my wife, when has it ever

seemed like we were a family who had a warm and fuzzy Christmas?"

I giggle. It's true, of course. I can't picture them around a tree opening presents the way my family does every Christmas morning. Our reserved family gets very loud at Christmastime.

He's been doing that a lot lately...calling me his wife. It's weird, and I want to ask him why he's saying it all the time, but I don't.

"It's my favorite." My face gets pink with the confession. I've been doing this a lot lately too...sharing parts of myself.

"Really?" He turns on his side, his face resting against his hand. "Tell me about it."

"Well, every Christmas Eve, we have a big supper of chicken and homemade noodles. It's the only time we all invade the kitchen and we have a contest for who makes the best noodles."

He listens, rapt. "And who usually wins?"

"Jadon. Sometimes Mother...Jadon is the best at everything."

He rolls his eyes. "He's secretly very egotistical, isn't he..."

I look at him like he's crazy. "Jadon? No, that's what makes him all the more special. He's truly, deeply *good*."

"There's nothing wrong with a little ego."

"Yeah, you keep telling yourself that, buddy."

He reaches out and grabs me, his fingers tickling my sides. I try to get away and he just tickles another part of me.

"Stop," I wheeze. "I can't breathe."

He lets go and our laughter dies down. He stares at me for a long moment then slowly leans in to kiss me. I shift out of the way and stand up, looking across the fields of endless flowers. Luka stands up and moves behind me.

"I'm sorry I hurt you, Eden."

"You were right—you warned me. It's not like I didn't know what was coming, I just got swept up in us for a minute...I've learned."

He leans his head on my shoulder. "*I've* learned."

The conversation is steering out of my comfort zone and thankfully, he seems to sense it.

I can't help but think it isn't realistic to trust any feelings when we're shut away from the rest of the world and only have a dysfunctional family surrounding us. It's natural we would bond somewhat when we're together all the time. That doesn't mean it's anything close to love, certainly not for him.

As for me, it takes everything inside me not to give in to his pull.

"So after the noodles, then what?"

"We sing Christmas carols near the tree...and after everyone has gone to bed, Mother sneaks the presents into the stockings."

"You still have a stocking?"

I smile at his shock. "We all have stockings, even my parents."

"Your parents really love each other, don't they?"

"Yeah...they do. The only snag they've ever had was before I was born and it's a big one. My mother is not kind to Jadon because of it..."

I've said too much and fortunately, both of our phones vibrate and save me from spilling all of our family's drama.

"We should get back. We have to go over the details of the charity with Mother."

Cece and Mara are waiting in the living room when we get there.

"Where have you been?" Mara snaps.

"We're here now." Luka shrugs. He moves a pillow to make sure I have room to sit down.

Mara's eyes narrow. "What's going on? You two are awfully chummy lately."

"Don't you worry about us," he says. "Another night caught partying?" He tuts quietly and it makes her squirm with discomfort. She looks at Cece, who is giving her the evil eye.

"What now, Mara?"

She glares at Luka. "Nothing—I-I just went to a party last night and the photographers made things look worse than they really were."

"How the photographers make things look is what matters," Cece cries. "When will you learn? It's why you have to be beyond cautious, so they can't misconstrue."

I keep my mouth shut but feel gratitude for a mother who worries more about what is really going on with her kids, and less about how we are perceived.

"Thanks, *brother*." Mara sits back, crossing her arms over her chest.

I can see her wheels turning and it brings an uneasy feeling over me.

"If you could all just cooperate and not bring any unnecessary negative press on us, that would be really great."

"The press is obsessed with my wife," Luka says.

I want to elbow him in the gut, but he's already blabbing more.

"They love her. She's created quite the following and—did you see? They're calling her the people's princess."

"Luka, stop," I whisper.

"What does that even mean? We're all for the people," Mara says.

"If you got to know them like she has, the media would be less inclined to show your bad side."

Mara tugs on her hair and smirks. "I don't have a bad side."

Cece flings her notes on the table. "Enough, you two. We have work to do."

The night of the charity, I try to send Luka to his own room so I can get ready. Ever since I was sick, he spends a lot of time in here. I always make him go to his room when we're getting tired so he doesn't fall asleep in here, and he pulls the wounded puppy act. Even now, he's lingering, his arms on the top of the doorjamb as he watches me put on the finishing touches of my makeup. When I start twisting my curls into something manageable, he steps in closer.

"I don't know how you do that." He holds a curl between his fingers and kisses it.

I feel heat rise from the tips of my toes to the curl he's kissing. My body has never stopped wanting him—it's safe to say I want him more than ever. Sexy, bad boy Luka brought me to a steady burn; sexy, sweet Luka brings me to a raging inferno.

"Are we matching tonight?" he asks.

That's become a running joke because we've matched for every event without even trying. Even when we're just hanging out—classes or going into town—we coordinate.

"We'll have to see. What fun would it be if we planned it?" I scoff.

He stares at my mouth and grins. "I know at least a dozen things that would be fun if we planned them...would you like to hear just one?"

By the look in his eyes, I know that I would love to hear it and that it's the last thing I *need* to hear. "No."

He steps closer and inhales my hair and my neck. "I feel like I'm lying in the farsynthia fields...are you drugging me, Mrs. Catano?" His lips brush against my neck and I squeeze my thighs together, closing my eyes to catch my breath.

"I assure you, I am not."

He lets go of me and my body feels desolate. "Soon, beautiful."

I open my eyes and he's gone. I try to steady my fingers to finish my makeup and have to redo my lipstick three times.

Luka Catano consumes me.

He sets my soul on fire.

I don't know what I'm going to do.

CHAPTER TWENTY-NINE

"Another day, another formal," Basile is saying when I step into the foyer.

He and Luka pause when they see me and both grin so wide.

"Well, well. Look who's bringing the legs into royalty. Luka, are you ready to go down in history as the husband of the legs?"

"Fuck. Yes." Luka's eyes roam over me until I'm squirming and I walk toward the two of them, willing my heated cheeks to die down.

I asked Teresa to make a short dress for this event, unheard of around here for these formal affairs, and am pleased with the results. Red with off the shoulder sleeves, the bottom falls into two flouncy tiers. It's fun and festive and I almost saved it for the ball but didn't want to waste it on the family.

It looks like it wouldn't have been wasted based on Luka and Basile's reaction. I reach out and straighten Luka's red tie, biting the inside of my cheek to keep from groaning.

"Are you sure you're not conspiring with Teresa?"

"I swear." He looks down at me and puts his hands on my shoulders, giving each cheek a kiss. "I swear you get more beautiful every day."

"Oh, gross. Seriously, you guys are making me ill," Mara says, coming to a dead stop when she sees what I'm wearing. "You can't go in that. It's not—"

"She can and she will," Luka interrupts. "Come on, let's go before we're late."

"I'm waiting for my date."

"Who is it tonight?" Basile asks.

She rolls her eyes, but they're gleaming. I wonder what she's up to. "You act like I'm a slut..."

Basile shoots her a droll expression and she huffs, waving her hand at all of us.

"Just go already."

"I thought Elias was out of town," Luka says. He puts his arm around her and she leans into him.

"He is—" She swallows hard. "I haven't heard from him in a while."

Luka frowns. "Does he know you're going out with... whoever this mystery guy is?"

She straightens. "I hope he sees my face all over the Internet tomorrow and suffers."

She talks the talk, but really, she looks devastated. I almost feel a tiny bit of sympathy for her—almost.

We get in the car, Basile sitting across from us, and head to the Sanchuron Hotel. It overlooks the bluffs and is a stunning display of architecture full of history and elegance. I've been dying to go inside since the first time I saw it.

I'm relieved to have Basile as a buffer in the car. With the way Luka has been getting more comfortable with his suggestive comments lately and our history in cars, I was a little worried with how this night would go. He looks somewhat edgy, but when I ask if anything is wrong, he leans into my ear.

"I live in a constant state of discomfort when you're around...even when you're not. If you so much as lean that pretty ass into my cock tonight, I'm going to explode." He leans back and grins, his eyes on my mouth.

I swallow hard and he grins wider. I have to look away.

When we arrive at the hotel, the cameras are primed for us. Harmi opens the door and Luka steps out first then holds his arm out for me to take. I look up at him and feel my courage return with his touch. We walk toward the building as the photographers go wild and I turn and wave one last time before we go inside. A low cheer goes up and builds and I laugh, feeling overwhelmed.

"They love you," Luka whispers.

It's as if we've stepped back in time once we're inside. Gold inlays are in the wall and ceiling, antique furnishings of exquisite craftsmanship are strategically placed. We're ushered to the ballroom where flowers and lights create a dreamy effect. We've only just sat at our table when Mara and her date walk up. I hear Luka's exclamations of surprise and look up.

"What are you doing here?" I stand up and rush to Jadon, hugging him tight. "It's so good to see you. Tell me you aren't really Mara's date," I whisper in his ear.

"Technically I am, but really I'm just here to check on you," he whispers back. He leans away and holds both of my hands. "Look at you. Marriage looks fantastic on you."

Mara sighs loudly and we all look at her.

"How did you manage to keep this a surprise?" Luka asks.

"When it comes to your wife, I'm always scheming," she says sweetly.

I don't miss the daggers she points my way with her eyes. "Well, this time you've outdone yourself. What a perfect surprise!"

If she thinks I'm worried my brother will fall for her act, she's in for a rude awakening. She must have had that in mind because she looks disappointed in my joy.

Jadon sits on one side of me and Luka on the other. He fills me in on everything that's happening at home. He's been given more responsibilities and hates it, and Ava is becoming quite the little swordsman.

"I bet Mother loves that."

We laugh and he takes a drink of wine. "Oh, you have no idea. It's helped turn her attention off of me, which is nice." He sobers and I put my hand on his arm.

"Is everything really okay at home? Luka spoke with his father about us coming for the holidays. Do you think it's safe?"

His eyes light up. "I do. How soon can you get there?"

Luka leans forward. "I was going to tell Eden tonight, but I may as well say it now...we leave next week and we'll be there the whole month."

I turn to him, wide-eyed, and throw my arms around him. "Are you sure? We don't have to stay for—"

"I got us out of it." He leans his head against mine and we cackle like two little kids.

Mara and Jadon speak at the same time.

"Do I even want to know—" Jadon laughs.

"Knock it off, you guys. You're embarrassing me—" Mara snaps. "Oh look, there's Nadia." Her voice is back to syrup and I freeze, backing away from Luka.

He turns my chin to face him again and stares at me. "Don't shut me out."

I lift my chin up and out of his hand and turn to Jadon. "I'm really glad you're here."

Nadia walks up to the table a few minutes later—I know it's her before I even see her by the way Luka stiffens next to me. He tries to grab my hand under the table and I yank it away. I don't need his guilt.

It feels like every eye is on us as she hugs Mara and turns to look at Luka and me. "Hello," she says in her lilting accent. She really is stunning.

"Have you ever been formally introduced to my wife, Eden?" Luka asks.

Nadia gives me a strained smile and I don't return it. "Hello, Eden," she says quietly. "Luka, I wondered if I might have a word with you regarding the charity we did for MS last year. They'd like us to—"

"As I said in my email to you, I'm not interested." His words are so cold, the whole table stops and looks at him. You could hear a pin drop.

She looks flustered. "If I could just speak with you—"

"No, Nadia." He stands up and holds his hand out for me to take.

I take it numbly and he wraps his other hand around it, as if to guard me.

"It's over, Nadia," he says quietly. "It's been over and you need to stop this insane pursuit. I was stupid to not see what I had in front of me." He looks at me and I blink, wondering if I'm hearing him right.

Nadia presses her lips together and when I look at her, I can almost see the wheels turning in her head. Whatever she's processing, she clears her throat and gets her composure back.

"Got it," she says. "Public functions are never the time

nor the place, are they?" The flirtatious look she throws Luka is not lost on anyone within view.

She does not buy one word he's saying. And it hits me full-force that neither should I.

I try the rest of the night to engage, but my emotions are all over the place. Luka and I have gotten so much closer lately and even to myself, I've claimed that I was happy with the way it is, that I'm not going to let him in...keep him at a safe distance and protect my heart, all that.

I've been such a fool.

The hope was building inside me all along.

One night with Nadia around crushes all of that.

I need to make sure I never forget: this marriage is based on protection and financial gain.

Nothing more.

CHAPTER THIRTY

I dance with Jadon and Luka and get through the night. Jadon is by far the best part of the night. When I hug him goodbye, I start to cry.

"You're coming next week," he says. "Ava will be so excited."

"It's just hard that this is what our lives have become... grateful for short visits and surprise trips."

He gives me one more hug. "I know. You belong in Farrow, even though it does look as if you're warming up to Niaps. Or maybe just warming up to Luka." He pulls away and grins, his smile dropping when he sees more tears.

Luka is behind me, but he's giving us privacy, so I'm able to speak to Jadon freely.

"I think it's all an act. He's been doting and sweet and—now that I think about it, it makes way more sense than thinking he's actually fallen for me."

Jadon looks over my shoulder. "The way he's staring at you right now, and every other second of the night, I'm gonna have to disagree with you, little sister." He leans closer. "I don't think he's just fallen, I think he's completely sunk. Not even trying to swim above water, sunk."

"You really think so?"

"I'm about 112% certain."

Luka moves behind me then. "I'm sorry to cut this short, but they're wanting a picture of all of us." He motions behind Jadon to the photographers waiting.

We all turn and loop arms, smiling, while their cameras click.

Mara wraps her arms around Jadon and whispers something in his ear. I roll my eyes. I want him to shut her down so bad, but he just looks amused as he pulls away.

After we say goodbye to Jadon, I turn to Luka. "Can we leave now?"

He puts his arm around me and pulls me into his side. "Mara's not the only one with a surprise tonight."

"Uh-oh. Will I like it?" I look up at him and he looks sheepish.

"I don't know."

"Spill. This is making me nervous."

"Okay, come on. I'll let you see for yourself..."

He leads me away from the people and a guard escorts us to a back elevator. We get in and I hold my hand out.

"What did you do?"

He grins. "Just wait."

The elevator climbs to the top floor and we step into a hall leading to the penthouse suite. He opens the door and I gasp. Floor-to-ceiling windows with the city lights sparkling over the water, a grand piano sits close-by, plush couches and pillows make the otherwise formal suite look more inviting.

"It's beautiful."

"I thought you might need a break from the Catano

estate." He puts his hands in his pockets and tries to read my reaction. "Is this okay?"

"It's more than okay, but Luka—I'm not sure what you're expecting from me."

"Honestly? I want far more than I'm expecting." He smiles and I relax a little bit. "But you don't have to do anything you don't want to do. I just want to enjoy our time together here, in this beautiful place, outside the claustrophobic walls of my house."

"Are you gonna hurt me?" I whisper. "If I let you in, will you destroy me?"

He frowns and rubs his hand across his face. "Fuck, Eden. I never want to hurt you. I never meant to hurt you in the first place. This is a fucked-up situation. But I can assure you that my motives are honorable." His voice is pleading and he looks urgent, like he's begging for me to hear him and believe him.

"Honorable." My lips quirk up. "I like it when you get riled up."

His eyes lift and he looks at me with a growing fire. "I can get a lot more riled up than this, trust me."

"Yeah?"

"Yeah. Let me tell you...you are an ache in my chest that never goes away. I try to run and you're there. I try to fill the empty hole you've left inside me and it never works. I try to stay busy and distract myself and I can't because I'm always wondering what you're doing!" His voice is rising and he grabs me and pulls me against him. "You've completely wrecked everything."

I grin and he tilts my chin up so I can't look away.

"You don't have to say yes tonight, but...I hope you'll give me another chance. I want that more than anything. Do you believe me?" he whispers.

"I want to."

"What can I do to convince you?"

I close my eyes and feel his lips brush across my eyelids, my cheeks, my ear, my neck. I shiver and he smiles against my skin.

"Let me show you..."

I can't think straight, much less come up with reasons to stop him when he's making me delirious. He could be saying all the right things or he could mean them with all his heart, but either way, at this point, I deserve a night of seduction.

I can deal with the fallout later if there is one.

When his lips track their way back up my jawline and get near my mouth, I groan and tilt my face so his lips meet mine.

"I've been dying to kiss you for so long now," he says against my lips. His tongue traces my bottom lip. "This mouth is my downfall. *You* are my downfall. I'm willing to dive headlong into oblivion as long as you're on the other side."

He devours me then, his tongue raiding mine with sweeping strokes. For the way he's working my mouth, the rest of him stays chaste. His hands aren't roaming, just holding me in place like he can't get his fill.

I eventually take off his jacket and still, he keeps his hands on my face or around my waist. Coming up for air, I back away and look at him, chest pounding out of my skin.

"What do you want, beautiful?" He's breathing hard too. He pulls my fingers up to his mouth and kisses each one, sucking on my last finger.

I close my eyes and when I open them, I feel light-headed. "I want everything you're offering."

"I'm yours," he says. "Whether we stand here kissing all

night or I take you in every position against every surface of this suite, I'm yours."

I push my hair to the side and turn my back to him. He puts his hands on my bare shoulders and kisses the exposed skin on my back before slowly unzipping my dress. I pull down the sleeves and the dress drops to the floor. I hear his sharp intake of breath and smile.

"It's a good thing I didn't know this was underneath that dress all night. I wouldn't have been able to function."

I guess the red thong and going braless was the right choice.

"Brace yourself," he says and he picks me up and carries me to the bedroom, placing me carefully on the huge bed overflowing with pillows. "I'd like our first place to be here. I will worship you and then I'll fuck you into tomorrow in the shower. What do you say?"

He reaches between my legs and feels the wet lace.

Satisfaction covers his face and he nods. "Yeah, I'm thinking you agree."

He rips the lace off of me and buries his face between my legs, his tongue doing deeds that I can't fathom. He stays right there for I don't even know how long...however long it takes for me to scream his name and then he keeps going until my head is thrashing on the pillow again. All of a sudden, his mouth is gone and he drives into me with one long thrust. I scream again and he goes completely still while I pulse around him.

"Be still," he whispers. "Tell that pussy of yours to settle down so I don't blow my load before we even get started."

"You have the dirtiest mouth," I moan.

"If I said everything I thought, you'd run."

"And yet here I am, pinned underneath you."

He grins and starts moving again, his hair a whirlwind

around him after I held onto him for dear life. "You feel too good," he moans. "I'm not gonna last, it's been too long."

I feel a sick satisfaction that he's coming undone. If that's what he even means. I push the thought aside and let my body enjoy the sensation of him filling me up completely. I don't think anything in the world could feel as good as this does right now.

His pace quickens and he leans up on both elbows. "Are you ready? I don't want to do this without you."

He slams into me, and the bed drives into the wall again and again and again. Faster, faster, faster. I've never felt like this. I close my eyes, sinking fast.

"Look at me," he demands. "This is you and me right here, no one else, nothing else exists but you and me."

I cry out and he follows, a sharp moan before whispering into my hair, "You're mine, Eden Catano. Whether you want to be or not, you're mine." His lips reach my ear. "And I'm yours."

CHAPTER THIRTY-ONE

Luka makes good on his promise and then some. In the early hours of the morning, we drag a blanket onto the balcony and while the sun comes up, he rocks into me from behind.

Throughout the night each time before he pulls out, he's whispered, "This was my favorite time."

He says it again now, and I sleepily say, "Mine too," before falling into an exhausted sleep.

A few hours later, I wake up to him moving me back to the bed.

"The sun was getting too strong out there. I don't want you to get sunburned."

I kiss his arm and go back to sleep. When I wake up, he's not next to me and I feel a sinking dread. Did I make a mistake?

I stretch in bed and love every tired muscle, grinning when I think about all the ways we had sex last night. I think my favorite was the last time...just when I think it can't get any better, each time exceeds the last. The dining room table was fun too though...

He comes in a few minutes later, pushing a cart of food.

"Basile set all of this up for us. He paid off the guy who brought us up last night, food for today...dinner tonight. We're set to stay for a few nights if you'd like."

"Sounds good to me." I sit up and he grins when he looks at me.

"Your hair is extra crazy right now."

"That last shower and then sleeping on it." I laugh, suddenly shy, remembering the two times we were in the shower. "How are you awake right now?"

"I have enough stamina for the two of us." He winks. "Hungry?"

He lifts the lids and there are waffles and omelets and fruit.

"Coffee and then I can function again."

He pours a cup of coffee and hands me the cream and sugar. When I take my first sip, my eyes close and I groan.

"There she is." He chuckles and I open one eye. "I live for your moans." He leans down and kisses me, putting my coffee aside and leveling his face with mine. "Last night was legendary. Did all of that really happen?" His eyes widen and so do mine.

I nod.

"I thought so. What the fuck? Today we'll have to outdo that...I don't know...are you up for the challenge?"

I shake my head.

He straightens and puts my coffee back in my hand. "Here, drink up. You have to get some energy."

His phone starts vibrating on the bedside table and he lifts his head up to the ceiling. "I made Basile swear he wouldn't disturb us." He picks up his phone and frowns. "Well, this is cryptic. He says we need to get home as soon as possible."

"He doesn't say why?" I shift to the side of the bed and put my feet on the floor, taking one more sip of coffee. "Can we at least eat?"

"Let me call and see what's going on." He dials the number and waits. "No answer. Why don't you eat and I'll keep trying to reach him."

I shovel in a few bites and feed him a few, but we're both too anxious to keep eating.

"I think we should get home. If everything is okay, we can always come back later today, right?" I have a déjà vu moment the second the words are out of my mouth.

He nods. "Yeah, I think you're right. I'll make sure Harmi's ready."

I'm sad to leave our sanctuary, but the promise of coming back makes it a little easier. I grab one of the muffins and pick off bites for both of us as we're going down the elevator. The man who led us up last night is there waiting and I wonder if he got any sleep. He takes us through the office hallways and out the back where Harmi is waiting.

Harmi nods briskly and drives us back to the estate in a hurry. I hold on and Luka asks him to slow down more than once. A sense of foreboding builds the closer we get. Basile still hasn't answered his phone. When we pull into the driveway, Brienne is waiting and she ushers me out, her face solemn.

"Do you know what's happening?"

"No one will tell me anything," she whispers.

Luka threads his fingers through mine and kisses my hand before opening the door to go inside. His parents, Basile, and Mara are there, like they've been waiting for us to arrive. Cece steps toward me and puts her hands on my shoulders, leading me away from Luka and into the living room where she sets me down on the couch.

"What's going on?" I ask, looking behind me for Luka.

He sits on the other side of me and looks at Titus. "Will someone please tell us what is happening?"

"There was an accident early this morning—" Titus begins.

My hand goes straight to my throat. "Jadon—is Jadon okay?"

"As far as we know, your brother and sister are fine." Titus clears his throat and clasps his hands together. "Eden, I am sorry to tell you this...so sorry. Sweetheart, your father was killed in a car accident this morning."

I jump up and Luka does too, his arm around me and I shrug it off. I turn around wildly. "What do you mean? No, that can't be right. It wasn't him. No...that can't be true." I shake my head and look at Luka, my eyes blurring so much I can't see his features. "Basile, tell me. I will only believe it if you say it. This has to be some kind of sick joke." My face crumbles and Basile holds me up as I fall toward him.

He hugs me to him and says quietly, "I'm sorry to say that it is true. We made sure there was proof before telling you."

The agony that pours out of me—I can't keep it in. Luka helps me back to the couch and tucks me into this arms. I cry and beat my fists into his chest.

"I can't breathe." I look at him panicked. "Get me out of here. Please."

He doesn't hesitate, he lifts me up and carries me out of the room.

When we reach my room, he sets me down on the bed and looks at me with all the despair I feel in his eyes.

"I need to go home. I need to see my family. Where is my mother? Why isn't she telling me this?"

"I'll arrange it immediately. We'll go as soon as possible."

"Is this really happening? A car wreck? My father has the most responsible driver. I—"

He strokes my hand while I ramble. All the thoughts are flooding my mind at once.

"I wonder if Jadon knows yet—he probably wasn't even home when it happened. I need to get home to Ava. She needs me." I start hyperventilating again and he helps me gradually slow my breathing.

Basile peeks in the room and says, "The jet can take you home as soon as you're ready. We will be following when we know about the funeral arrangements."

I sob into my hands and nod.

"Thank you, Uncle," Luka says. "She'd like to go right away."

He walks over to Basile and I know he's trying to say it so I don't hear, but I do.

"Are we sure...does this all check out as an accident? Alidonia didn't have anything to do with this, right?"

"It's been filed as an accident due to icy roads," Basile says under his breath.

I wipe my face and look at both of them in a daze. "You have everything to gain now that my father isn't in power."

The color drains out of Luka's face. "You don't think we—"

I stand up and move toward him, wiping my nose. "Sebastian has never once had a wreck. He wouldn't allow them to go anywhere if he thought it was too risky, and if he deemed it safe, then it was. My father has always trusted him with all of us. And who would gain from this besides Alidonia? You."

"If there were any foul play involved, it would be Vance

Farthing, not my father!" Luka looks at me in a panic and then turns to his uncle. "Right? Tell her we had nothing to do with this."

Basile tightens his lips together and bows his head. "The tension between our three countries has been tumultuous at best. We are not directly involved—I can't imagine Titus ever sinking to that level—but to say we are not indirectly involved, I cannot."

My blood runs cold. "That is a lot of nothing you're spewing, Basile. I think maybe you don't fully know what your family is capable of."

"Eden, please don't jump to this...let's get you home and find out more about it." Luka holds his hand out to me and when I don't take it, he drops it limply. "I vow to you that if I find out my father is involved, I will make him pay. You have my word."

"Again with your word." I shake my head and turn around, numbly gathering my bag. I place my phone in the side pocket and pass them, standing by the door. "I have everything I need at home. I'm ready to go." I look at Luka. "You should wait and come with your family."

"You are my family," he says.

My eyes fill with tears again.

"I'm coming with you."

CHAPTER THIRTY-TWO

The flight home is long and fitful. I lie on the bed, my back to Luka, unable to stop the tears from falling. He holds me until I sit up and need to breathe and then I lie back down again, feeling like I'm going to lose it if I have to stay on this plane for another second.

Neither of us talk. I eventually fall into a restless sleep, exhausted from our night together and all the crying I've done since. I wake up to the pilot saying we're about to land. We go into the main cabin and buckle up. Brienne sits there stoically and asks if I need anything. I shake my head and thank her.

Before we get off the plane, Luka puts his hand on my shoulder. I turn to look at him.

"I want to be whatever you need. I'll follow your lead, but know that I'm here and I want to walk through this with you."

I bite my bottom lip to keep it from trembling so hard and nod. "Thank you, Luka." A tear spills over and he wipes it with his thumb.

I turn around and we walk off the Catano family jet. A

driver that I don't recognize picks us up and also Perez, my father's right hand. Perez hugs me and his eyes fill with tears as he expresses how sorry he is.

The roads are clear and I wonder again about the ice Sebastien supposedly lost control on...it doesn't ring true. But I don't bring it up in the car; there will be time for that once I'm home.

Home...I can't believe I'm back. I was so excited to bring Luka here and now that we're here, everything feels *wrong*.

"It's beautiful," he says quietly as we drive through the snow-tipped mountain peaks.

When we pull up to our estate, every room in the house is lit up, something my mother usually doesn't allow. Brienne stands protectively by me as I get out of the car and when I step inside the door, I fall into Ava's waiting arms. Mother comes up behind her and puts her arms around both of us.

When Mother realizes Brienne is standing there, she goes to her and holds out her arms. Brienne hugs her hard and it's the first time I've seen her cry. Luka stands near me, and when Mother lets go of Brienne, he reaches out to her.

"Lady Kathryn, I can't tell you how sorry I am. Please let me know what I can do to help."

"You can start by finding out who did this."

He flinches but nods. "I won't rest until I do."

"So you're certain—" I can't even finish the words, but my mother nods.

"You and I both know Sebastien didn't lose control of the car. It's being looked into as we speak, and justice will be served. It's the only ho—" Her face twists in pain and she puts her head in her hands, sobbing.

Ava and I surround her and the rest of the day is spent that way. Stops and starts of tears in mid-sentence in the quiet lulls, and any time it hits any of us individually, we rally around the other and cry together. Jadon returns home in the evening and the tears start all over again.

Later that night, I am about to head to my room for the night when I hear Jadon and Luka down the hallway. Their tone is quiet but urgent. I stay on the stairs and listen.

"Have you seen anything to make you suspicious?" Jadon asks.

"I've been so wrapped up in your sister lately, so no." He tugs on his hair in frustration and leans closer to Jadon. "Something Basile mentioned has me uneasy, though. He said something about not being able to say we were directly involved...but he couldn't fully say if there was an indirect involvement. At the time I didn't think it made any sense. That he was just talking off the top of his head the way he does sometimes, you know? But now I wonder if he was telling me exactly what he thought."

"That your father had something to do with it...and of course someone else did the dirty work, meaning how would we ever prove..."

"Exactly."

"*Fuck!*" Jadon explodes. He wipes his eyes and stares down at the floor.

I round the corner and Luka has his arm on Jadon's shoulder looking at him intently. He looks the most sincere he's looked since I've known him and I sag against the wall, the relief overwhelming me. I want to believe him. I want to believe with everything in me that he didn't know anything about this. He hears me and turns around, rushing over when he thinks I'm about to fall.

"I'm okay," I tell him. "I'm just...thank you for not listening to me earlier, for coming with me. I-I'm glad you're here."

Jadon puts his hand on my arm and gives me a tear-filled smile. "This one cares about you a lot," he says. He smirks despite his watery eyes. "Don't ever go easy on him though. He needs to be kept on his toes."

"Hey!" Luka stands up taller and puffs his chest out, but he's grinning.

Jadon chuckles and then they both sober up just as quickly. "You should get some rest. It will be utter chaos the next few days. Sleep. I will handle as much of the funeral arrangements as Kathryn would like, but I would imagine she has a plan for how she'd like it to go already."

"Let me worry about her." I don't want him to suffer any additional pain right now. My mother is hardest on her stepson.

He gives me a weak smile. "You just worry about you. It's a long trip from Niaps and we can't have you getting sick again."

I hug him. "Always thinking of everyone else first. You just made the same trip I did. I love you. No matter what Mother might say to you in the upcoming weeks, Father was proudest of you and he had every reason to be. You are the noblest man I know."

He lowers his head and struggles to keep his composure. "I can't believe he's gone."

When I take Luka to my room, I turn awkwardly to show him where he can put his things, where the bathroom is...

the towels. He comes up from behind me and puts his arms around my waist.

"I'll make myself at home, don't worry. The way you and your family love each other is beautiful."

I lean my head back against his chest and feel the tears starting up again. He sees my face in the dresser mirror and turns me around.

"Let's get you to bed. You must be exhausted."

I don't have it in me to argue. I want a bath. I feel like I should check on my mother and Ava again…I need to see a picture of my Father…all these random thoughts pour through my mind all at once. But I listen to him and take his hand as he leads me to bed.

He strips me down to my underwear and pulls back the covers. I crawl into bed and he covers me up. He takes his shirt and pants off and gets in next to me, pulling my back against his chest. I cry until I fall asleep and he holds me the entire night.

The next few days are a blur. I feel as if I'm sleepwalking through all of it. The funeral director comes to the house to make everything easier on us, and although his casket and resting place are already decided based on our lineage, we can choose the flowers, song selections, who speaks and who does not. My father's hand and a few other advisors are staying close even though they are not given much say in these decisions.

My brother has always been favored among the people and it drives my mother crazy. I have to set my foot down about him speaking because otherwise neither of them would agree to it. My mother because she isn't ready for him to become the king, and Jadon because he doesn't want to further aggravate her.

"It's important that they hear from you, Jadon. You will be the one leading us and it's a necessary progression. I know it's hard, but it's what Father would expect of you; it's what the people expect of you."

"Kathryn, can you agree to that?" he asks.

She blows her nose and looks down at the table. "Yes."

Once the day arrives and I'm sitting in the vast church that is filled to overflowing, I think it fully hits me that my father is dead. It still doesn't seem possible, but it does feel real. The pain is acute. I swallow back the tears and keep my head down. The whole service is televised, which just feels like a horrific way to treat a grieving family, but Mother didn't contest it for the sake of those who weren't able to attend...so they could feel part of it too.

Titus, Cece, and Mara arrive and each kiss my cheek. I thank them for coming and they take a seat behind our family. I decide to bury my distaste of them for at least the day and focus on my family. It's hard to do when I turn and see Mara dotting her nose with her handkerchief for the sake of the camera on her. *I just can't think about them today*, I tell myself.

Luka holds my hand and keeps me supplied with tissues. I don't know what I would've done without him. He's been a shoulder—a literal, physical shoulder—that has sometimes been the only thing holding me up.

I hear the songs that I suggested, and I hear phrases from the speaker, but Jadon is really the only one who captures my attention when he speaks.

"A man cannot truly be a great man without honor, and our father and king, Neil Safrin, was a man with the utmost honor. Kind to a fault, yet bold when he needed to be—he knew when to discipline us at home and when to extend mercy—just as he has with this country. Far too soon, he was taken from us, along with his faithful driver, Sebastien, who was by his side for forty years. But he will never be forgotten, and instead of mourning his passing, which is inevitable, I know my father would want us to celebrate his crossing into the next life. To be absent from the body is to be present with the Lord and besides ruling this country to his greatest ability and caring for his family, that was his greatest hope. To one day meet his maker with open arms. Rest now, Father. We will hold your memory safe here for as long as we live. Until I reach the other side, farewell for now."

There is not a dry eye in the house as Jadon steps down from the grand staircase and walks back to his seat.

Within the week, the coronation takes place and my brother is crowned king of Farrow, ruler of our land and household.

CHAPTER THIRTY-THREE

It's been two weeks since my father died and beyond putting his arms around me each night and holding me, Luka hasn't touched me. Even during the day, he is attentive yet keeps his distance. At first I appreciated it and needed the space, but for the past couple of days, it's made all my doubts about him resurface. He's been spending more time on the phone, and he seems antsy, which makes me feel bad for keeping him here when we're all so melancholy.

After lunch he's especially quiet, only smiling here and there at Jadon and Ava bantering back and forth. I excuse myself to my room and he comes in a few minutes later, assessing my mood.

"I feel like you're always checking me out to see if I'm about to have an epic breakdown; you're on pins and needles all the time. I can't take it!" I sound much harsher than I intended, but once I've said it, I realize I mean it.

"I...you're probably right. I'm sorry."

"And that—you've never apologized so much in your life. You don't need to start now!" I'm yelling at him and he's staring at me, eyes huge. "Just stop watching me. Don't even look at me," my voice drops to a whisper, "I mean it."

A small smile starts at the corner of his mouth and then grows. "I can't *not* look at you. I mean, have you seen you?"

I turn away from him but not before he sees me smile. It falls away when I think about what I need to say. I don't want to, but it's the right thing.

"You should go home." I turn around and face him again. "I need to be here with my family and I can't fully focus on them when I'm worried if you're okay. Not that you're acting like you need anything—you've been wonderful actually. But I want to spend the holidays with them, maybe come back when a little time has passed."

His left hand grabs onto his right shoulder and he's quiet for a moment. Finally, he nods. "I don't want to go, but I think you're right. There are some things that need to be looked into at home and I can't really be effective doing it from here."

The air whooshes out of my chest. I didn't even realize I was holding my breath those few seconds. I'm devastated that he agrees with me so quickly yet glad he's being truthful.

"When will you leave?" I ask.

"Well, there's a good chance that I'd just prolong going because it'll be hard to leave you, so I should probably head out tomorrow. Not put it off."

My eyes blur and I blink, hoping he doesn't notice. Too late. His arms grip mine and he looks concerned.

"Or whenever you say. I don't have to leave tomorrow."

"I hate how I'm like a water faucet that won't turn off." I laugh and wipe my face. "No, you're right. Tomorrow would probably be best. It will be a busy week with getting Mother moved into her new quarters."

"Are you sure she won't regret making such a hasty decision?"

"No, once she sets her mind on something, good luck trying to change it."

My mother hasn't wanted to stay in the room she slept in with my father, and by right, it's Jadon's now anyway. I doubt he will even change rooms, although his guard says it would be safer. It's caused a few arguments, but Jadon can be stubborn when he wants to be.

Mother will be moving into the west wing, an area of the estate that never gets used.

"I actually think she's looking forward to diving into a remodeling project."

"Maybe it'll be good for you too."

I sigh. "We sound like an old married couple talking right now."

I plop down on the bed and fall back. He sits next to me and does the same thing and turns his head sideways to look at me.

"I'm just trying to be the calm. If you need me to be the storm, I can turn it up." He grins when he says it and I see the twinkle in his eyes that has been missing since we got here.

"How would you turn it up, if I needed it?" I turn to face him and he does the same, tracing a line down my cheek and neck.

"How raging do you need the storm to be?"

"Lightning, thunder, power outage, pouring down so hard you can't see in front of you..."

"Quite a storm." He licks his bottom lip and grips my chin between his two fingers. "It's already brewing," he whispers. "You better protect yourself. Can't hold back much longer."

I lean into his hand when he brushes back my hair.

"Are you sure you're ready for this?"

I nod.

"Let's get this dress off of you. I need to feel your skin. There's been way too many clothes between us in bed every night." He unzips the back and I lift my legs so he can pull it all the way down. "Get on your hands and knees and let me make you forget for a while."

And he absolutely delivers.

The next morning I'm still sleeping when he leans over and kisses my cheek.

"Take care of yourself, Eden," he whispers. "I'm sorry I have to go. Goodbye, I'll miss you."

I'm half asleep, but when I come to as he shuts the door, I sit up in a panic. That was not an *I'll see you soon* goodbye, but a *goodbye*.

I feel sick all day. I can't concentrate on anything anyone says to me and walk around the house listlessly. Every time the grandfather clock chimes, I do the countdown in my head.

Five hours until he's home.

Four.

Three.

Two.

One.

He should be home by now.

He's been home at least an hour.

Two.

Three.

Four.

Five.

When I go to bed that night and check my phone for the thousandth time, I convince myself it would be okay to check in with him. We've never really talked on the phone or texted, so it feels strange.

Checking to make sure you got home safely...

It's midnight my time when he answers.

Made it!

I can't go to sleep after that. *Made it?* Is that really all he's going to say?

I lie awake most of the night, wishing I was in his arms. There are no tears left to cry and all I want is for him to hold me.

When a full week has passed and he's made no effort to communicate—I can't eat, I can't sleep. Brienne hovers worse than Mother, trying to make me eat something, but it just comes back up.

When she comes in on Monday morning and won't look me in the eye and doesn't mention food, I know my worst fears are coming true.

I resist looking online all day. I stay away from Brienne in case I'm tempted to ask what she knows, but before bed, against my better judgment, I pick up my laptop.

I can't fight the truth any longer.

The first picture is of Luka and Nadia leaving the hotel we stayed in the night of the charity function. His fingers are threaded through hers and they're huddled together.

The next article shows a series of her exiting the castle, so the shots are not the best, but it's clearly her leaving after sleeping over. Luka hugging her goodbye, kissing her, and leaning over the car door when she gets in.

A glutton for punishment, I wipe the tears that are dripping off my chin and keep going. One more, from last night.

He's got her on his shoulders in the ocean and Mara is nearby laughing like she doesn't have a care in the world.

I throw my laptop against the wall and scream. Brienne comes running in and sits down on the bed, nervous and unsure of what to do. I fall into her arms and she holds me until I pass out from exhaustion.

Hell.

I'm in hell.

I gave my body to a monster. Not just once or twice, but countless times.

He fed my cravings like I was starving, and I was—I wanted him beyond all reason.

And in return I spoonfed my soul to him at the expense of all sanity.

I knew who he was. Didn't I?

I'm so confused because I thought he grew. I thought my love for him changed him.

Love.

I never even told him I loved him. He never came close to telling me he loved me.

And what woman has ever changed a man?

I've been so incredibly stupid.

Jadon comes to my room the next night after I've not shown up for any meals.

"He's not worth this, Edie. You have to get up and fight. You can't let him win."

"Was I crazy? Blind? Stupid? You thought he cared for me, right? He told you he did?"

He puts his head down and looks back up at me with such sorrow, I feel bad for bringing more pain on him.

"I believed him with everything in me. I-I don't even know what to say. I've been the worst judge of character."

He wraps his arms around me and my eyes fill, my skin aching with rawness as the tracks fall down my face.

"Please forgive me. I will get you out of this. I swear to you, Eden, you won't stay married to that bastard."

CHAPTER THIRTY-FOUR

As news of our open marriage fills the airwaves and TV hosts discuss it over coffee on their morning shows, I fold more and more inside myself.

It takes effort to get myself out of bed in the morning; to listen to Ava, who is trying so hard to distract me; to help my mother move everything to the west wing; to go through my father's things and box them up—it takes everything in me to *function*.

A few nights after I've seen the pictures, I get a phone call in the middle of the night. I'm awake. I'm always awake now. His face flashes across the screen and I debate not answering it, but like the pathetic person I am, I need to hear his voice.

I pick up the phone and don't say anything.

"Eden? Are you there?"

"I'm here." My voice comes out raspy because as soon as I hear his voice, I start crying. Again.

"I'm sorry, Eden. I'm so sorry."

"I don't need your empty apology. You told me from the beginning, I should've—"

I hold up the phone and it's dead. I'm not sure if he hung up on me or if the call dropped. When he doesn't call back, I assume he couldn't handle hearing my anguish.

I sit up all night, trying to figure out what to do.

It's been nice to be home and with my family, but I don't feel settled here. It's not the same. I came home a different person. I know I don't belong in Niaps either, although my blood craves the water. I miss the ocean almost as much as I miss Luka.

I decide after the holidays I will travel. Maybe even go back to Kings Passage. It would feel strange to be there without him, but I'd like to finish what I started. Or maybe I can see if Ms. Macardi would still come here without Luka.

I need new paint supplies...

My eyes drift shut and I think about all the things I want to paint. I need to paint the water.

———

My mother is in my room when I wake up, standing over me.

"Oh, I hope I didn't wake you. You've just been out for so long, I wanted to be sure you weren't sick."

"I finally slept," I say, mostly to myself. I stretch and then sit up. "I needed that."

"You've barely functioned for weeks now. I'm so worried about you."

"It's been weeks? Wow. It feels like moments and months all at the same time."

She smiles. "Christmas is the day after tomorrow. Your father loved Christmas most." She presses her lips together and we both tear up at the same time. "You've been through too much, losing your father and now your husband..." She smooths my hair back and wipes away one of my tears. "You fell for him, didn't you."

"I tried really hard not to, but yes...I did. Completely."

"Perhaps he needs to grow up, sow a few wild oats before settling down...the two of you are really young."

"I won't be here waiting should he decide to grow up."

"There's still a marriage agreement. All of his foolishness aside, you are his wife and he has an obligation to protect you."

"Where is the protection now? Father is dead. I'm here where I belong and if Alidonia or Niaps tries to take over our country, they'll have a fight on their hands. Jadon has more allies than Father ever did—did you know that? They trust him, they will fight for him, and he's prepared. You should believe in him. It would mean everything to him."

She turns away. "I'll have to take your word for it. Watching everything your father has built go into a mere child's hands. It's hard to watch."

"Jadon is five years older than me!"

She smiles. "As I said, a mere child."

I shrug. "He's older than Father was when he became king."

"True. And I hope with everything in me that you're right. Otherwise, our life as we know it is about to change even more. With Luka behaving like this, it creates more division between all of us, and our surrounding countries aren't going to know who to follow. Alidonia will have a way in." She shakes her head and puts her handkerchief to her nose. "I just don't know why it couldn't have been me instead..."

I throw my arms around her. "Never say that. If you are alive, you have a purpose. You are meant to be here and only you can do what you've been called to do. Never forget that."

She sniffles and when she pulls back, she's smiling. "You went and grew up while you were gone, I see."

"Who's the mere child now?" I smile. "Not me."

I think about Luka as we have the noodle contest. He would've enjoyed this even though we're drastically more subdued without Father here. The gaping hole my father has left is excruciating for all of us, but we press on. I'm proud of my mother for trying.

I think about him as we get up before the sun on Christmas morning and open presents.

I think about Luka when I see all my new art supplies and his eyes are the only eyes I can paint.

I think about him with every canvas I hide away because it's him. He stands in the water, he looks back at me, he smiles with mischief, he sobers and that moment just before he kisses me...I paint it all.

I think about him when I paint over his image, slashing red and black paint in bold strokes. The blue in his eyes stares back at me until I swish, swish, swish that brush right over him until it's like he was never there.

It's the end of January before I realize I never made any resolutions and I decide to do so. Resolutions that do not involve Luka Catano. Well, everything seems to revolve around him, but soon, that won't be the case.

I resolve to take care of myself. I'm still not eating much, but it's getting easier.

I resolve to paint whenever I feel like crying. I've painted a *lot*.

I resolve to not let any man ever consume my heart again.

That one will take longer to accomplish, but I vow to myself that I will wipe my heart clean of Luka.

"I have a meeting with the future queen of Alidonia, Delilah Farthing," Jadon announces at supper that night.

My mother's fork clatters to her plate and we all stare at him.

"She will be coming here. We will speak peacefully and hopefully restore relations between us. The king is dying and it will be her who carries on. I'm hopeful." He holds his glass up for us to celebrate and we all numbly lift our glasses.

It's just the five of us, counting Brienne.

"Are you sure this is wise?" I ask.

"I know no other way to forge peace than to offer it willingly. We will see if she accepts."

"When is she coming?"

"Next month."

My mother gets up and leaves the room in a rush.

Jadon lowers his head and digs into his plate.

"Just keep talking to her, Jadon. It'll get better."

He doesn't say anything but smiles at me before glancing back down at his food.

After dinner, Ava and I go out and stand on the balcony and look at the stars and lights of our city.

"Did you miss the cold while you were away?" she asks.

"No," I laugh, "no, I never did. I did miss you though." I turn to her and she grins.

"It was nice having the house to myself. I could get into your things without being yelled at..."

I push her in the arm and she jumps back, laughing.

"I hear your phone ringing sometimes in the night. Why do you not answer it?" She huddles in closer to me now and I watch as our breath drifts up into the clouds.

"I don't want to hear anything he has to say." That's not true. I'm tempted to answer every time he calls in the night. But I'm not strong enough. Not yet.

"What if he's calling to say he made a mistake?"

"It's far too late for that."

She nods. "It's a shame. He seemed to be genuinely good under all that beauty."

I look at her, always surprised by the wisdom in my baby sister. "I thought so too," I whisper.

"I know you're trying—I see what it takes for you to be so strong every day—but you don't have to, you know? You're home. This is where you're allowed to feel whatever you feel."

"How did you get so smart?" I put my arm around her and pull her closer.

"I'm Jadon's and Father's favorite and they've passed on all the brains to me." She tries to hold back her laugh but can't. When I look at her, her eyes are shining.

"You don't have to be strong either," I whisper. "This is your safe place."

"It isn't the same, is it? It doesn't feel as safe anymore."

"I think that's part of how we know we're becoming adults. We've always had to be far older than our years; it comes with being part of a royal family. No hiding behind childhood any longer..."

"Well, I fucking hate it," she says.

"Ava!" I look at her wide-eyed and she stares back defiantly.

"Well, I *do*."

"Me too," I finally concede. "I hate it too."

CHAPTER THIRTY-FIVE

Early the next morning, Jadon knocks on my door. I answer, barely able to focus on him. He laughs when he sees me.

"I'm sorry to wake you up. I just wanted you to see this before I leave. I have to fly out in half an hour." He hands me a folder. "Let me know what you think of it. I'll be back around eleven tonight."

I flip open the folder and my eyes widen. "Oh. Okay. Thank you."

"Love you." He kisses me on the cheek. "Go back to bed."

I grin and shut the door, crawling back into bed with the folder.

Termination of Marriage...

I read through the paperwork that states that I am seeking to terminate the marriage due to irreconcilable differences. *That's what they all say, isn't it.* Everything seems to be in order, even down to citing where the contract we had could only be broken should one or both parties engage in adultery. Luka must have known about that loophole and saw it as his way out. Or he thought his family would cover for him the way they've covered their own infidelities for years.

The very last paragraph is what shakes me and I want to run after Jadon and dance in the hallways.

The countries of Farrow and Alidonia are in the process of ongoing peaceful negotiations and request that Niaps join them in moving forward.

My mind is blown. How was my brother able to accomplish this in such a short amount of time? I need to know what he's sacrificed to make this happen. Ongoing peaceful negotiations and they haven't even met yet? What is he not telling me? I'll have to pull it out of him tonight when he gets back.

I set the papers down and fall back to sleep smiling.

Maybe now I will be able to move on.

I practically pounce on Jadon when he gets home. It's actually morning and he looks exhausted but brightens up when I barrel into him.

"I take it you're happy about the documents." He laughs, setting down his bag.

"Yes, how soon can we send them?"

"I will send it over now, if you like. You read it over carefully? You won't be compensated—that all went back into the oil rigs—but hopefully it's an agreement to stay civil and maintain peace for at least these years that I'm king."

"I don't want anything from him." I turn around and pinch my hand so I won't cry. "But tell me, how has this all happened with Alidonia so quickly? What did you do?" I look at him over my shoulder.

"Let me worry about that."

His eyes are so tired and he looks like he's carrying the weight of the world on his back. I decide to let it go. For now.

"Go to bed. Thank you, Jadon. You're saving my life."

"I will sleep better at night, knowing you're not part of that miserable family."

I haven't looked online to see what's happening with Luka in weeks. I'm tempted, always tempted. I also haven't stepped foot outside our estate. *Tomorrow I will stop being a recluse* is what I tell myself each day.

I wake up the next morning feeling rested despite it being five in the morning. I look around to see what woke me and my phone is vibrating on my bedside table. I pick it up.

Luka.

I set the phone back on the table and it starts vibrating almost as soon as it stops. And again and again...until I get up and start pacing. I turn the sound completely off and try to ignore it, but now I see it light up and still know when he's calling.

Finally, I cave.

"Hello?"

"Don't do this," he says.

"Why not?"

"The whole point was to not put your family in any danger. One person is already dead. I don't want to se—"

"Little good it did for us to be married if that were the case."

"Eden, listen to me—"

"No, you listen to me. The *point* was our fathers needed

something only the other could give. We now have the money to keep things running smoothly here, thanks to you; you have access to our oil and other resources. That's what our marriage accomplished. Alidonia is the wild card and now they're listening to my brother. Your father should do the same. The day I stop being your wife will be the happiest day of my life. You know why? I will be completely rid of you in every way."

"I'm sorry you feel that way." His voice is quiet and I raise my eyes to the ceiling and shake my head.

"What game are you playing, Luka? You know what, I don't even want to know. Don't call me again. Jadon has worked this out and you need to sign the papers, end of story. We can put an end to this joke of a marriage."

"Please listen—"

I hang up on him and power off my phone. I don't have to listen to him for another second.

After all of my restraint with not seeking out information about him, I give into the pull after our conversation. His tone...he didn't sound like his normal cocky, arrogant self. He sounded flat and weary.

The pictures don't lie though. His smile is just as bright, if not brighter, as it ever was with me. He has the charm turned up full-throttle in every picture with Nadia by his side. And there are dozens of pictures.

It's still a topic of controversy: *how could he do this to his wife and right after she lost her father?* and *well, he's just like every other prince who's been able to have his cake and eat it too.*

When I go to breakfast, Mother and Ava are already eating. On the wall next to where I usually sit is a dartboard with Luka's face on it. The target is dead center on his nose. They both are quiet as they watch my reaction. I stare at it and then them, bending over and laughing until I hurt. They start laughing too and the rest of the breakfast, every time I look over and see that dart in his nose, I cackle.

"What is all this racket?" Jadon comes in smiling. When he sees the dartboard, he loses it too and picks up one of the other darts, nailing Luka right in the forehead.

I still cry at night. Every night. Even if I go to bed feeling happier than the day before, when I get under the covers and remember how his arms felt around me in this very bed, the way I felt protected and even cherished at times, I grieve for the loss. It might not have been what I thought it was, but I *felt* every moment of it.

Now that it's gone, I realize how much richer my life felt with Luka.

Even it was a lie.

Sometimes I wish I hadn't learned the truth and could keep pretending. Anything to feel his arms around me again.

But when I wake up, the anger comes back with the sunrise. It's a gift. Otherwise, I'd be in Niaps fighting for a chance.

My first public outing since my father's death is the parade they do every year for his birthday. Typically, I ride through the streets in a horse-drawn carriage, waving and smiling as people cheer. This year I watch from the balcony of the cathedral next to my family. The mood is more somber than in past years, but there's still a festive feeling in the air.

As the last dancing team goes by, we go our separate ways. I decide to go to one of my favorite cafes and get a hot chaider. I can't remember the last time I had one—I used to live on them in the coldest months.

I'm walking down the snowy streets and feel the photographers' presence as I always have when I'm out, but I'm caught off guard when one of them jumps out next to me and starts walking beside me.

"You startled me." I laugh, clutching my chest.

"It's good to see you again, Mrs. Catano."

I glance up, startled, and it's Juan Salvo. "What are you doing here?"

He holds up his camera. "I must always follow the beauty."

I laugh. "You didn't have to come all this way. There's plenty of beauty in Niaps."

"None like yours."

I stop walking and face him. "I'm sure you get many women to fall for those lines, but to me? They're simply that and nothing more. What do you want, Juan?"

He shrugs. "I would like to take your picture."

I hold out my arm. "Well, here I am. Take one."

"I would like you to pose for me. Alone. In the snow."

We reach my cafe and I turn to walk down the cobbled path. He rushes to open the door for me.

"You should try the chaider here. It's amazing."

"Okay," he says, grinning. "So, yes? You will let me take your picture?"

"Sure. It's time for a new portrait. I won't be Mrs. Catano for much longer."

His eyes light up. "So the rumors are true..."

"Never pay attention to rumors, Juan."

I try to pay for my drink, but the barista insists on giving it to me. I put the money in her tip jar instead and she smiles gratefully.

I sit at a table in the back and Juan sits across from me without asking. I widen my eyes at him and he just laughs.

"We're friends, yes?"

"I don't really know you."

"Yes, but we have spent time together. When I photograph someone, I feel I know them on an intimate level." He leans across the table, getting closer and closer, and I have a flashback of Luka kissing me across the table.

I stand up and slosh out a little bit of the chaider when I pick it up. Juan follows closely behind.

"You're making me uncomfortable."

"That is not my intention."

"I don't know what your intention is, but you need to back off. I'm not in a generous mood these days."

He sighs. "Fine. We will take pictures here in the square, yes? There's still snow around. This is not the location I would've chosen, but it will do."

I look at him for a few moments and my shoulders sag. "Set up an appointment with our house manager for some time this week. I will give you half an hour."

"That will be perfect. An hour would be better, but—"

I level him with a look and he holds up his hands.

"Perfect," he says, smiling. "It will be just perfect."

CHAPTER THIRTY-SIX

The weather is still brisk, but the sunlight is beginning to last longer. After a winter where the most sunlight we got was somewhere around six hours, the days of more light make it feel like spring is coming. And it is, even if that means the snow doesn't go anywhere for a while yet.

Juan sets up his tripod in the forest of snow. I'm wearing a long white dress and a white cape and my red hair and lips are a shock against the backdrop of white trees. Brienne is standing guard under a nearby tree and has a general look of annoyance. I don't think she likes Juan very much. We are just outside the gardens of the Safrin estate and he's already scheming for more time.

"We agreed to half an hour," I remind him, staring into the distance. I forget he's even there until he tells me to turn toward him.

"You're preoccupied today. Is everything okay?"

"I'm fine."

Luka's voice telling me he doesn't believe me when I say I'm fine mocks me as Juan reminds me to lift my shoulders.

By the afternoon, there are pictures online of me with Juan in the cafe. The picture of him leaning forward as far as he can is the one that's talked about the most. There are a few pictures of us in the woods, but those aren't taken as seriously since he's known for his photography. The speculation is high that Juan is the one I've chosen as a rebound from Luka. He's the one I'm finding solace in—it's all so ridiculous that I put it out of my mind. It'll die down soon enough since I won't be seeing Juan again. I think he got all the shots he needed.

My mother isn't happy about the pictures, though.

"You're not divorced yet. It isn't proper to be seen with another man."

"I wasn't doing anything wrong. You want to see wrong, look at Luka's pictures with Nadia. Juan just showed up here. He wanted to take photos of me and that's what he did." I shrug. "I can't help what other people turn it into. Nothing happened."

"I'm sure he intended on making something happen." She tuts and glares at me.

"Mother! Even if that was his intention—*nothing happened.*"

"You just make sure nothing does until your papers are signed and everything is legally over. We can't afford to ruffle feathers. And even after it's legal...do you really think you'll be ready to date anyone right away? Sweetheart..." She shakes her head. "Guard your heart."

"I don't feel like I'll ever be ready for love again. You don't need to remind me of my broken heart."

Her lips press together and she reaches for the teapot. "Would you like some tea?"

"Tea will not make me feel better right now."

"Rum?"

"Rum would help."

———

I sit up in bed, panting, terrified.

"Who's there?"

I move to turn on the light and a hand stops me. I start to scream and a hand covers my mouth.

"It's me. Please don't scream."

He removes his hand.

"What are you doing sneaking in here in the middle of the night, Luka? You could've been shot!" I whisper-shout, but even with that, he holds a finger up to my lips.

"No one can know I'm here. Do you swear you won't tell a soul?"

"If you'll tell me honestly why you're here, I swear."

"I can't sign the divorce papers. I need you to trust me and stop pushing me to sign them. Can you do that?"

"No."

He takes my hand and I yank it away. His sigh fills the room.

"Just let me turn on the light. The guards outside will think I'm up reading or something."

He doesn't say anything, so I turn it on.

His eyes roam over me like he hasn't had water in years. Greedy, thirsty...full of lust and exhaustion and pain. I don't understand any of this.

"You look awful. Tell me what's going on."

"I don't have much time. I just need you to quit hounding my lawyers about the papers. And stay the hell away from Juan Salvo while you're at it."

My eyes narrow on him. "Juan? That's what this little break-in is about? Are you mad? Every time I turn on the TV or open my laptop, I see pictures of you with Nadia, and you want to monitor my behavior with Juan?"

I stand up and his eyes trail down the front of my gown, which of course makes me heated. I groan in frustration.

He puts his hand on mine again. "Be quiet," he pleads. "I took a risk in coming here. Please listen to me."

"I'm listening, but you're not really saying anything."

He stands up and grabs hold of my arms. He lowers his head and kisses me hard. I'm so shocked at first I kiss him back, like I'm as starved as he is. My senses suddenly rush back and I push him away as hard as I can. He stumbles back and steps forward again.

"You lay another hand on me and I will kill you myself."

He stops mid-step, his eyes filled with hurt, and I feel my body drain of all energy. I start to cry and he comes back toward me, putting his arms around me and hugging me. I let him this time. I cry and cry and cry and he bears the weight.

When I'm all cried out, he lifts me in his arms and places me on the bed.

"I'm sorry," he whispers. His head lowers to his chest and he doesn't look at me for a long time. He opens his mouth to speak and closes it. He looks as if he's carrying the weight of the world on his shoulders, far from the boy I met at Kings Passage.

I want to shake him until he gives me answers.

He broke my heart—what does it matter whether I'm with Juan or not?

Why is he sorry when he willingly chose her?

But it looks like I won't be getting any answers today. He turns off my light and stands by the window. After ten minutes or so, he climbs out and I'm left with more questions than ever.

Seeing him stirs everything up again. Not that I was even close to better, but I had begun to at least function. Now I'm back to where I started, except maybe even more tormented. He just doesn't make sense. That's the answer I keep going back to.

He wants what he cannot have and the moment he gets it, he's gone.

Juan comes to the house to show me the pictures. My mother and Brienne stand in the hallway disapprovingly as he makes up an excuse to why he's there.

"I approved it with your house manager. I needed you to see these exquisite pictures." The words rush out of him; he knows he's on borrowed time. "You should choose one for me to make into a massive portrait. I can show you my favorites."

He did do a good job. I look like fire against the snow.

"I wonder if we could go out for chaider again?" He leans in, whispering.

"That wasn't a date."

"Oh no, I know, but...it was nice."

Thinking of Luka's warnings, I grab my coat. "I'll be back later," I tell my mother. She starts to say something but stops and I hurry out of there before she gets her voice back.

Brienne rushes after us. "I'll drive."

"Oh, that's okay. I have my car..." Juan stops when he sees her expression and nods. "Sure, you drive."

I glare at her defiantly and she stares right back. I'm so tired of constantly having eyes on me. Even hers.

I don't argue, instead climbing in the back of the car and glaring out the window.

Juan's chatter fills the entire drive. He is enchanted with this country and tells me every reason why on the short drive.

"I think I might make this my home base," he finishes.

Brienne is parking and she turns to look at Juan. "She's married, you know. I can show you his picture if you'd like... he's quite good-looking."

Juan laughs loudly and I just want to get out of this car.

"I took the best pictures of them together. Believe me, I know." He leans in closer to Brienne. *"Where is he now?"*

Her face gets red and I hop out of the car before she blows. She's usually even-tempered, but the anger is pouring out of her right now. If I were Juan, I'd run.

She follows us into the cafe and I order her a chaider as a peace offering. She smiles kindly at me and then goes back to piercing holes through Juan's skull.

Juan and I sit at the same table as the last time and he leans his face against his hand as he looks at me.

"So many hoops to jump through just to be alone with you, Eden Catano. S*emi*-alone."

"I'm not sure what you're expecting."

"Not much. Just a chance to see you again."

"Juan...it's not a good idea. I'm too complicated and...taken."

"Ah, still taken, huh. The boy is a fool to let you out of his sight."

"The biggest fool. Now which picture is your favorite?"

He lights up and pulls out his portfolio, showing me his top three. I choose one and he sighs like I've made the best choice.

"Should I send a life-size print of this one to your

husband?" His eyes are twinkling as he says it and I wish I could take everything he's offering. It's tempting to let him distract me for a while.

I laugh. "No, that won't be necessary. He doesn't deserve to see this."

"Remember that when he comes crawling back. Has he even tried?" He leans forward, both arms on the table and I feel a prickle of something. I don't want to acknowledge it at first, because I'd be forced to admit I was momentarily blinded by yet another man's charm, but my intuition is still intact.

"How much are they paying you?" I lean forward and stare him down until he sits back in his chair, laughing and shaking his head.

"What?"

"You heard me. How much?" I glare at him until he squirms.

Brienne walks up then. "Is there a problem here?"

"This bastard was sent to spy on me. Find out who it is." I look at Juan then and get in his face. "And the answer is no. He hasn't. Why don't you go running back to whoever hired you and tell them that."

I walk outside and Brienne follows, carrying a dangling Juan by the arm. I'd give anything for her strength. She takes him around the back of the cafe and I stand by the car, waiting until she's done her thing.

She comes back wiping her bloody hands on her pants.

"Is he okay?"

"I didn't hurt him too badly." She grins and shrugs. "He can walk away, so I'd say he's doing all right. He's working for Titus."

"I knew it. But why?"

We get in the car and I sit in the front with her. She

faces me and puts her fingers to her lips for me to be quiet. We don't talk the whole way home. My leg is bouncing up and down with the effort it takes.

As soon as we arrive at the house, she looks through the car until she finds a recording device and smashes it. She still doesn't say a word until we get in the entryway and she's found another.

"That should be it since these are the only two places he's been. I'll have the others do a more thorough search." She motions for me to follow her back outside. "Until then, watch what you say."

"Brienne, he was here last night—Luka," I whisper.

"I know." Her eyes crinkle up with her smile. "I'm the one who helped him get in."

CHAPTER THIRTY-SEVEN

"Why would you do that?" I trail Brienne as she goes back inside.

"I need to go shower." She holds up her bloody hands and smirks.

"Not so fast." I follow her to her room, which is next to mine and when I begin to walk inside, she tucks her head and looks at me with surprise. I come to a full stop. I've never entered her room and want to always be respectful of her space. It's an odd relationship where she constantly calls me Lady Eden, which is like her holding up a giant wall between us at times; yet, I trust her with my life.

"You can come in," she says, opening her door wider. She quickly goes through her room and when she comes up with nothing, she relaxes. "This is probably the safest room in the house for talking."

"You really think the house is bugged? By Juan?"

"I guess it's possible that Luka could've bugged the house, but I don't believe he did. If he did, I think he'd have a good reason."

"Why did you let him in to see me? For that matter—

why do you trust him at all?" I chew the outside of my lip, something my mother never lets me get away with.

"Quit chewing your lip. It'll bleed."

I sigh. "It's like having two mothers around. How old are you anyway?"

"I'm twenty-three. Old enough." She goes into her bathroom and washes her hands.

"You're barely older than me!" I raise my voice so she can hear me over the water. "And don't get me off the subject."

She doesn't answer until she comes out of the bathroom, drying her hands.

"I don't know why I let Luka in. He seemed desperate to see you and I thought you deserved to hear him out. And he warned me about Juan."

"What? Why didn't you tell me?"

"I wanted to see if he'd try anything. But you didn't even really need me—you figured him out for yourself. It was a proud mama moment."

She laughs and I realize how rarely she laughs. I feel a pang of guilt that I haven't tried harder to get to know her. It must be lonely watching out for a family who isn't your own. I remember my mom saying something had happened with Brienne's family and I'm ashamed that I never bothered to ask more about it.

"Thank you for watching out for me, Brienne. I'm really fortunate to have you in my life."

"It's my highest honor, Lady Eden."

"You know, I've said it about a million times, but I really wish you'd just call me Eden."

"That would feel disrespectful."

I laugh. "The last thing anyone would call you is disrespectful. You are always the epitome of proper, and you don't have to be with me. I consider you...a friend."

She goes completely still and looks down, her hands gripped tightly. When she raises her head, there are tears in her eyes. "Thank you, Eden. I consider you a friend too."

I press my lips together and try to keep my tears from spilling over. I take a shaky breath. "And thank you for getting Luka past the other guards. You're right—I did need to talk to him. Not that he told me anything..."

"I can't forget the way he looked at you." She sighed. "It almost made me believe in love."

"Love?" I spit out. "Uh, no. After all he's done, I hardly think he loved me. But after seeing him, I did wonder if maybe he really did...care. Maybe. I don't know. It's all so confusing."

"I don't think it's over. There's a reason he came. Don't you think? And there's a reason Titus sent Juan to check things out. Something's going on."

I want to agree with her, but I can't help but think if Luka wanted me, he'd be here right now. Not with Nadia.

"None of it makes sense." I walk to the door and look back. "We're a good team."

"We are." She leans against a chair and looks like a portrait herself.

I get back into the groove of being home. It still feels strange to be back, but with each week, I find a new normal. I help Mother with the charities she runs and spend time with Ava when she's done with her classes. When I'm not with them, I take online college courses and paint. I gave up on the thought of Ms. Macardi. I don't want to put her in an

awkward position when she's on Titus's payroll. I consider
going back to Kings Passage, but that would put *me* in an
awkward position. I do think about Tysa and even Thad on
occasion and wonder what they're doing. I left in such a
hurry and never looked back. Tysa probably thinks I'm a
terrible person, dropping off like that.

The only time I ever was allowed to enjoy a short
glimpse of freedom was at Kings Passage and later at Luka's
home. I'd really like to change that.

I've spent many days in the city and nearby villages,
taking food to the workers and handing out coats for those
in need. I've never gone and painted them. So one day
when I have nothing else I'm required to do, I let Brienne
know my plan.

"It's the perfect day for it. Shouldn't be too cold," she
says.

"I know it would be better to wait during the midnight
sun, when there's endless sunlight, but...I can't wait!"

We drive to one of my favorite streets, where the shops
and restaurants are built into a cliff. The mountains still
have snow on them, but it's melting. Spring always brings
people out by the droves. It's like we all awake from a deep
sleep.

I set up my easel in a park and the first person to notice
me is a little girl. She walks up and starts chatting before
I've even looked up.

"Whatcha doin'?"

I glance at her around my easel and she's holding onto a
ragged teddy bear.

"I'm going to paint for a bit. Would you like me to paint
you?"

I look around for her mother but don't see anyone. I
frown and turn around, searching for Brienne. She's

standing near the entrance of the park. I motion for her to come over.

"Where is your mother?" I ask.

"I don't have a mother. But my dad is over there." She points and I look but don't see him.

"Are you sure he's over there?"

She pokes her lips out and looks at me like I'm crazy. "Yes! He fell asleep while I was playing."

Sounds like a real winner. I look again and I can barely make out a body lying on the grass. "Okay, well, why don't I paint you and when he wakes up, we can take it to him."

She claps her hands together, barely making any sound around the bear.

When Brienne gets close, I lean over and ask her to go check out the guy. I start painting while the little girl talks my ear off. Brienne comes back a few minutes later, while I'm engrossed in the drawing.

"We need to leave," she says.

"What—" I look up and she's as close to panicked as I've ever seen her.

"Something doesn't feel right. No one was over there."

"I don't think we should leave her alone." I look at her and she's fidgeting. I sigh. "Did you make that up about that man being your father?"

"He asked me to do it," she said.

"Who?"

"He didn't say his name. But he gave me ten scrupas to ask you to paint my picture."

"Are your parents nearby?"

"My grandmother is right over there." She points and I see a woman crocheting in a rocking chair across the street.

"Eden," Brienne urges. "Let's go."

I give the little girl her painting and she grins. I guess the whole trip wasn't for nothing, to see her smile.

We walk to the car and get inside. Before Brienne turns the key in the ignition, she looks to me, eyes huge. "Get out of the car!"

I don't hesitate. We both jump out of the car and run. We're halfway down the street when the car explodes in a huge crashing flame. We stand there, breathing hard, watching the car burn.

"We need to get out of here!" Brienne yells.

She makes a few phone calls and we run a few blocks to meet a guard. A couple of other guys from our security team go to what's left of the car and look for any sign of who could've done this in the surrounding area. The little girl describes the man but has very little to offer about his description. On the way home, I call Jadon.

"The car I was in just blew up."

"*What?* Where are you now?" he yells.

"I'm on my way home with Brienne. She has a few guys from the security team on it. What else should we do?"

"Are you hurt?"

"No, Brienne saved my life."

"I'll be sure to thank her when I see her. For now, *get home.* I'll call the police and alert them that this is going on. I needed to call them about Juan anyway. Do you think he was involved in this?"

"I can't figure out why he's involved in *any* of it. He's a successful photographer, high profile...I don't get it."

"It's time for a confrontation with Titus. Do you want in on that?"

"I wouldn't miss it for the world."

CHAPTER THIRTY-EIGHT

I expected Luka to check on me after news spread world-wide about the attempt on my life. I hate to admit it, even to myself, but I did. I wanted him to. Needed to hear his concern for me. If nothing else, just to know that I did matter to him in some way.

But nothing.

And it makes everything that much more painful.

To top it off, now I'm paranoid about going anywhere. Everyone is trying to convince me that now that the guards are on high alert, they'll protect me, but it's too little, too late. The damage is done.

We're easing into summer slowly but surely and the days are getting longer. It's the time of year when I'm usually outside nonstop into the wee hours of the morning because it's still light outside. Now I go to the roof and wish for the stars and the dark sky. Anything to commiserate with how lonely I feel.

I need something—anything—to be darker than me.

I can't figure out what to do. It feels like until Luka signs those papers, I'm in limbo. And even when he does, what then? After being groomed a large part of my life to be his wife, I'm at a loss on what to do with my life and feel like I'm supposed to have it figured out.

I'm still reeling with the loss of my father too—we all are —and that has everyone more on edge than usual.

So, when Jadon announces that the Catano family will be coming here for a gathering to discuss peaceful negotiations, that sends me into a tailspin more than ever.

"When? Why here? Do you really trust them not to knock one of us off while they're here?" I'm standing in front of Jadon's desk, heels clicking on the hardwood floor as I walk back and forth, back and forth. He catches me off guard when he starts pacing with me.

"What are you doing?"

"Just seeing if it works." He grins.

I smack his arm and he jumps out of the way before I can hit him again.

"Next week. I want them in our territory. And no, I don't trust them, but I hardly think they'll try anything in our home. That being said, they will be checked for weapons, bugs, and so will their guards. We will have a nice dinner and talk like civilized humans."

"Luka is the only civilized one of all of them, and look how he's turned out. If his mother and sister show up, it should be quite the show."

"They better all show up. I have a few choice words to say to each of them."

I rub my hands together and he laughs. "You having choice words—I can't wait."

I work alongside our cleaners during the week leading up to the dinner, then do yoga for hours at a time at night, needing desperately to keep myself grounded but clear-headed. My brain wants to obsess over all the what-ifs and it's taking every ounce of willpower I possess to avoid going down that path.

I do plan my outfit carefully. It's one thing to be the woman scorned, but if I show up at this dinner and am not dressed to perfection, I may as well not even go at all.

Shallow? Check.

Hoping to make him suffer, even if it's just a little? Check. Check.

The end result is a black shorts set with red embroidered flowers across the chest and along the side of the shorts...with a flash of my midriff showing. It's not too low but short enough to drive Luka crazy. Unless all of that was fake. It sure didn't feel fake when he drove into me so hard it took our breath away...

My hair is down and in loose waves around my face. No twists or braids, just simple, so it doesn't look like I'm trying too hard.

Half an hour before they're scheduled to arrive, I have a panic attack in my room. I lower my head between my legs and am breathing heavily when Ava bursts through the door.

"They're here," she gasps. "What are you doing?"

I look up and she's breathing almost as hard as I am.

"Panicking."

"Why?" She frowns at me.

She has no concept of what it's like to worry what people think of her or to let a guy consume her.

"I hope you always stay this way," I tell her, exhaling through my mouth.

"Did you hear me say they're here?"

"Yes, but I'm *trying* to calm down first. Why are they early?"

"Trying to catch us off guard would be my guess."

"You need to always stay smart too."

She comes over and puts her hand on my forehead. "Are you getting sick?"

I brush her hand off and she giggles. "Losing a touch of the rottenness would be okay." I hold up my fingers to show her just how much.

"You look fucking amazing," she says when I stand up.

"Would you stop already with the sailor's mouth? It does not suit you."

"You just told me to never change."

This time she's prepared for when I try to swat her backside and jumps away, cackling.

"Come on. I can't wait for him to get an eyeful of you tonight." She leans in my face on her tiptoes. "*Make him suffer.*"

"Sounds like we're on the same wavelength, little one."

I hear him before I see him and my heart begins thumping in triple time. Then I hear Mara's voice and I cringe. Brienne exchanges a look with me and it's like she's swallowing something bitter. I'm not the only one who finds Mara so distasteful.

I enter the room with Ava by my side, Brienne close behind. Everyone stops to look at me: my mother and Jadon, Luka, his parents, and Mara. Just an intimate gathering amongst family. I nearly giggle and have to shove it down. I feel a manic laugh building up in me and that never ends well.

Cece offers her hand to me and I take it, kissing her on both cheeks. I do the same when Titus offers his hand and the look in his eyes gives me chills. He takes in my outfit and when his eyes reach mine, I'm disgusted by the lust I see in them. I pull my hand away and wish I could go wash it right then. Has he always looked at me that way and I never noticed?

I ignore Mara and look at Luka.

"No kisses for me?"

It's as if we've stepped back in time and it's our first night at Kings Passage, when he was too cool to be bothered with me but didn't mind spewing out seductive words to put me under his spell. I don't know what I expected, but it wasn't this. He's so far from the guy who snuck into my bedroom and the man I knew in Niaps.

"Never again." I turn from him and go stand next to Jadon.

"Yeah, right." Mara makes a noise of disbelief behind me, something between a snort and a huff. "You're not even going to say hello to me?"

"Hello."

Her mouth drops and she stares at her mother, apparently thinking if she glares at her long enough, her mother will defend her. It doesn't happen.

Jadon motions for us to sit at the dining table and the five-course meal begins. First, our camembert cheese with red wine, followed by smoked salmon and bleu cheese on a crisp cracker, mini waffles with a caramelized whey cheese, lamb, and mashed potatoes (I stick with the waffles), and cloudberries and cream with coffee.

Jadon and Titus keep conversation going, discussing the stock market and concerns about crops worldwide with the amount of snow we had this year, and for them, the heat.

Luka sits across from me and avoids looking at me. My outfit was a waste on him because other than when I walked into the room, he's studiously listened to his father or stared at his plate. I think about all the times he's eaten the meat off of my plate and looked like he wanted to devour me, and I feel a rush of sadness.

Why did I agree to be here for this? It backfired on me because he obviously feels nothing.

As soon as I'm done with my dessert, I stand up and excuse myself. Luka's head jerks up and it's the only time I've seen a reaction from him. The next second his face is wiped clean of all expression and I leave the room before the tears start to fall.

I'm almost to the bedroom when I hear him call my name. I stop but don't turn around.

He comes up behind me and whispers in my ear, "It will be over soon."

"What will be over? It'd be over now if you'd just sign the papers."

He shakes his head. "Soon. Trust me."

My body sags and I want to lean my back against his chest, but I don't. "Just do it and get it over with already."

I start to walk away and he follows, grabbing my arm before I go into my room. "Eden, wait—"

"You didn't even check to make sure I was okay after I was nearly killed, Luka, and you want me to—"

He shakes his head and I don't finish my sentence. He looks down the hall, almost as if he expects someone to be listening. Brienne stands there, and he relaxes.

"I know it sounds insane to ask this of you, but know I wouldn't without good reason."

"You've spoken in riddles the past two times I've seen you. I'm tired, Luka. I'm not cut out for this game." I open my door and turn around leaning against the doorframe. "Make my life a little easier and divorce me already."

He looks down the hall again. "I need to get back. I wish you'd come back in..."

"And watch you ignore me again? No, thank you." I stand up straight and step back. "Goodbye, Luka."

CHAPTER THIRTY-NINE

I have a hard time settling into sleep. I jump up when I hear the car start outside and watch as Luka and his family drive away. It feels like another door shutting to us and our ending, even though I still share his name. I don't know why he insists on stretching this out.

Jadon peeks his head in my room and sees me staring out the window.

"Are you okay?"

I nod, clinching the material of my robe between my fingers. "I will be." I turn to face him. "Did you find out anything?"

"This night further cemented the fact that I do not trust Titus Catano. He claims he had nothing to do with our father or this latest threat, and that he only wants to maintain a peaceful relationship, despite the ongoing differences between you and Luka."

"My relationship has nothing to do with it. If he had anything to do with Father, it was when things were good between Luka and me. Maybe that's what he felt threatened by..."

Jadon looks through me; I can tell his thoughts are rushing through his head. It's the look he gets when all the pieces are coming together for him, and usually when it does, it's a profound revelation. I want to push him—plead with him to tell me what he's thinking—but I know better. He has to work it all out before he'll spill.

"I need to look over some paperwork, do some kingly things." He waves his hand and smirks, trying to snap out of his thoughts. "Just wanted to make sure you're okay. And also," he hesitates for a long moment, "I'm sorry to ask this of you, but can you stay put until we get to the bottom of this with the car explosion?"

"That could be forever! It's finally getting nice out—I need to be outside."

"Be outside here, where we have more of a handle on security. It won't be long."

Luka's words come back to me. *It will be over soon.*

What aren't you telling me, Jadon? I want to ask him so badly, but I know by the determination in his eyes that I won't be getting anything out of him tonight.

I turn back to the window. "It must be nice having control of all of us. Holding all the answers inside and keeping the reins on us. Must be really nice."

He puts his hand on my shoulder. "Don't be like that. You know that's not what this is."

"You may not see it that way, but I have been a trained puppet my whole life, simply by being born a woman. This is where it ends. You are my king and I respect you as my king and brother, but I will not let anyone pull my strings anymore. Not you, not Mother, and not the Catano family."

He grins. "I think you might have finally grown up, Edie. Just don't forget to use caution and wisdom while you're trying out those wings."

I roll my eyes. "Yeah, yeah. Go do your kingly things and let me sleep."

He kisses my cheek and leaves me alone.

Despite all my bold talk about doing whatever I want, I stay in the house for the next two weeks, only going outside on our patio in the mornings and on my balcony at night. I paint in the sun-room off of the patio and embrace the solitude. I create a series of ocean landscapes and continue the series that I try to keep hidden from prying eyes—all of Luka. Everyone leaves me alone for the most part. I see them at dinner but otherwise keep to myself. I feel the need to heal by myself and to take time before trying to figure out the next step. I'm still in limbo and it's still driving me crazy, but I'm gaining more peace inside with each passing day. At least that's what I tell myself: all of this solitude has to be helping.

It changes the next morning when Ava pounds on my door at eight in the morning. I was up all night painting and didn't go to bed until five, so I yell at her.

"Go away!"

"I have to show you something!"

"Show me later," I moan into my pillow.

She stalks in anyway, completely ignoring me, and throws the newspaper at me. I crack an eye open and glare at her but then look at the paper. She has it folded so I can only see Luka and Nadia.

All I see are the words: *New baby for the clandestine couple*...and I don't even read the rest. It shows them leaving the hospital and I get up and run past Ava to the bathroom, throwing up.

"You have to do something about this. He's making you look like the biggest fool." Ava gets a wet washcloth and hands it to me when I'm done.

"You think I don't know that?" I croak. "What do you suggest I do? He won't sign the papers."

"Show this to your lawyer and I think this will get you out of it."

"It might not even be true." I lean my head against the wall. "But I'll try. You're right. I have to do something. You could've told me when I was fully awake, though."

"Look, I know you're going through a lot, working things out and all that, but you can't stay in that room painting the days away."

"Jadon told me to stay put. Someone tried to kill me, in case you forgot!"

"I could never forget that, but this with Luka needs to be put to rest. You deserve at least that much."

I nod and get to my feet. "You're right. I've been wallowing too long."

"You said it, not me." She grins.

I flick her with a towel and she jumps out of the way.

While I'm grabbing my toothbrush, she adds, "So I called your lawyer and he should be here in half an hour."

"Ava!"

"What? Someone has to be proactive around here."

"Not your place."

"You weren't getting it done." She shrugs, and in spite of being furious with her, I love her for looking out for me.

I take a quick shower and take a picture of the headline. Not letting myself think about it too much, I send it with a text to Luka.

This seals the deal. Thanks for that. My lawyer will be finalizing our divorce with or without you.

After I've sent it, I hope that I'm right.

A few nights later, I'm at dinner and my lawyer has just left. He says my divorce should be final within the month. Luka never responded to my text and it's just as well. Brienne rushes in the dining room, face flushed.

"I think you need to see this." She's out of breath and motioning for us to follow her into the living room.

I get up and follow her and so does Mother and Jadon. Ava is the last to enter the room. The TV is on and there's a breaking story.

"What's going on?" I haven't seen what is so important yet, it's just reporters waiting at a courthouse. "Wait, is that Niaps?" It is.

I squeeze my hands together when I start to shake, feeling in my gut that this is big. And I don't have to wait long. The doors open and Titus is led out in handcuffs, guards surrounding him and he's shuffled to a waiting car. The reporter quietly gives the play-by-play.

"It appears that the Niapsian king, Titus Catano, has been arrested for conspiracy of murder on two counts. What this means for the throne is still in question, as far as how soon Prince Luka will take the title...and the prince has been in the news a lot lately himself. What does this mean for the royal family?"

They talk and talk and talk, but I'm stuck on *conspiracy of murder on two counts*. So it is true.

Everyone turns to see my reaction, but I have to move. I leave the room and go outside. If he's responsible for the threat on my life, I don't have a reason to be afraid. I walk for at least an hour, mulling over every possibility.

When I get back to the house, I grab my phone and walk out on my balcony.

I'm tired of waiting. I call Luka.

He answers on the first ring and says these four words: "I'm coming to you."

CHAPTER FORTY

It's early the next morning before he arrives and I haven't slept at all. Jadon and I are the ones who let him in, even Brienne hasn't gotten up yet and she's always up before I am. The house is quiet and I'm glad that Jadon and I are together for this.

Luka looks as exhausted as I feel. He's lost weight, something I hadn't fully noticed when he was here the last time because of his suit, but without his jacket over his button-down shirt and black pants, it shows. He has a bag slung over his shoulder and it looks heavy.

He moves toward me, as if to hug me and I step back.

"Right," he says, holding his hands up.

Jadon leads us to his office and shuts the door. He motions for Luka to sit down and folds his hands together. "Give me one good reason why I should be trusting you inside this house."

"I'll give you several reasons. I'm the one who turned in all the evidence against my father. I'm prepared to show you all of it." He holds his bag up.

Jadon motions for him to get on with it and Luka pulls out a large file and sets it in front of Jadon.

"I left here because things weren't sitting right with me about your father. Things *my* father said in the months leading up to that. The way he was so obsessed with our marriage and tried to be involved in our relationship. In ways I never told you about," he says to me. "Basile and I started meeting regularly when I went back...somewhere different each time and without a tail unless we wanted it. He was in agreement with me and ready to see my father pay for not only this but things he's done in the past. I finally learned the depths my father could go to and when he hired Juan and your car exploded within days of him being here, I was truly terrified that I wouldn't have enough on him to keep him from doing this again...until he succeeded."

He bows his head and rubs his eyes and when he looks up again, the exhaustion in his face is almost more than I can take. Everything in me aches to comfort him and I end up sitting on my hands to keep from doing just that.

"How were you able to prove it was him?" Jadon cuts to the chase.

"After we came here for that farce of a dinner party, he was overly cocky. He was after me all the time about cutting ties with you once your father..." He clears his throat and swallows hard. "Can I just say...I know what my family has done can never be forgiven...but no one is sorrier than I am that my family is the cause of such an unspeakable act." His eyes fill with tears. "I haven't been able to rest, knowing that my father committed this crime against you and your family. If he'd succeeded with you—" He looks at me and shakes his head.

The sorrow in his eyes, the guilt; he's drowning in it.

"Nadia was able to secure papers that I couldn't get my hands on. After the explosion, she acquired phone records of his conversations with Juan before and after he was here, and in that second conversation, Juan said a name that made everything come together. Caulder Farthing."

Jadon slams his hand on the desk and I jump.

"Fuck!" he yells.

"Who is he in relation to the king in Alidonia?" I ask, unsure of how this all ties together. It's a blow to Jadon, that much is obvious. Being the female that I am, I'm still stuck on Nadia.

"He's the nephew and right hand to the king." Jadon goes through the file, his forehead creased with worry. "I'm supposed to meet with Delilah, the king's daughter, as soon as the king passes, to negotiate new terms. It keeps getting delayed. This will change everything."

"Your father was working with Alidonia to destroy us?" It all finally makes sense to me. Except one thing. "Why did he push so hard for us to get married?"

"Yes, he was working with Alidonia." Luka's face is grim, but he looks at us boldly. "And he got what he wanted from our marriage. Once he had access to all your resources, he was done. He just didn't expect me to—" He turns to me and touches my hand, causing goose bumps to scatter across my skin. His jaw ticks before he continues. "It's a relief to finally say all of this out loud. To you. I'll spend the rest of my life trying to give my family a better name, a name to be proud of."

"You said there were several reasons to trust you. This is huge, I'll grant you that." Jadon's voice is low and measured, as if it's taking everything in him to carry on this conversation. "Name another."

"I've realized I'm in love with your sister," Luka says it

to Jadon, but when the words are out, he looks at me, his eyes gleaming.

I feel like my heartbeat is going to pound me into the ground.

"I know I don't deserve her in any way, but I love her and I'll do anything to protect her." This time he's facing me when he says it, his voice soft.

"Even sleep with your ex-girlfriend?" Jadon asks coldly.

My face heats, but I can't look away from Luka. He swallows hard.

"I'm not proud of the things I did to get to the truth. I was being watched night and day, I had to make it look convincing. It felt like the whole world was my audience and one wrong move would wreck all the progress I'd made."

His eyes are pleading with me now. "This isn't the time or place, but when you fully hear me out, I will fall on my knees and beg your forgiveness...or anything else it takes." He clasps his hands together and I realize they're shaking. He clears his throat. "I didn't think I could trust Nadia at first. Once I realized I could, she began helping me and it made the difference. She is an ally, but that is all. She's one-hundred-percent clear on my feelings for you."

I have a lump in my throat that I'm trying really hard to ignore. I look at the ceiling and will my tears away.

"Eden has my support in whatever she decides. She shouldn't have to subject herself to you or your family for one second longer." Jadon's crystal blue eyes level Luka and for someone who is unfailingly kind, he looks like he could kill Luka with a single thrust of a sword.

"I agree. I will do whatever you wish, whether that means moving on with the divorce, or worshipping the ground you walk on for the rest of my days." A faint smile touches Luka's lips, but he quickly sobers. "I didn't feel I could explain until I had enough proof to put my father away and the assurance that you were safe. I haven't felt that until now, with my father behind bars. The country of Niaps is already in the process of overthrowing him and I will be sworn in this weekend."

"You've given us a lot to consider," Jadon finally says. He looks at me, his eyes questioning, but I can't form a rational sentence yet.

He loves me.

His father killed my father.

His father tried to kill me.

He loves me.

Not Nadia.

Could that really be true?

"I'd like time to look over this folder. I'm grateful you brought it—I recognize that you wouldn't have had to and did so as a show of good faith. Thank you. It's still really hard to swallow that my sister is married to the son of the man who killed our father. That will take time to work through, for all of us. Whether Eden ever can is up to her."

Jadon stands and opens the door. Luka and I both stand up and walk out. I hesitate after Jadon shuts the door and Luka touches my arm.

"Can we talk?"

"I really don't know what to say. I'm...stunned? If that's even the word? This is a lot to take in and I want to believe you, but you've kept me in the dark for so long. Any word or *clue* in this time would've helped..."

"I thought begging you not to sign the papers was a clue. I thought the way I looked at you spoke volumes...I worried I was being too obvious. The dinner here—torture. I knew the way I looked at you would give me away, so I just... didn't."

I start walking toward the sunroom.

"Can I?" He falls into step beside me.

I nod.

"When I left here and returned to Niaps months ago, I realized almost immediately that my room was bugged. I left them in place and tried to use it to my advantage. But that meant things with Nadia went further than I wanted them to."

I grit my teeth. "I'm sure that was very difficult."

He turns me toward him and his eyes are fiery. Not with anger but maybe something like righteous fury.

"I'm too young to have trouble in that department and yet I did. I managed to keep her happy up until a certain point and then she started wondering why I wouldn't seal the deal...do you really want to hear this?" His voice sounds agonized and I glare at him.

"No, I don't want to hear this, but I think I have to," I snap at him.

"I was afraid, Eden. Your father was dead. My father was getting careless and I was so afraid of what he'd do next. I didn't want to leave the house for fear of missing something important, so except for the rare outing with her, all of my interactions with Nadia were at the house. When she started wondering out loud what was wrong with me, and I knew we were wired, I did it...I had sex with her. I'd do it again if it meant saving you."

"How noble of you."

He grasps both of my arms and puts his forehead against mine. "No one has ever been in my heart before. No one. Until you. You have buried yourself down into the depths of me and there is nothing I can do to get you out.

I've tried. I resisted. You know better than anyone how long I resisted. But you are in every moment I breathe. Your face, your skin, your body next to mine infused with me...there's no escaping. I didn't want to run from it when I left you to go find out the truth, and yet it was agonizing to play a part after I'd come to that realization. All I wanted was you. I swear to you. And no one could tell you that better than Nadia. Whatever it takes, I want to prove it to you. Will you give me a chance?"

I back away from him and his hands drop to his sides.

"Is she pregnant?"

CHAPTER FORTY-ONE

I walk away, suddenly not sure if I want to hear his answer. I walk into the sun-room and he's right behind me. When we get inside, I realize my mistake. In my bleary state this morning, I didn't hide the painting of him. In the middle of the ocean, the castle, the farsynthia fields, Luka's likeness stands front and center. He stares at the paintings, walking closer to inspect every detail. When he gets to the one of him, he shakes his head.

"I can't believe how talented you are. Your artwork should be in museums for everyone to appreciate. I feel like I'm in the presence of greatness." He turns around, and the sincerity in his eyes shakes me. "No, she's not pregnant. I've only ever gone bare with you. Ever."

I let out a deep exhale.

"It was the last card in my hand. I was getting desperate to wrap things up. He mentioned often the fact that if you'd been pregnant, it would have been perfect—sort of the only hitch to his plan, so to speak." He scoffs, a disgusted look on his face. "There's no way in hell I'd ever let him get close to our child."

My blood heats when he says those words and it's as if he knows. He reaches out and his fingers skate across my arm.

"Turns out I didn't need it. The phone records were in my hand right after that headline went public and it was exactly what we needed."

"You must have gotten closer to Nadia through all of this, though. I can't believe that you'd have sex with her, go through all of this, and not have feelings for her."

"I didn't keep having sex with her—it happened once before she wanted to know what the fuck was wrong with me. I took her to a hotel and told her I'd pay her to keep her mouth shut. She didn't want the money," he adds.

"This is all hard to believe. She's one of Mara's best friends. Mara has been dying for the two of you to get together all this time. The way Nadia looked at you when we were at school and in the photos—even when I saw her in person last—I don't buy that she doesn't want you."

"She'd actually met someone she really liked before I came back. She thought she was in love with me until we were together again, but I'm not the same person I was when we were together, and neither is she. I needed her help and feel bad for manipulating the situation. I've apologized to her for that. She was relieved when we didn't work —honestly, she was. Hopefully once she explains things to him, they can work it out. And she's willing to talk to you too, if you ever need more answers."

I twist my hair around a finger and tug. He stills my hand after a few minutes and steps closer. "I know it will take time, but do you think you can see a future for us? Do you love me even a little bit?"

Every time he says the word *love*, my heart jolts and I feel the need to grab onto something before I go down.

"Sometimes we love, but it's to our detriment. That's how my love for you has felt—painful, one-sided, and incapacitating. It hasn't been a healthy love."

"If you know my love for you is true, do you think that could change? That the...love...you feel for me could be perfected and grow?"

"I don't know." My lips tremble and I put my head in my hands. The tears that have been barely hanging by a thread, pour out of me, and he's there to witness my ugly spiral.

"I'm so sorry," he whispers, taking me in his arms and holding me.

I stand there for a long time, enjoying the strength of his arms around me, feeling his heartbeat against mine. I've missed him so much. When the air between us intensifies, I lean back and he bends down, his lips brushing against mine. I want to kiss him back, I really do.

"I can't do this." I push him away. "I need time."

I walk to the door and he stands there surrounded by my artwork and the sunlight. I wish I could paint the look on his face right now. It would be the most beautiful piece yet.

"I understand," he says quietly. "I'd like to have a chance to speak to the rest of your family, but even after I go home, I will be there waiting for you. Praying with everything in me that you will find me when you're ready. I need you by my side, Eden. There is no obligation for us to be together anymore. That ended long ago. This is between you and me. *You* are the one I want. And I hope to God I'm the one you want. I'm ready to work hard to build your trust in me. For as long as it takes."

I leave him there and run into Brienne on the way to my room. She takes a look at my face and follows me inside. I sit down on the bed and she stands in front of me, waiting. Eventually, I tell her everything, and she paces as she listens. When I finish with our talk in the sunroom, she smiles.

"You're smiling? Why? I haven't decided anything."

"I think your heart decided long ago." She ducks when I throw a pillow at her and laughs as she dodges the second one too. When she makes sure I'm not throwing another, she crosses her arms over her chest. "Do you want to believe him?"

"With everything in me."

"That's a good start."

When my mother comes into my room a few hours later, I take one look at her face and know Luka managed to weasel his way into her heart. Her eyes are dreamy and she sits down on the bed with a sigh.

"He risked everything to bring the truth to light and to keep anything from happening to you...it's such a brave risk he took!" She clutches her throat and wipes a few tears away.

"It doesn't bother you that it's his father who took Father from us?" I can't keep the incredulous tone out of my voice.

"Of course it does." She turns to me and takes my hand, her tone softening. "We don't have a say about the family we're born into. By doing the right thing, he risked his whole future and proved himself to this family. I could lump him in with his father and hate him with the same hatred, or I can thank him for his sacrifice. I choose to be grateful." She pats my hand. "And when he talks about his love for you, I believe every word he says. You've won his heart, Eden. The love of a woman can change the worst of men. And you do love him, don't you?"

My eyes well with tears and spill over. She clutches my hand tighter.

"Don't spend too much time mulling over everything that's happened. He's made mistakes, big ones, but I believe he did them for the right reasons." She stands up and walks to the door, turning around to look at me once more. "Anything worth saving goes through a few battles first, it's just the way of life. If you decide to fight for this man, the biggest battle will be behind you, no matter what you face."

I stand up. "I need to see him. Where is he?"

"Oh sweetheart. He left, not even an hour ago. I thought you knew that. He said he wanted to see you again but thought he'd done enough damage for one day."

I sit back down on the bed and cry until no tears are left.

She pats my back and when the tears begin to ease up, she says, "There, there. He is staying in town for a day or two though." She gives me a sly grin.

"Why didn't you tell me?" My voice is hoarse from crying.

"I wanted to see how invested you are..." She nods. "I think he stands a good chance."

I wipe my face. "When did you get so twisted?"

She leans against the wall and laughs. It's the hardest I've heard her laugh since Father passed away. I smile in spite of myself.

"I wanted to know if you truly love him. Love breaks

you apart and puts you back together. It wouldn't really be love if it didn't. Go and see him."

"I can't. Not yet. But I will."

CHAPTER FORTY-TWO

I don't go.

Every time I take a step out of my room to go see him, I think about all that's happened. Maybe it's denial or maybe it's acceptance, but for two days I'm paralyzed.

On the third day, he knocks on the door and Brienne lets him in. She comes to find me in my room and I'm standing at my window, having seen him get out of the car.

"Prince Luka is here to see you."

"I saw that. What does he want?"

"Other than wanting to see you, I'm not sure." She smirks when I growl at her. "Why don't you come and find out?"

"The women in this household are conspiring against me." Everyone but Jadon has tried to push me to go see him; he's stayed steadfast about me deciding for myself, and that's why he's my favorite. I smile and turn so Brienne can't catch it, but I'm too late.

"Hurry. You've made him wait long enough."

"Ava told me to make him suffer and then changed her

tune after seeing his swoony face. You're all a bunch of turncoats."

Brienne shrugs. "He is a beautiful man...and quite convincing."

I roll my eyes and check in the mirror to see if I should really go out like this. I look like I've spent three days crying.

"Don't—" Brienne taps my shoulder. "He should get a look at what you've been through too. You saw him—he looks like he's been through a war. You've been right there with him."

I groan again and shuffle out the door, making my way slowly down the stairs. I wrap my arms around my stomach and feel it grumble with hunger pains.

I step into the living room and he rises when he sees me, rushing to stand in front of me. His eyes are full of concern and he stretches his hand out but drops it at the last second.

"You belong with me," he whispers. "Tell me you know it's true."

I swallow hard and nod. "I know it's true." I close my eyes and he touches my face, pulling me closer.

His shoulders sag and he takes a deep breath. "I wanted to come in here, demand that you come home with me, but I'm not your king, I'm your lover, your fool, your forever if you'll have me. I'll do anything to make you happy."

"Do you really mean that?" I whisper.

"I don't give you my word anymore because that hasn't meant much...but I plan on changing that. One day you will believe me because I will give you my *everything*. Starting now."

He puts his hands on my face and lowers his head to kiss me. I stand on my tiptoes to be level with him, wrapping my arms as tightly around him as they'll go. His hands roam my body like he's becoming reacquainted in fast forward, but it's still not fast enough.

Someone clears their throat just as he's picking me up and I've wrapped my legs around his waist. I pull back, drugged. Jadon stands in the doorway with his hands on his hips.

"Working things out, I take it. You have my blessing, but for the love of God, take it to the bedroom." His eyes are twinkling as he says it and he laughs when I flush and bury my head in Luka's neck.

Luka grins and we walk past Jadon. "Thanks, brother," Luka says.

He carries me to my bedroom, having to pass my grinning mother, sister, Brienne, and every other employee who works at the house, along the way. Once we're in my room, he shuts the door and leans me up against it.

"Is this really happening right now?" His eyes are light and smiling and he looks the happiest I've ever seen him. He's looking at me like he *loves* me.

I pull his mouth to me and kiss him hard. Our kiss is a promise, it answers every question that still lingered.

He sets me down and gives me a slight push backward, his eyes already doing their drag down my body. His fingers slide my loose top down my shoulder and he unbuttons the top two buttons that cause it to slide the rest of the way down. The skirt is simple to tug down too and he looks pleased with himself when I'm standing there in my panties and bra. I point at his clothes and he grins, getting right to work undoing his pants.

"Are you ready to be thoroughly fucked?" he whispers once he's taken off his shirt. He steps forward and undoes my bra with one flick of his fingers, grinning when it drops to the floor. "I'd like to take back that statement about not being your king...in the bedroom."

"Oh? You think you can be demanding in bed and get away with it?"

"Take off those panties and lie back on that bed. Let me see what I've been missing."

My pulse races and I bite down on my lip to keep from smiling. I do what he asks.

"I can see how wet you are. Have you missed me? I can't wait to sink inside you." He closes his eyes when he touches me and then plunges his finger inside. "So ready."

His tongue dives into my mouth and his finger keeps time, both plunging in and out and making me greedy for more. He puts a second finger in, then a third, his thumb caressing me on the outside. In one second, he pulls out and slides into me instead, filling me far more than his three fingers could. I gasp into his mouth and he never stops kissing me, his hands everywhere, while he thrusts hard and fast.

"You feel too good," he moans into my mouth. He leans back and looks at me, his eyes baring his soul and reflecting back what I feel for him. He stills and lowers back on me, chest to chest. "I love you."

"I love you too," I whisper.

He runs his hands through my hair as he twitches inside me but doesn't move right away.

"I don't want to ever live without you again," he says, the pain showing up in his face again. "Please stay. Stay with me."

A tear rolls back into my hair and he wipes it away.

"I'm not going anywhere."

When I say those words, his shoulders relax and he starts moving again. Each thrust gets more urgent until we're both sweating and breathing hard. My eyes start to roll back in my head and he's right there.

"Look at me, let me see you when you come."

I struggle to keep my eyes open. It feels too good. He groans when I clench around him and it sets him off.

I'm out of breath and so is he, but we still kiss and it isn't long before he's driving into me again.

"I'll never get enough of you. Ever." His eyes are resolute and he loves me again and again until I can't think straight.

The next morning when I go into the bathroom, my lips are red and puffy and my neck and breasts have hickeys. My hair is going in every direction and I look like I've been in a fight. Luka comes up behind me and looks at me in the mirror, his arms wrapping around my waist as his chin rests on my shoulder.

"Ahh, thoroughly fucked," he says, grinning. "It's my favorite look on you. You are wearing me everywhere."

I put my arm around his head and turn my face to the side to kiss him. "There are probably a few places you missed."

"Let me find them." He picks me up and sets me in the bathwater he ran fifteen minutes ago before discovering places he'd missed then. It doesn't matter that the water isn't as hot as I like it. He'll have me hot in seconds.

Our walk into the dining room is embarrassing. Ava does the slow clap and Brienne can't stop laughing at that.

Mother flushes and doesn't make eye contact. It's a good thing Jadon isn't here or I'd die.

"Thank you for letting me back into your home." Luka puts a napkin on his lap and takes the bowl of scrambled eggs Mother offers him.

"Thank you, thank you," Ava mimics, and I drop my fork, reminded of the times in the night that I thanked Luka for hitting just the right spot with his tongue.

I glare at Ava and Brienne loses it again. For someone so stoic, she sure has found her laughter at my expense. I glare at her too.

Luka nods and grins at Ava, looking pretty pleased with himself. I turn my glare to him.

"What? I personally love gratitude," he whispers loud enough for the whole table to hear. "This breakfast is delicious," he adds when my glare intensifies. "I've missed our breakfasts together."

"It's good to have you back," Ava says, her voice normal this time. "When do you have to leave?"

"Today, I'm afraid." He looks at me when he says it and I see the fear in his eyes, even after the night we had.

"I'm going with him." I look around the table and see the pride in each of their faces. They're happy for us.

"What can we do to help?" Brienne asks. Then, "You know I'm coming with you, right?"

I grin at her. "You better. I can't do this without you."

I look at Luka and feel the excitement building in my chest.

I actually feel like I'm going home—with my husband—ready to face the future.

CHAPTER FORTY-THREE

When we reach the Catano estate in the middle of the night, the house is quiet and I'm glad I don't have to face his mother or sister just yet. Luka checks his phone as I take off my makeup and slip into one of the gowns I grabbed from my room next door, still set up with all of my things.

"How did you manage to leave my room intact? I can't believe Hanna didn't get rid of it all the minute you came back without me." I walk into the room and he's watching something.

"Look at this." He holds up his phone and someone else has come forward saying they have more information about Titus. "He'll be in prison for a long time."

I hope.

He's deep in thought for a moment and then seems to snap out of it. "I said you'd get suspicious if you came back here and found your things missing..."

"I'm glad it worked. It meant less time packing at home and more time...in bed."

"Come here. I can't wait to have you back in my bed."

He pulls me on top of him. "Oh, and Hanna was fired once I found out she was the one who planted the bugs."

"This just gets more and more bizarre."

"Let's talk about you being in my bed again."

Cece and Mara steer clear of me the first few days I'm back. The day before the coronation, Luka and I are eating breakfast when we finally see them.

Neither of them acknowledges me and barely look at Luka.

"So this is how it's going to be?" Luka asks. "Father deserved to pay for what he did. Eden is my wife and I love her."

"What about Nadia?" Mara asks, picking at her food and sending hate vibes my way.

"Ask her. She'll tell you everything. I've never loved Nadia. You loved the idea of us more than either of us ever did. I needed her help and she gave it, willingly."

He leans his elbows on the table and looks at both of them while they study their food. He slams a hand down on the table and his mother jumps.

"If I find out either of you had even the tiniest bit to do with any of this, I'll make sure you pay too. We are not a family of murderers and thieves."

"Hear, hear," Basile chants when he comes into the room. He smiles warmly at me and I return the smile. He's the one other Catano I'm happy to see.

"I won't let you or anyone else destroy our name," Luka continues. "And if you can't be respectful and courteous to my wife, you can get the fuck out of this house. That can be my first job as king, throwing you both out of here and banishing you to Baelle."

Cece pales and Mara gasps.

"We just need time to adjust to everything," Cece says, pressing her lips together. She looks at me and nods. "Eden...welcome back."

"Thank you."

"Mara?" Luka prompts.

"Welcome back," she mutters.

Luka picks up his fork and we all eat in silence.

The next morning, Brienne joins us for breakfast and when Mara walks in, she comes to a standstill.

"What are you doing here?"

"You remember Brienne? She's been here with me all along, last time too." I look at Brienne and the coldness on her face surprises me. What am I missing?

"Oh, I remember her, but she at least stayed hidden in the shadows. You don't belong in here. This is for family only." Mara's lip curls and she sits down, snapping her fingers at Chelsea to pour her coffee.

"Brienne is my family. Don't ever let me hear you speak to her that way."

Mara sits there and fumes but doesn't say another word. Brienne looks at me with gratitude, and I vow to get to the bottom of whatever is going on between them later.

The coronation of Luka Elvais Catano is a beautiful and majestic affair. I watch in awe as the crown is placed on his head and he goes through the rituals of the Niapsian people. We're standing on a cliff with the ocean roaring behind us and there are people standing nearby and in boats on the water, watching him become their king. When it's official and he's pronounced King Luka Catano of Niaps, a cheer erupts and the sound is deafening.

Luka's eyes find mine and he looks so happy, so complete. I hardly recognize him from the boy I met at Kings Passage.

"I love you," he mouths the words to me and I sigh.

"This is where you can tell me I was right," Basile says under his breath. "Anyone who can't see that the boy is mad for you is blind."

I smile and he shakes his head.

"You're nearly as stubborn as he is."

"Oh, you've got that right. This should be fun," Jadon throws in.

"Don't you start," I mutter under my breath. "You're supposed to be here to show your support, not throw in your two cents about my personality."

"I *am* here for support," he replies. "And stating the obvious."

"I can't wait to see your children torment you with their bullheaded wills." Basile claps his hands and then falls into step behind Luka with Cece and Mara flanking him on either side.

Luka holds his hand out to me and I join him. A crown is placed on my head and I am pronounced Queen Eden Catano of Niaps—Queen! It will take me a while to get comfortable with the title.

When the applause dies down, we gradually make the procession down the cliff and back to the church. A feast is prepared outside and we eat and drink and dance under the stars. I look for Brienne and find her leaning against the wall. Elias walks by her and says something and she flushes. He throws his head back and laughs and Brienne ducks her head. Mara walks up to Elias and loops her arm through his, pulling him away. He looks over his shoulder at Brienne and the look in his eyes surprises me.

"Do Elias and Brienne know each other?" I'm in Luka's arms under a canopy of lights.

"They've probably met at the house. Elias has been there often and will be working with me now."

"Hmm."

"What are you thinking?"

"Some of Mara's hostility toward Brienne is starting to make sense."

"I want to talk about us." He nuzzles my neck. "Do you remember the first thing I said to you?"

I lean back to look at him, trying to remember exactly what he said. I start to grin and he nods.

"You remember." He kisses up my jaw and I shiver.

"I remember."

"Hello, future," he whispers.

He spins me until I'm breathless and when the people remaining begin to clap and cheer, he tilts me back and I curtsy when I come back up.

"Hello, future," I whisper back.

This time we seal it with a kiss.

EPILOGUE

Twenty-five years later

"Are you ready for this?" Luka asks, grabbing me and pulling me back into bed with him.

"I won't be if you don't let me get up."

"We just had Selene yesterday, right? It feels like yesterday. I'm not ready for her to get married. There's still time to talk her out of it, isn't there?" He sits up and I push him back on the bed, crawling on top of him.

His hands find my backside and he groans. "You are the best negotiator in the whole wide world, Mrs. Catano. Get me on my back and I will give you whatever you want."

I place him right where I want him, deep inside me, and he grins.

"Anything you wish..." he whispers.

I rock back and forth, amazed that after all these years, the spark between us only grows.

"You will give our daughter away today and be nice to George. He's the love of her life and perfect for her. No more talking her out of it nonsense, okay?" I pick up speed and his eyes light up.

"You're playing so dirty. I love it."

"Do we have a deal?"

He flips me over and lifts my knees against his chest, driving into me harder. "You do not play fair."

I go still and he frowns.

"Yes, we have a deal. Now, let's forget about this wedding for a while. I have things I need to do." He moves faster and faster, until I can't remember what we were negotiating.

He's sweeter when we're getting ready in the bathroom later. I think he's actually excited about this wedding, although he'd never admit it. When he puts his jacket on and helps me zip up the back of my dress, his fingers tickle my neck as he moves my hair back into place.

"You are the most beautiful woman in the world, Mrs. Catano. I can't believe I was lucky enough to capture you."

"You captured me back then and every day since. Turns out our parents did one thing right," I tease, turning around to face him. Knowing anything related to his parents will always be a touchy subject, I quickly move on. "I am so proud of who you are and the family we've created together. Three kids, a new son-in-law in a few hours, a country who still adores you. I'm grateful every day that we chose one another when we could've let it all crumble."

"You know when I feel most grateful?" He kisses my cheek. "When you crawl into bed next to me every night. I live for that moment when we're done with the insanity of our day, ruling the world and keeping this family on track, and we come together between the sheets."

I put my hand on his cheek and kiss him. "It's my

favorite too. Keep this up, and tonight, you're going to get very lucky."

"I'll make it worth your while, I swear."

We lose track of time, swaying back and forth in our bedroom overlooking the water.

He's my home and I am his.

Our love has changed the world, one country at a time.

It's taken patience and building relationships with people we might not have chosen, had we not forged peace between Farrow and Niaps.

It gives me hope for our world's future.

"Let's go to this wedding," he whispers. "The sooner it's over, the sooner I can take this gorgeous dress off you."

I laugh. "I hope you never lose your dirty mind."

"Never," he vows as he takes my hand.

I always forget someone in this section and feel terrible. Hopefully, I'll get close this time. There are so many people in my life that I'm grateful for—the list is vast...far longer than this one.

Thank you, Nate, Greyley, and Indigo for your constant support and love. I love you so much and thank God every day for you.

Thank you, Dad, for your love. I really hope you didn't read this one. Matter of fact, skip the whole series, PLEASE. Love you!

Thank you, Christine Estevez and Jennifer Mirabelli for cheering me on throughout this process, for being the ultimate support team. I couldn't have done it without either of you!

And Christine, for the things you do for me on a daily basis as my assistant—I would be lost without you.

Thank you, Darla Williams, for giving this your wise eyes. Invaluable. Love you!

Thank you, Christine Bowden, for your unwavering encouragement. You just seem to know what to say and do, even from across the world. I love you!!

Thank you, Wander Aguiar for the fantastic photograph of Alex Clagett and for being SO EASY to work with.

Thank you, Hang Le, for this amazing cover and for being so delightful.

Thank you, Dani Sanchez, for your help!

Thank you to the following friends who I love dearly and who cheer me on in various ways, book related and otherwise: Tosha Khoury, Courtney Nuness, Priscilla Perez, Jesse Nava, Steve and Jill Erickson, Staci Frenes, Ashleigh Still, Savita Naik, Kira Fennell, Kell Donaldson, Claire Contreras, Maria Milano, Holly Ray, Christine Brae, and all my loves at Grace Place...

Thank you to the Asters group! I love you!

Thank you, Tarryn Fisher, for forcing me to watch Game of Thrones. And for all the other stuff too.

Thank you to the bloggers out there who work tirelessly on authors' behalf—I appreciate you so much!

And to all the readers out there who read my work no matter what I write, I'm especially grateful to you. To you who have given my work a chance for the first time, thank you so much.

XO,
Willow

EXPOSED (KINGDOMS OF SIN #2)

Chapter 1: Mara

Today is the worst day of my life.

Even worse than the day my father went to prison for murder, which was right up there. Today is the day my brother Luka becomes king and that whiny, pansy wife of his will be crowned right alongside him. This was never supposed to happen, not like this.

My father might be a lot of things, but he is *not* a murderer.

I love my brother, I really do, but ever since Eden, Princess of the North and all that is cold and pale, got under his skin, he has become a different person. He's betrayed our family, and all for his gain. It's crazy too, because I've always done everything I could to earn my parents' approval, while Luka has always had it without even trying. If anyone should be bound by honor, it seems it would be him.

I watch the crown being placed on his head and choke

back the tears that threaten to fall. It's like I don't even know him anymore. He used to be fun, always up for trouble, and he got a kick out of my presumed bad behavior.

At least I thought he did.

He would've never, *ever* turned his back on our family like this.

It's all *her* fault.

Now he feels like a stranger. Maybe neither of us ever really knew one another at all.

He's never known what I'm truly capable of.

I think my father knew. My mother might know too. It's why they've always had Luka look out for me, cover me, keep me in line. He's younger than me, but you'd never know it. Technically, I should be mad that he was ever born. It got in the way of me becoming queen, with the firstborn son always taking over the monarch, and the daughter only inheriting the throne should a son not be born. I should hate him, but he was the best thing that ever happened to me.

The day Luka was born, I finally had the freedom to be me.

It might have been used against me at times—this freedom—but I've been grateful for it nonetheless.

And now, with the way my brother has turned against us and embraced his foreign wife, I fear that liberation is over. Forever.

I feel eyes on me and my skin prickles in awareness. I look up and sure enough, Elias Lancaster is watching me. Sometimes I think he might see the real me too. It's part of what intrigues me about him and part of what makes me keep my guard up.

I've loved Elias Lancaster for as long as I can remember. He will be mine one day soon, but a couple of things have to change first:

He needs to be convinced he belongs with me.

He needs to realize he's good enough for me.

Two things that I'm not worried about, not with the way his eyes skate down my skin like they wish they could unwrap me and lay me bare. *It's only a matter of time, dear Elias.*

I don't care what he does for a living—he's doing exactly what he's always wanted, being an advisor to the king—but for some reason, he thinks I need more.

It's been a while since Elias has made a move besides being an attentive flirt whenever we're together. I'm getting tired of waiting.

He has no reason to work for the attention of whatever woman he wants. He walks into a room and is instantly swarmed. It's disgusting. He stands taller than the other men in the room, except for Luka. His brown hair and blue-grey eyes and constant smile draw the attention of everyone in the room. The dimple makes sure the attention stays. It's the only time I wish he wasn't so beautiful: when everyone else notices it and he's *not* by my side. I try my best to stand apart by ignoring him until he finds me. And he *always* comes to find me.

He's wealthy enough to be dangerous but not so wealthy that he isn't still a bit hungry for more. It keeps him on his toes and he likes playing hard to get.

I, for one, am up for the challenge, but I intend on playing hard to get right back.

He motions for me to step forward and I put my hand through my mother's arm, separating to stand on either side of Uncle Basile as we follow the processional. The people who surround us on each side look at my mother and me skeptically, something that never happened until my father was accused. I shiver with some of the expressions that stare back at me.

The walk down the cliff is hot and I wish I'd worn thinner material, especially when we continue the celebration outside. I stand along the sidelines, turning down everyone who asks me to dance. Finally, I turn away and walk toward the food. I just can't shake the mood I'm in, but when Elias comes into my line of sight, I smile in spite of everything. My smile drops when he doesn't return it. But then I realize he's looking past me and doesn't even seem to notice that I'm standing right in front of him. I turn to see what has his attention and I frown.

Brienne Jarvis, my sister-in-law's shadow, is standing against the stone wall, tapping her right foot to the music.

I turn back to Elias, thinking he's surely spotted me by now, but he's moved past me and is moving toward Brienne.

My ears burn and I put my hand on the table to steady myself. What the hell?

I watch as he stops near her and says something, which causes her to laugh and flush a delicate shade of pale pink.

That slutty ox!

Besides us both having blond hair, we're about as opposite from one another as you can get. She's nearly six feet tall and although I guess I can see how some might consider her attractive, she doesn't have an ounce of personality. I'm only five foot three, but I have more personality in my big toe than she does in her entire stretched out body. She does look strong and extremely fit, but what man wants a woman who can carry *him* to bed? I shudder at the thought of her carrying Elias. What could he possibly see in her?

In the past when I've seen him at parties, flirting with whoever was hanging on his arm at the time, I simply encouraged whoever was paying attention to me at that moment and Elias was there before I had to do much at all. But seeing as how I've sent everyone away tonight with my crabby disposition, I'm all alone.

It's because of the day. That's what I tell myself. I wouldn't normally put myself out there like this, knowing it could backfire with Elias, but the turmoil of the past few months has taken its toll on me. I don't stop to overthink it, I storm over to Elias and Brienne and slide my arm through his, pulling him away.

I glare at Brienne and my heart thuds when he turns back to look at her.

"Was it really necessary to be so rude to her?" he asks, patting my hand despite his words.

The way Brienne seemed to dare me with her eyes, I think *yes, it was necessary*.

"After all I've been through today, the least you can do is dance with me."

"Fair enough." He smiles and I know all is forgiven.

I give him a smug smile in return and he laughs.

"You are too beautiful for your own good, Mara Catano. And I seem to fall for it every time."

I sigh as I step into his arms, already feeling so much better as we begin to slowly sway. But I can't leave well enough alone. "When you say you fall for it, do you mean you fall for me?" I feel his body stiffen slightly and I pull back to look in his eyes. "We've played this game for so long, Elias. Don't you ever get tired?"

He stops swaying and studies me. "If you only knew." His finger traces my jaw and moves to my lips. I go completely still, willing him closer, but he breaks the moment with his next words. "You don't know what you want."

"Oh, I absolutely *do* know what I want." I lean in closer to him and he backs away.

"It's impossible to know what you want when you don't even know who you *are*." He drops his hands and takes another step back, bowing slightly. "Thank you for this dance. I should go make sure your brother is enjoying his party."

I stand, mouth open and fuming as he leaves me standing in the middle of the dance floor, feeling like a fool. It's like déjà vu all over again.

Click here to continue reading Exposed

ACKNOWLEDGMENTS

I always forget someone in this section and feel terrible. Hopefully, I'll get close this time. There are so many people in my life that I'm grateful for—the list is vast...far longer than this one.

Thank you, Nate, Greyley, and Indigo for your constant support and love. I love you so much and thank God every day for you.

Thank you, Dad, for your love. I really hope you didn't read this one. Matter of fact, skip the whole series, PLEASE. Love you!

Thank you, Christine Estevez and Jennifer Mirabelli for cheering me on throughout this process, for being the ultimate support team. I couldn't have done it without either of you!

And Christine, for the things you do for me on a daily basis as my assistant—I would be lost without you.

Thank you, Darla Williams, for giving this your wise eyes. Invaluable. Love you!

Thank you, Christine Bowden, for your unwavering

encouragement. You just seem to know what to say and do, even from across the world. I love you!!

Thank you, Wander Aguiar for the fantastic photograph of Alex Clagett and for being SO EASY to work with.

Thank you, Hang Le, for this amazing cover and for being so delightful.

Thank you, Dani Sanchez, for your help!

Thank you to the following friends who I love dearly and who cheer me on in various ways, book related and otherwise: Tosha Khoury, Courtney Nuness, Priscilla Perez, Jesse Nava, Steve and Jill Erickson, Staci Frenes, Ashleigh Still, Savita Naik, Kira Fennell, Kell Donaldson, Claire Contreras, Maria Milano, Holly Ray, Christine Brae, and all my loves at Grace Place...

Thank you to the Asters group! I love you!

Thank you, Tarryn Fisher, for forcing me to watch Game of Thrones. And for all the other stuff too.

Thank you to the bloggers out there who work tirelessly on authors' behalf—I appreciate you so much!

And to all the readers out there who read my work no matter what I write, I'm especially grateful to you. To you who have given my work a chance for the first time, thank you so much.

XO,
Willow

ABOUT THE AUTHOR

Willow Aster is a USA Today Bestselling author and host of Living in the Pages podcast. She lives in St. Paul, MN with her husband, kids, and rescue dog.

♡ Subscribe to my newsletter for updates.

♡ Listen to my podcast—Living in the Pages on the Website or iTunes.

♡ Join the Willow Aster Facebook Group (we have lots of fun in there and talk about things I don't talk about anywhere else).

Reviews mean the world to authors! If you enjoyed this story, please take the time to share a line or two. It makes all the difference.

XO, Willow

ALSO BY WILLOW ASTER

Standalones

True Love Story

Fade to Red

In the Fields

Maybe Maby

Lilith

The La Jolla Series

5,331 Miles

Miles Ahead

Kingdoms of Sin Series

Downfall

Exposed

Ruin

Preorder Pride

The End of Men Series with Tarryn Fisher:

Folsom

Jackal